DOGFIGHT!

One of the Vampyres went up in a cloud of flame . . .

The other Vampyre—Reynolds wasn't sure which—was firing its remaining missiles.

They were almost on top of each other. In the radarmap and the infrared they were. Only in the eyeslit was there still space between the two.

And then they were together. Joining. One big ball, orange and red and yellow, swallowing both Vampyre and prey, growing, growing, growing.

Reynolds sat almost frozen, climbing towards the swelling inferno, his laser firing ineffectively into the flames. Then he came out of it. And swerved. And dove. His laser fired once more, to wipe out a chunk of flaming debris that came spinning towards him.

He was alone. The fire fell and faded, and there was only one Vampyre, and the stars, and the blanket of cloud far below him. He had survived.

of the Vampyres"
.R. Martin

SPACE DOGFIGHTS

INTRODUCTION BY GORDON R. DICKSON

WITH ALGIS BUDRYS, CHARLES G. WAUGH, AND MARTIN HARRY GREENBERG, EDITORS

ACE BOOKS, NEW YORK

SPACE DOGFIGHTS

An Ace Book / published by arrangement with
the editors

PRINTING HISTORY
Ace edition / January 1992

ISBN: 0-441-53167-9

Ace Books are published by The Berkley Publishing Group,
200 Madison Avenue, New York, New York 10016.
The name "ACE" and the "A" logo
are trademarks belonging to Charter Communications, Inc.

PRINTED IN THE UNITED STATES OF AMERICA

10 9 8 7 6 5 4 3 2 1

Contents

Introduction

Gordon R. Dickson

With the entrance of combat aircraft into the fighting of World War I, 1914 to 1918, we began to hear on both sides references to "our *gallant* airmen."

—*Gallant*: "brave; high-spirited; courageous; heroic; of a noble bearing" says *Webster's Unabridged Dictionary*—

Why "*gallant*" airmen, then?

The artillerymen, the infantry in the trenches, the engineers—all had various complimentary terms addressed to them too. They were "heroic," they were "brave," and so forth. But there was a conspicuous absence of the word "gallant" in descriptions of them.

There was a reason for this. They were the toilers of war. The time had been when any soldier could be referred to as being gallant right up through the first part of the eighteenth century.

Then the word began to disappear, along with the development of more efficient weapons of destruction and mass battles. Now what was talked about was more the number slain or captured on each side than the individual actions of those who exposed themselves to death. Only in rare instances where an individual found himself alone facing a mass of enemy and behaved in a way that went beyond commendable into the extraordinary was the word "gallant" still used.

The gallant had all but died; but then, from 1914 to 1918, it was being revived for the pilots, who at first waved to their opposite numbers above the front-line trenches as they flew, then began to exchange pistol shots from their cockpits as their opposed aircraft passed, then progressed to mounted machine guns—and once more we began to have warriors who were spoken of as gallant.

x   Gordon R. Dickson

The reason for it all, and its application to this particular collection, is connected to the human instinctive system. Something that over a few thousand years we humans have come almost to deny. We can and do respond to our instinctive system in times of emergency or danger, but we usually rationalize our actions by coming up with a cognitive, a "thinking," reason.

Consequently, the reason for suddenly attributing gallantry to the embattled pilots of World War I and afterward, was obscured by the fact that, then and now, we reached for thinking reasons to use the word.

It seldom occurs to us that our responses are ones that go back to the beginning of human time.

In the beginning all fights were individual fights. Back in the Stone Age, when one tribe battled with an enemy, it became a series of single combats—one man against another, until one of those men went down; at which point the victor might be free to take on another opponent among the enemy tribesmen. One who also happened to be free at the moment.

Under these conditions it was easy to see that some fighters were more outstanding than others. So that the word that evolved down through history to describe the unusually praiseworthy actions of one of our warriors in single combat against an enemy warrior was "gallantry." It connoted, among other things, "nobility"—itself now a lost word in its original meaning.

"Gallantry" connoted an all-or-nothing meeting with at least an equal; and either a remarkable victory, or great bravery and skill shown even in defeat. This element of the word actually lasted up through the time of cavalry. There were horsed cavalry in combat in World War I; but they soon disappeared. They were pitifully vulnerable to the machine gun and other new improved modern weapons of the time.

To be shot down by massed fire from up to some hundreds of yards makes combat mass murder with little opportunity to show gallantry.

On the other hand, actual physical contact, above all the one-on-one battle in which two individuals meet and only one survives as victor, made it possible.

Now, suddenly with the cloth and wire aircraft of World War I, it became possible again. For aerial combat was essentially a throwback to the Stone Age, in that two met *a outrance*, as in medieval days.

What the airplane had revived in air warfare was the ancient duel between two individuals.

There is an instinctive response to the idea of the duel, particularly if not exclusively, on the part of males, who tend to see such an encounter in itself as proof of courage and possible nobility.

For in the duel, it was a situation in which everything was put on the board, including the life of the people engaging in it. It was a standard by which combatants could be measured; and until very very recent times—and we are not even yet free of them today—the willingness to engage in it was one measure of the one who engaged in it.

Therefore, the idea of the aerial duel lit the fuse of imagination in many earlier authors. An author's job, in the long run, after all, is to pluck the emotional strings of the reader with a story that evokes the music of his imagination.

The mere concept of the aerial duel did this. As a result, a great deal was written in the way of air-war stories for a period following World War I. As late as the 1930s and '40s there were still pulp magazines that were devoted exclusively to air-war stories; most laid back in the time of World War I, others laid in some far-off corner of the world, where for some reason ancient enemies of the air were meeting once again with their ships and their machine guns in one-on-one combat.

With the vanishing of the pulp magazines the air-war stories also vanished.

They reappeared in science fiction and fantasy, some years later, but with a difference.

It has always been the province of science fiction—and the fantasy from which it derived—to add an element of the unknown to what otherwise might be a here-and-now story. A sort of literary fourth dimension, without which it did not stand apart from fiction of the here and now. Often what once was, or what may be in the future or otherwhen, is used as a metaphor to make the story science fiction or fantasy.

As a result, the reader of this book will find in it a number of remarkable stories, all of them well researched and true in their depiction of early aircraft and aerial combat—but also in their application of that image to the later, modern world as we know it now.

This is done by a number of methods, from the familiar one (in science fiction) of someone who falls back through time into a

World War I situation—as a combat flier in Dean McLaughlin's "The Hawk Among the Sparrows," to Algis Budrys' "The Nuptial Flight of Warbirds," who sets up the parallel between the original early-twentieth-century wartime air battle and a comparable, very modern situation—which cuttingly compares the past real, with a present falseness.

But in each case the story touches on the strangeness, the response to the notion of gallantry under extreme pressure, of the original duelists of the air that were the World War I airmen; even if this is only implied—as in the narrator's building a perfect replica of a Fokker tri-plane as in Gene Wolfe's excellent "Against the Lafayette Escadrille"—to tell a story which draws on imagination in a different area, but with both areas reflecting the same intense longing for what can never be, for the narrator.

We are taken into a moment in the immediate future in "Night of the Vampyres" by George R. R. Martin, but the story is told within the action that was the one-on-one aerial action of the first warplanes, even though these particular warships are as viciously armed and powered as those we're familiar with today.

There are two things, therefore, for the reader to resonate to in all of these stories: One is the past loneliness and potential gallantry of single combat; the other is what the author wishes to tell us, in the unique literary mode of science fiction and fantasy, about ourselves, here in the present.

SPACE
DOGFIGHTS

NIGHT OF THE VAMPYRES

George R. R. Martin

The announcement came during prime time.

All four major holo networks went off simultaneously, along with most of the independents. There was an instant of crackling grayness. And then a voice, which said, simply, "Ladies and gentlemen, the President of the United States."

John Hartmann was the youngest man ever to hold the office of President, and the commentators were fond of saying that he was the most telegenic as well. His clean-cut good looks, ready wit, and flashing grin had given the Liberty Alliance its narrow plurality in the bitter four-way elections of 1984. His political acumen had engineered the Electoral College coalition with the Old Republicans that had put him in the White House.

Hartmann was not grinning now. His features were hard, somber. He was sitting behind his desk in the Oval Office, looking down at the papers he held in his hands. After a moment of silence, he raised his head slowly, and his dark eyes looked straight out into the living rooms of a nation.

"My fellow countrymen," he said gravely, "tonight our nation faces the most serious crisis in its long and great history. Approximately one hour ago, an American air force base in California was hit by a violent and vicious attack . . ."

The first casualty was a careless sentry. The attacker was quick, silent, and very efficient. He used a knife. The sentry died without a whimper, never knowing what was happening.

The other attackers were moving in even before the corpse hit the ground. Circuits were hooked up to bypass the alarm system, and torches went to work on the high electric fence. It fell. From the darkness, more invaders materialized to move through the fresh gap.

But somewhere one alarm system was still alive. Sirens began to howl. The sleepy air base came to sudden, startled life. Stealth now useless, the attackers began to run. Towards the airfields.

Somebody began to fire. Someone else screamed. Outside the main gate, the guards looked in, baffled, towards the base. A stream of submachine gun fire took them where they stood, hammering them to bloody death against their own fence. A grenade arced through the air, and the gate shattered under the explosion.

"The attack was sudden, well-planned, and utterly ruthless," Hartmann told the nation. "The defense, under the circumstances, was heroic. Nearly one hundred American servicemen died during the course of the action."

The power lines were cut only seconds after the attack got under way. A well-placed grenade took out the emergency generator. Then darkness. It was a moonless night, and the clouds obscured the stars. The only light was the flash of machine gun fire and the brief, shattering brilliance of the explosions around the main gate.

There was little rhyme and less reason to the defense. Startled by the sirens, troops scrambled from the barracks and towards the gate, where the conflict seemed to be centered. On either side of the fence, attackers and defenders hit the ground. A searing crossfire was set up.

The base commandant was as startled and confused as any of his men. Long, valuable minutes passed while he and his staff groped for the facts, and tried to understand what was happening. Their response was almost instinctive. A ring of defenders was thrown around the Command Tower, a second around the base armory. Other men were sent sprinting towards the planes.

But the bulk of the troops were rushed to the main gate, where the battle was at its fiercest.

The defenders brought up heavy weapons from the base armory. The shrubbery outside the base perimeter was blasted by mortars, blown apart by grenades. The attackers' hidden position was systematically pounded. Then, behind a wall of smoke and tear-gas, the defenders poured out of the gate, washed over the enemy positions.

They found them empty, but for corpses. The attackers had melted away as suddenly as they had come.

An order for search and pursuit was swiftly given. And just as swiftly rescinded. For over the machine gun fire and the explosions, another sound could now be heard.

The sound of a jet taking off.

"The attackers concentrated most of their forces against the main entrance of the air base," Hartmann said. "But for all its fierceness, this assault was simply a diversion. While it was in progress, a smaller force of attackers penetrated another part of the base perimeter, beat off light resistance, and seized a small portion of the airfields."

The President's face was taut with emotion. "The goal of the attack was a squadron of long-range bombers, and their fighter escorts. As part of our first line of defense to deter Communist aggression, the bombers were on stand-by status; fueled and ready to take off in seconds, in the event of an enemy attack."

Hartmann paused dramatically, looked down at his papers, then back up. "Our men reacted swiftly and valiantly. They deserve only our praise. They retook several planes from the attackers, and burned down several others during takeoff.

"Despite this courageous resistance, however, the attackers put seven fighters and two bombers into the air. My fellow countrymen, both of those bombers were equipped with nuclear weaponry."

Again Hartmann paused. Behind him, the Oval Office background dissolved. Suddenly there was only the President, and his desk, outlined against a blank wall of white. On that wall, six familiar sentences suddenly appeared.

"Even while the attack was in progress, an ultimatum was sent to me in Washington," Hartmann said. "Unless certain demands were met within a three-hour deadline, I was told, a hydrogen bomb would be dropped on the city of Washington, D.C. You see those demands before you." He gestured.

"Most of you have seen them before. Some call them the Six Demands," he continued. "I'm sure you know them as well as I. They call for an end to American aid to our struggling allies in Africa and the Mid-East, for the systematic destruction of our defensive capacities, for an end to the Special Urban Units that have restored law and order to our cities, for the release of thousands of dangerous criminals, for the repeal of federal restrictions on obscene and subversive literature, and, of course,"—he flashed his famous grin—"for my resignation as President of the United States."

The grin faded. "These demands are a formula for national suicide, a recipe for surrender and disgrace. They would return us to the lawlessness and anarchy of a permissive society that we have left behind. Moreover, they are opposed by the great majority of the American people.

"However, as you know, these demands are vocally advocated by a small and dangerous minority. They represent the political program of the so-called American Liberation Front."

The background behind Hartmann changed again. The blowup of the Six Demands vanished. Now the President sat before a huge photograph of a bearded, long-haired young man in a black beret and baggy black uniform. The man was quite dead; most of his chest had been blown away.

"Behind me you see a photograph of one of the casualties of tonight's attack," Hartmann said. "Like all the other attackers we found, he wears the uniform of the paramilitary wing of the A.L.F."

The photo vanished. Hartmann looked grim. "The facts are clear. But this time the A.L.F. has gone too far. I will not submit to nuclear blackmail. Nor, my fellow countrymen, is there cause for alarm. To my fellow citizens of Washington I say especially, fear not. I promise that the A.L.F. pirate planes will be tracked down and destroyed long before they reach their target.

"Meanwhile, the leaders of the A.L.F. are about to learn that they erred in attempting to intimidate this administration. For too long they have divided and weakened us, and given aid and comfort to those who would like to see this nation enslaved. They shall do so no longer.

"There can be only one word for tonight's attack. That word is treason.

"Accordingly, I will deal with the attackers like traitors."

"I've got them," McKinnis said, his voice crackling with static. "Or something."

Reynolds didn't really need the information. He had them too. He glanced briefly down at the radarmap. They were on the edge of the scope, several miles ahead, heading due east at about 90,000 feet. High, and moving fast.

Another crackle, then Bonetto, the flight leader. "Looks like them, alright. I've got nine. Let's go get 'em."

His plane nosed up and began to climb. The others followed, behind and abreast of him in a wide V formation. Nine LF-7 Vampyre fighter/interceptors. Red, white, and blue flags on burnished black metal, silvery teeth slung underneath.

A hunting pack closing for the kill.

Yet another voice came over the open channel. "Hey, whattaya figure the odds? All over they're looking. Betcha it gets us promotions. Lucky us."

That had to be Dutton, Reynolds thought. A brash kid, hungry. Maybe *he* felt lucky. Reynolds didn't. Inside the acceleration suit he was sweating suddenly, coldly.

The odds had been all against it. The kid was right about that. The Alfie bombers were LB-4s, laser-armed monsters with speed to spare. They could've taken any route of a dozen, and still make it to Washington on time. And every damn plane and radar installation in the country was looking for them.

So what were the odds against them running into Reynolds and his flight out over northern Nebraska on a wild goose chase?

Too damn good, as it turned out.

"They see us," Bonetto said. "They're climbing. And accelerating. Move it."

Reynolds moved it. His Vampyre was the last in one arm of the V, and it held its formation. Behind the oxygen mask, his eyes roamed restlessly, and watched the instruments. Mach 1.3. Then 1.4. Then higher.

They were gaining. Climbing and gaining.

The radarmap showed the Alfie positions. And there was a blur up ahead on the infrared scope. But through the narrow eyeslit, nothing. Just cold black sky and stars. They were above the clouds.

The dumb bastards, Reynolds thought. They steal the most sophisticated hunk of metal ever built, and they don't know how to use it. They weren't even using their radar scramblers. It was almost like they were asking to be shot down.

Cracklings. "They're leveling off." Bonetto again. "Hold your missiles till my order. And remember, those big babies can give you a nasty hotfoot."

Reynolds looked at the radarmap again. The Alfies were now flat out at about 100,000 feet. Figured. The LB-4s could go higher, but ten was about the upper limit for the fighter escorts. Rapiers Reynolds remembered his briefing.

They wanted to stick together. That made sense. The Alfies would need their Rapiers. Ten *wasn't* the upper limit for Vampyres.

Reynolds squinted. He thought he saw something ahead, through the eyeslit. A flash of silver. Them? Or his imagination? Hard to tell. But he'd see them soon enough. The pursuit planes were gaining. Fast they were, the big LB-4s were no match for the Vampyres. The Rapiers were; but they had to stay with the bombers.

So it was only a matter of time. They'd catch them long before Washington. And then?

Reynolds shifted uneasily. He didn't want to think about that. He'd never flown in combat before. He didn't like the idea.

His mouth was dry. He swallowed. Just this morning he and Anne had talked about how lucky he was, made plans for a vacation. And beyond. His term was almost up, and he was still safe in the States. So many friends dead in the South African War. But he'd been lucky.

And now this. And suddenly the possibility that tomorrow might not be bright. The possibility that tomorrow might not be. It scared him.

There was more, too. Even if he lived, he was still queasy. About the killing.

That shouldn't have bothered him. He knew it might happen when he enlisted. But it was different then. He thought he'd be flying against Russians, Chinese—enemies. The outbreak of the South African War and the U.S. intervention had disturbed him. But he could have fought there, for all that. The Pan-African Alliance was Communist-inspired, or so they said.

But Alfies weren't distant foreigners. Alfies were people, neighbors. His radical college roommate. The black kids he had grown up with back in New York. The teacher who lived down the block. He got along with Alfies well enough, when they weren't talking politics.

And sometimes even when they were. The Six Demands weren't all that bad. He'd heard a lot of nasty rumors about the Special Urban Units. And God knows what the U.S. was doing in South Africa and the Mid-East.

He grimaced behind the oxygen mask. Face it, Reynolds, he told himself. The skeleton in his closet. He had actually thought about voting A.L.F. in '84, although in the end he'd chickened out and pulled the lever for Bishop, the Old Democrat. No one on the base knew but Anne. They hadn't argued politics for a long time, with anyone. Most of his friends were Old Republicans, but a few had turned to the Liberty Alliance. And that scared him.

Bonetto's crackling command smashed his train of thought. "Look at that, men. The Alfies are going to fight. At 'em!"

Reynolds didn't need to look at his radarmap. He could see them now, above. Lights against the sky. Growing lights.

The Rapiers were diving on them.

Of all the commentators who followed President Hartmann over the holo networks, Continental's Ted Warren seemed the least shell-shocked. Warren was a gritty old veteran with an incisive mind and razor tongue. He had tangled with Hartmann more than once, and was regularly denounced by the Liberty Alliance for his "Alfie bias."

"The President's speech leaves many questions still unanswered," Warren said in his post-mortem newscast. "He has promised to deal with the A.L.F. as traitors, but as yet, we are unsure exactly what steps will be taken. There is also some question, in my mind at any rate, as to the A.L.F.'s motivation for this alleged attack. Bob, any thoughts on that?"

A new face on camera; the reporter who covered A.L.F. activities for Continental had been hustled out of bed and rushed to the studio. He still looked a little rumpled.

"No, Ted," he replied. "As far as I know, the A.L.F. was not planning any action of this kind. Were it not for the fact that this attack was so well-planned, I might question whether the A.L.F. national leadership was involved at all. It might have been an unauthorized action by a group of local extremists. You'll recall that the assault on the Chicago Police Headquarters during the 1985 riots was of this nature. However, I think the planning that went into this attack, and the armament that was used, precludes this being a similar case."

Warren, at the Continental anchordesk, nodded sagely. "Bob, do you think there is any possibility that the paramilitary arm of the A.L.F. might have acted unilaterally, without the knowledge of the party's political leaders?"

The reporter paused and looked thoughtful. "Well, it's possible, Ted. But not likely. The kind of assault that the President described would require too much planning. I'd think that the whole party would have to be involved in an effort on that scale."

"What reasons would the A.L.F. have for an action like this?" Warren asked.

"From what the President said, a hope that a nuclear threat would bring immediate agreement to the A.L.F.'s Six Demands would seem to be the reason."

Warren was insistent. "Yes. But why should the A.L.F. resort to such an extreme tactic? The latest Gallup poll gave them the support of nearly 29% of the electorate, behind only the 38% of President Hartmann's Liberty Alliance. This is a sharp increase from the 13% of the vote the A.L.F. got in the presidential elections of 1984. With only a year to go before the new elections, it seems strange that the A.L.F. would risk everything on such a desperate ploy."

Now the reporter was nodding. "You have a point, Ted. However, we've been surprised by the A.L.F. before. They've never been the easiest party to predict, and I think—"

Warren cut him off. "Excuse me, Bob. Back to you later. Correspondent Mike Petersen is at the A.L.F.'s national headquarters in Washington, and he has Douglass Brown with him. Mike, can you hear me?"

The picture changed. Two men standing before a desk, one half slouched against it. Behind them, on the wall, the A.L.F. symbol; a clenched black fist superimposed over the peace sign. The reporter held a microphone. The man he was with was tall, black, youthful. And angry.

"Yes, Ted, we've got you," the reporter said. He turned to the black man. "Doug, you were the A.L.F. presidential candidate in 1984. How do you react to President Hartmann's charges?"

Brown laughed lightly. "Nothing that man does surprises me any more. The charges are vicious lies. The American Liberation Front has nothing to do with this so-called attack. In fact, I doubt that this attack ever took place. Hartmann is a dangerous demagogue, and he's tried this sort of smear before."

"Then the A.L.F. claims that no attack took place?" Petersen asked.

Brown frowned. "Well, that's just a quick guess on my part, not an official A.L.F. position," he said quickly. "This has all been very sudden, and I don't really have the facts. But I'd say that was a possibility. As you know, Mike, the Liberty Alliance has made wild charges against us before."

"In his statement tonight, President Hartmann said he would

deal with the A.L.F. as traitors. Would you care to comment on that?"

"Yeah," said Brown. "It's more cheap rhetoric. I say that Hartmann's the traitor. He's the one that has betrayed everything this country is supposed to stand for. *His* creation of the Special Suuies to keep the ghettos in line, *his* intervention in the South African War, *his* censorship legislation; there's your treason for you."

The reporter smiled. "Thank you, Doug. And now back to Ted Warren."

Warren reappeared. "For those of you who have flicked on late, a brief recap. Earlier this evening, an American air base in California was attacked, and two bombers and seven fighter planes were seized. The bombers were equipped with nuclear weaponry, and the attackers have threatened to destroy Washington, D.C., unless certain demands are met within three hours. Only an hour-and-a-half now remain. Continental News will stay on the air until the conclusion of the crisis . . ."

Somewhere over western Illinois, Reynolds climbed towards ten, and sweated, and tried to tell himself that the advantages were all his.

The Rapiers were good planes. Nothing with wings was any faster, or more maneuverable. But the Vampyres had all the other plusses. Their missiles were more sophisticated, their defensive scramblers better. And they had their Vampyre fangs: twin gas-dynamic lasers mounted on either wing that could slice through steel like it was jello. The Rapiers had nothing to match that. The Vampyres were the first operational Laser/Fighters.

Besides, there were nine Vampyres and only seven Rapiers. And the Alfies weren't as familiar with their planes. They couldn't be.

So the odds were all with Reynolds. But he still sweated.

The arms of the V formation slowly straightened, as Reynolds and the other wingmen accelerated to come even with Bonetto's lead jet. In the radarmap, the Rapiers were already on top of them. And even through the eyeslit he could see them now, diving out of the black, their silver-white sides bright against the sky. The computer tracking system was locked in, the warheads armed. But still no signal from Bonetto.

And then, "Now." Sharp and clear.

Reynolds hit the firing stud, and missiles one and eight shot from beneath the wings, and etched a trail of flame up into the night. Parallel to his, others. Dutton, on his wing, had fired four. Eager for the kill.

Red/orange against black through the eyeslit. Black on red in the infrared scope. But all the same, really. The climbing streaks of flame that were the Vampyre missiles intersecting with a descending set. Crisscrossing briefly.

Then explosion. The Alfies had rigged one of theirs for timed detonation. A small orange fireball bloomed briefly. When it vanished, both sets of missiles were gone, save for one battered survivor from the Vampyre barrage that wobbled upward without hitting anything.

Reynolds glanced down. The radarmap was having an epileptic fit. The Alfies were using their scramblers.

"Split," said Bonetto, voice crackling. "Scatter and hit them."

The Vampyres broke formation. Reynolds and Dutton pulled up and to the left, McKinnis dove. Bonetto and most of his wing swung away to the right. And Trainor climbed straight on, at the diving Rapiers.

Reynolds watched him from the corner of his eye. Two more missiles jumped from Trainor's wings, then two more, then the final two. And briefly, the laser seared a path up from his wingtips. A futile gesture; he was still out of range.

The Rapiers were sleek silver birds of prey, spitting missiles. And suddenly, another fireball, and one of them stopped spitting.

But no time for cheering. Even as the Rapier went up, Trainor's Vampyre tried to swerve from the hail of Alfie missiles. His radar scrambler and heat decoys had confused them. But not enough. Reynolds was facing away from the explosion, but he felt the impact of the shock, and he could see the nightblack plane twisting and shattering in his mind.

Reynolds felt a vague pang, and tried to remember what Trainor had looked like. But there was no time. He twisted the Vampyre around in a sharp loop. Dutton flew parallel. They dove back towards the fight.

Far below a new cloud of flame blossomed. McKinnis, Reynolds thought, fleetingly, bitterly. He dove. The Alfies got on his tail. The goddamn Alfies.

But there was no way to be sure, no leisure to consider the question. Even a brief glance out the eyeslit was a luxury; a dangerous luxury. The infrared scope, the radarmap, the computer tracking systems all screamed for his attention.

Below him, two Alfies were swinging around. The computer locked on. His fingers moved as if by instinct. Missiles two and seven leapt from their launchers, towards the Rapiers.

A scream sounded briefly from his radio, mingled with the static and the sudden shrill cry of the proximity alarms. Something had locked on him. He activated the lasers. The computer found the incoming missile, tracked it, burned it from the sky when it got within range. Reynolds had never even seen it. He wondered how close it had come.

A flood of bright orange light washed through the eyeslit as a Rapier went up in flame in front of him. His missile? Dutton's? He never knew. It was all he could do to pull the Vampyre up sharply, and avoid the expanding ball of fire.

There were a few seconds of peace. He was above the fight, and he took time for a quick glance at the infrared. A tangle of confused black dots on a red field. But two were higher than the rest. Dutton; with an Alfie on his tail.

Reynolds swung his Vampyre down again, came in above and behind the Rapier just as it was discharging its missiles. He was close. No need to waste the four missiles he had left. His hand went to the lasers, fired.

Converging beams of light lanced from the black wingtips, to bite into the Rapier's silver fuselage on either side of the cockpit. The Alfie pilot dove for escape. But the Vampyre minicomputer held the lasers steady.

The Rapier exploded.

Almost simultaneously there was another explosion; the Alfie missiles, touched off by Dutton's lasers. Reynolds' radio came alive with Dutton's laughter, and breathless thanks.

But Reynolds was paying more attention to the infrared and the radarmap. The radar was clear again.

Only three blips showed below him.

It was over.

Bonetto's voice split the cabin again. "Got him," he was yelling. "Got them all. Who's left up there?"

Dutton replied quickly. Then Reynolds. The fourth surviving Vampyre was Ranczyk, Bonetto's wingman. The others were gone.

There was a new pang, sharper than during the battle. It had been McKinnis after all, Reynolds thought. He'd known McKinnis. Tall, with red hair, a lousy poker player who surrendered his money gracefully when he lost. He always did. His wife made

good chili. They'd voted Old Democrat, like Reynolds. Damr
damn, damn.

"We're only halfway there," Bonetto was saying. "The LB-4
are still ahead. Picked up some distance. So let's go."

Four Vampyres weren't nearly as impressive in formation a
nine. But they climbed. And gave chase.

Ted Warren looked tired. He had taken off his jacket and loosene
the formal black scarf knotted around his neck, and his hair wa
mussed. But still he went on.

"Reports have been coming in from all over the nation on th
sighting of the pirate planes," he said. "Most of them are clearl
misidentifications, but no word has yet come from the adminis
tration on the hunt for the stolen jets, so the rumors continue t
flow unabated. Meanwhile, barely an hour remains before th
threatened nuclear demolition of Washington."

Behind him a screen woke to sudden churning life. Pennsylva
nia Avenue, with the Capitol outlined in the distance, was choke
with cars and people. "Washington itself is in a state of panic,
Warren commented. "The populace of the city has taken to th
streets en masse in an effort to escape, but the resulting traffi
jams have effectively strangled all the major arteries. Many hav
abandoned their cars and are trying to leave the city on foot
Helicopters of the Special Urban Units have been attempting t
quell the disturbances, ordering the citizens to return to thei
homes. And President Hartmann himself has announced that h
intends to set an example for the people of the city, and remain i
the White House for the duration of the crisis."

The Washington scenes faded. Warren looked off-camera briefly
"I've just been told that Chicago correspondent Ward Emery i
standing by with Mitchell Grinstein, the chairman of the A.L.F.'
Community Defense Militia. So now to Chicago."

Grinstein was standing outdoors, on the steps of a gray
fortress-like building. He was tall and broad, with long black hai
worn in a ponytail and a drooping Fu Manchu mustache. Hi
clothes were a baggy black uniform, a black beret, and an A.L.F
medallion on a length of rawhide. Two other men, similarly
garbed, lounged behind him on the steps. Both carried rifles.

"I'm here with Mitchell Grinstein, whose organization has bee
accused of participating in this evening's attack on a California ai
base, and the hijacking of two nuclear bombers," Emery said
"Mitch, your reactions?"

Grinstein flashed a vaguely sinister smile. "Well, I only know what I see on the holo. I didn't order any attack. But I applaud whoever did. If this speeds up the implementation of the Six Demands, I'm all for it!"

"Douglass Brown has called the charges of A.L.F. participation in this attack 'vicious lies,'" Emery continued. "He questions whether any attack ever took place. How does this square with what you just said?"

Grinstein shrugged. "Maybe Brown knows more than I do. We didn't order this attack, like I said. But it could be that some of our men finally got fed up with Hartmann's fourth-rate fascism, and decided to take things into their own hands. If so, we're behind them."

"Then you think there *was* an attack?"

"I guess so. Hartmann has pictures. Even he wouldn't have the gall to fake *that*."

"And you support the attack?"

"Yeah. The Community Defenders have been saying for a long time that black people and poor people aren't going to get justice anywhere but in the streets. This is a vindication of what we've been calling for all along."

"And what about the position of the A.L.F.'s political arm?"

Another shrug. "Doug Brown and I agree on where we're going. We don't see eye to eye on how to get there."

"But isn't the Community Defense Militia subordinate to the A.L.F. political apparatus, and thus to Brown?"

"On paper. It's different in the streets. Are the Liberty Troopers subordinate to President Hartmann when they go out on freak-hunts and black busting expeditions? They don't act like it. The Community Defenders are committed to the protection of the community. From thugs, Liberty Troopers, and Hartmann's Special Suuies. And anyone else who comes along. We're also committed to getting the Six Demands. And maybe we'd go a bit further to realize those demands than Doug and his men."

"One last question," said Emery. "President Hartmann, in his speech tonight, said that he intended to treat the A.L.F. like traitors."

"Let him try," Grinstein said, smiling. "Just let him try."

The Alfie bombers had edged onto the radarmap again. They were still at 100,000 feet, doing about Mach 1.7. The Vampyre pack would be on them in minutes.

Reynolds watched for LB-4s, almost numbly, through his eyeslit. He was cold and drenched with his own sweat. And very scared.

The lull between battles was worse than the battles themselves, he had decided. It gave you too much time to think. And thinking was bad.

He was sad and a little sick about McKinnis. But grateful. Grateful that it hadn't been him. Then he realized that it still might be. The night wasn't over. The LB-4s were no pushovers.

And all so needless. The Alfies were vicious fools. There were other ways, better ways. They didn't have to do this. Whatever sympathy he had ever felt for the A.L.F. had gone down in flames with McKinnis and Trainor and the others.

They deserved whatever they had coming to them. And Hartmann, he was sure, had something in mind. So many innocent people dead. And for nothing. For a grandstand, desperado stunt without a prayer of success.

That was the worst part. The plan was so ill-conceived, so hopeless. The A.L.F. couldn't possibly win. They could shoot him down, sure. Like McKinnis. But there were other planes. They'd be found and taken out by someone. And if they got as far as Washington, there was still the city's ring of defensive missiles to deal with. Hartmann had had trouble forcing that through Congress. But it would come in handy now.

And even if the A.L.F. got there, so what? Did they really think Hartmann would give in? No way. Not him. He'd call their bluff, and either way they lost. If they backed down, they were finished. And if they dropped the bomb, they'd get Hartmann—but at the expense of millions of their own supporters. Washington was nearly all black. Hell, it gave the A.L.F. a big plurality in '84. What was the figure? Something like 65%, he thought. Around there, anyway.

It didn't make sense. It couldn't be. But it was.

There was a knot in his stomach. Churning and twisting. Through the eyeslit, he saw flickers of motion against the star field. The Alfies. The goddamn Alfies. His mind turned briefly to Anne. And suddenly he hated the planes ahead of him, and the man who flew them.

"Hold your missiles till my order," Bonetto said. "And watch it."

The Vampyres accelerated. But the Alfies acted before the attack.

"Hey, look!" That was Dutton.

"They're splitting." A bass growl distorted by static; Ranczyk.

Reynolds looked at his radarmap. One of the LB-4s was diving sharply, picking up speed, heading for the sea of clouds that rolled below in the starlight. The other was going into a shallow climb.

"Stay together!" Bonetto again. "They want us to break up. But we're faster. We'll take out one and catch the other."

They climbed. Together at first, side by side. But then one of the sleek planes began to edge ahead.

"Dutton!" Bonetto's voice was a warning.

"I want him." Dutton's Vampyre screamed upward, into range of the bandit ahead. From his wings, twin missiles roared, closed.

And suddenly were not. The bomber's lasers burned them clean from the sky.

Bonetto tried to shout another order. But it was too late. Dutton was paying no attention. He was already shrieking to his kill.

This time Reynolds saw it all.

Dutton was way out ahead of the others, still accelerating, trying to close within laser range. He was out of missiles.

But the Alfie laser had a longer range. It locked on him first.

The Vampyre seemed to writhe. Dutton went into a sharp dive, pulled up equally sharply, threw his plane from side to side. Trying to shake free of the laser. Before it killed. But the tracking computers in the LB-4s were faster than he could ever hope to be. The laser held steady.

And then Dutton stopped fighting. Briefly, his Vampyre closed again, climbing right up into the spear of light, its own lasers flashing out and converging. Uselessly; he was still too far away. And only for an instant.

Before the scream.

Dutton's Vampyre never even exploded. It just seemed to go limp. Its laser died suddenly. And then it was in a spin. Flames licking at the black fuselage, burning a hole in the black velvet of night.

Reynolds didn't watch the fall. Bonetto's voice had snapped him from his nightmare trance. "Fire!"

He let go on three and six, and they shrieked away from him towards the Alfie. Bonetto and Ranczyk had also fired. Six missiles rose together. Two more slightly behind them. Ranczyk had let loose with a second volley.

"At him!" Bonetto shouted. "Lasers!"

Then his plane was moving away quickly, Ranczyk with him.

Black shadows against a black sky, following their missiles an
obscuring the stars. Reynolds hung back briefly, still scared, sti
hearing Dutton's scream and seeing the fireball that was McKir
nis. Then, shamed, he followed.

The bomber had unleashed its own missiles, and its lasers wei
locked onto the oncoming threats. There was an explosion; sever;
missiles wiped from the air. Others burned down.

But there were two Vampyres moving in behind the missile:
And then a third behind them. Bonetto and Ranczyk had thei
lasers locked on the Alfie, burning at him, growing hotter an
more vicious as they climbed. Briefly, the bomber's big lase
flicked down in reply. One of the Vampyres went up in a cloud c
flame, a cloud that still screamed upwards at the Alfie.

Almost simultaneously, another roar. A fireball under the win
of the bomber, rocked it. Its laser winked off. Power trouble
Then on again, burning at the hail of missiles. Reynolds flicked o
his laser, and watched it lance out towards the chaos above. Th
other Vampyre—Reynolds wasn't sure which—was firing it
remaining missiles.

They were almost on top of each other. In the radarmap and th
infrared they were. Only in the eyeslit was there still spac
between the two.

And then they were together. Joining. One big ball, orange an
red and yellow, swallowing both Vampyre and prey, growing
growing, growing.

Reynolds sat almost frozen, climbing towards the swellin
inferno, his laser firing ineffectively into the flames. Then h
came out of it. And swerved. And dove. His laser fired onc
more, to wipe out a chunk of flaming debris that came spinnin
towards him.

He was alone. The fire fell and faded, and there was only on
Vampyre, and the stars, and the blanket of cloud far below him
He had survived.

But how? He had hung back. When he should have attacked
He didn't deserve survival. The others had earned it, with thei
courage. But he had hung back. He felt sick.

But he could still redeem himself. Yes. Down below, there wa
still one Alfie in the air. Headed towards Washington with it
bombs. And only he was left to stop it.

Reynolds nosed the Vampyre into a dive, and began his grin
descent.

• • •

After a brief station identification, Warren was back. With two guests and a new wrinkle. The wrinkle was the image of a large clock that silently counted down the time remaining while the newsmen talked. The guests were a retired Air Force general and a well-known political columnist.

Warren introduced them, then turned to the general. "Tonight's attack, understandably, has frightened a lot of people," he began. "Especially those in Washington. How likely is it that the threatened bombing will take place?"

The general snorted. "Impossible, Ted. I know what kind of air defense systems we've got in this country. They were designed to handle a full-fledged attack, from another nuclear power. They can certainly handle a cheap-shot move like this."

"Then you'd say that Washington is in no danger?"

"Correct. Absolutely none. This plan was militarily hopeless from its conception. I'm shocked that even the A.L.F. would resort to such a foredoomed venture."

Warren nodded, and swiveled to face the columnist. "How about from a political point of view? You've been a regular observer of President Hartmann and the Washington scene for many years, Sid. In your opinion, did this maneuver have any chances of practical political success?"

"It's still very early," the columnist cautioned. "But from where I sit, I'd say the A.L.F. has committed a major blunder. This attack is a political disaster—or at least it looks like one, in these early hours. Because of Washington's large black population, I'd guess that this threat to the city will seriously undermine the A.L.F.'s support among the black community. If so, it would be a catastrophe for the party. In 1984, Douglass Brown drew more black votes than the other three candidates combined. Without these votes, the A.L.F. presidential campaign would have been a farce."

"How will this affect other A.L.F. supporters?" Warren asked.

"That's a key question. I'd say it would tend to drive them away from the party. Since its inception, the A.L.F. has always had a large pacifist element, which frequently clashed with the more militant Alfies who made up the Community Defense Militia. I think that tonight's events might be the final blow for these people."

"Who do you think would benefit from these desertions?"

The columnist shrugged. "Hard to say. There's the possibility

of a new splinter party being formed. And President Hartmann,
I'm sure, will enjoy a large swing of support his way. The most
likely possibility would be a revival of the Old Democratic Party,
if it can regain the black voters and white radicals it has lost to the
A.L.F. in recent years."

"Thank you," said Warren. He turned back to the camera, then
glanced down briefly at the desk in front of him, checking the
latest bulletins. "We'll have more analysis later," he said. "Right
now, Continental's man in California is at Collins Air Base, where
tonight's attack took place."

Warren faded. The new reporter was tall and thin and young.
He was standing before the main gate of the air base. Behind him
was a bustling tangle of activity, several jeeps, and large numbers
of police and soldiers. The spotlights were on again, and the
destruction was clearly evident in the battered gatehouse and the
twisted, shattered wire of the fence itself.

"Deke Hamilton here," the man began. "Ted, Continental
came out here to check whether any attack did take place, since
the A.L.F. has charged that the President was lying. Well, from
what I've seen out here, it's the A.L.F. that's been lying. There
was an attack, and it was a vicious one. You can see some of the
damage behind you. This is where the attackers struck hardest."

Warren's voice cut in. "Have you seen any bodies?"

The reporter nodded. "Yes. Many of them. Some have been
horribly mangled by the fighting. More than one hundred men
from the base, I'd estimate. And about fifty Alfies."

"Have any of the attackers been identified?" Warren asked.

"Well, they're clearly Alfies," the reporter said. "Beards, long
hair, A.L.F. uniforms. And many had literature in their pockets.
Pamphlets advocating the Six Demands, that sort of thing.
However, as of yet, no specific identifications have been
announced. Except for the airmen, of course. The base has
released its own casualty lists. But not for the Alfies. As I said,
many bodies are badly damaged, so identification may be difficult. I think some sort of mass burial is being planned."

"Deke," said Warren, "has there been any racial breakdown on
the casualties?"

"Uh—none has been released. The bodies I saw were all white.
But then, the black population in this area is relatively small."

Warren started to ask another question. He never finished his
sentence. Without warning, the picture from California suddenly
vanished, and was replaced by chaos.

"This is Mike Petersen in Washington," the reporter said. He was awash in a sea of struggling humanity, being pushed this way and that. All around him fights were in progress, as a squad of Special Urban Police, in blue and silver, waded through a crowd of resisting Alfies. The A.L.F. symbol was on the wall behind Petersen.

"I'm at A.L.F. national headquarters," he said, trying valiantly to stay before the cameras. "I—" he was shoved to one side, fought back. "We've got quite a scene here. Just a few minutes ago, a detachment of Special Urban Police broke into the building, and arrested several of the A.L.F.'s national leaders, including Douglass Brown. Some of the other people here tried to stop them, and the police are now trying to make more arrests. There's been—damn!" Someone had spun into him. The cops were using clubs.

Petersen was trying to untangle himself from the battle. He looked up briefly and started to say something. Then something hit the camera, and suddenly he was gone.

Reynolds was very much conscious of being alone. He was at 60,000 feet and dropping rapidly, ripping through layer on layer of wispy cloud. In an empty sky. The Alfie was somewhere below him, but he couldn't see it yet.

He knew it was there, though. His radarmap was acting up. That meant a scrambler nearby.

His eyes roamed, his thoughts wandered. It was one-on-one now. There might be help. Bonetto had radioed down when they first sighted the bandits. Maybe someone had tracked them. Maybe another flight was on its way to intercept the bomber.

And then again, maybe not.

Their course had been erratic. They were over Kentucky now. And they'd been up high, with scramblers going to confuse radar. Maybe their position wasn't known.

He could radio down. Yes. He should do that. But no, come to think of it. That would alert the Alfie. Maybe they didn't know he was behind them. Maybe he could take them by surprise.

He hoped so. Otherwise he was worried. There were only two missiles left. And Reynolds wasn't all that sure that a Vampyre could take on an LB-4 one-on-one.

Loose facts rolled back and forth in his mind. The lasers. The bomber had a big power source. Its laser had a range nearly twice that of the smaller model on the Vampyre. With a bigger computer to keep it on target.

What did he have? Speed. Yes. And maneuverability. And maybe he was a better pilot, too.

Or was he? Reynolds frowned. Come to think of it, the Alfies had pretty much held their own up to now. Strange. You wouldn't think they'd be so good. Especially when they made elementary mistakes like forgetting to throw in their scramblers.

But they had been. They flew almost like veterans. Maybe they were veterans. Hartmann had discharged a lot of A.L.F. sympathizers from the armed forces right after his election. Maybe some of them had gone all the way and actually joined the Alfies. And were coming back for revenge.

But that was three years ago. And the LB-4s were new. It shouldn't have been all that easy for the Alfies to master them.

Reynolds shook his head and shoved the whole train of thought to one side. It wasn't worth pursuing. However it had happened, the fact was the Alfies were damn good pilots. And any advantage he had there was negligible.

He looked at his instruments. Still diving at 40,000 feet. The LB-4 still below him somewhere, but closer. The radarmap was a useless dancing fuzz now. But there was an image on the infrared scope.

Through the eyeslit, he could see lightning flashes far below. A thunderstorm. And the bomber was diving through it. And slowing, according to his instruments. Probably going to treetop level.

He'd catch it soon.

And what then?

There were two missiles left. He could close and fire them. But the Alfie had its own missiles, and its laser net. What if his missiles didn't get through?

Then he'd have to go in with his own lasers.

And die. Like Dutton.

He tried to swallow, but the saliva caught in his throat. The damn Alfie had such a big power source. They'd be slicing him into ribbons long before he got close enough for his smaller weapon to be effective.

Oh, sure, he might take them, too. It took even a big gas dynamic laser a few seconds to burn through steel. And in those few seconds he'd be close enough to return the attentions.

But that didn't help. He'd die, with them.

And he didn't want to die.

He thought of Anne again. Then of McKinnis.

The Alfies would never reach Washington, he thought. Another flight of hunters would sight the LB-4, and catch it. Or the city's ABMS would knock it out. But they'd never get through.

There was no reason for him to die to stop the bomber. No reason at all. He should pull up, radio ahead, land and sound the alarm.

Thick, dark clouds rolled around the plane, swallowed it. Lightning hammered at the nightblack wings, and shook the silver missiles in their slots.

And Reynolds sweated. And the Vampyre continued to dive.

"The question of what President Hartmann meant when he promised to treat the A.L.F. like traitors has been resolved," Ted Warren said, looking straight out of millions of holocubes, his face drawn and unreadable. "Within the last few minutes, we've had dozens of reports. All over the nation, the Special Urban Units are raiding A.L.F. headquarters and the homes of party leaders. In a few cities, including Detroit, Boston, and Washington itself, mass arrests of A.L.F. members are reported to be in progress. But for the most part, the S.U.U. seems to be concentrating on those in positions of authority with the Community Defense Militia or the party itself.

"Meanwhile, the Pentagon reports that the bandit planes that the A.L.F. is accused of taking have been tracked over Kentucky, heading towards Washington. According to informed Air Force sources, only one of the hijacked bombers is still in the air, and it is being pursued by a interceptor. Other flights are now being rushed to the scene."

Warren looked outcube briefly, scowled at someone unseen, and turned back. "We have just been informed that the White House is standing by with a statement. I give you now the President of the United States."

The image changed. Again the Oval Office. This time Hartmann was standing, and he was not alone. Vice-President Joseph Delaney, balding and middle-aged, stood next to him, before a row of American flags.

"My fellow patriots," Hartmann began, "I come before you again to announce that the government is taking steps against the traitors who have threatened the very capital of this great nation. After consulting with Vice-President Delaney and my Cabinet, I have ordered the arrest of the leaders of the so-called American Liberation Front."

Hartmann's dark eyes were burning, and his voice had a marvelous, fatherly firmness. Delaney, beside him, looked pale and frightened and uncertain.

"To those of you who have supported these men in the past, let me say now that they will receive every safeguard of a fair trial, in the American tradition," Hartmann continued. "As for yourselves, your support of the so-called A.L.F. was well-intentioned, no matter how misguided. No harm will come to you. However, your leaders have tonight betrayed your trust, and your nation. They have forfeited your support. To aid them now would be to join in their treason.

"I say this especially to our black citizens, who have been so cruelly misled by A.L.F. sloganeering. Now is the time to demonstrate your patriotism, to make up for past mistakes. And to those who would persist in their error, I issue this warning; those who aid the traitors in resisting lawful authority will be treated as traitors themselves."

Hartmann paused briefly, then continued. "Some will question this move. With a legitimate concern for the American system of checks and balances, they will argue that I had no authority for deploying the Special Urban Units as I have done. They are right. But special situations call for special remedies, and in this night of crisis, there was no time to secure Congressional approval. However, I did not act unilaterally." He looked towards Delaney.

The Vice-President cleared his throat. "President Hartmann consulted me on this matter earlier tonight," he began, in a halting voice. "I expressed some reluctance, at first, to approve his proposed course of action. But, after the President had presented me with all the facts, I could see that there was no realistic alternative. Speaking for myself, and for those Cabinet members who like me represent the Republican Party, I concur with the President's actions."

Hartmann began to speak again, but the voice suddenly faded on the holocast, and a short second later, the image also vanished. Ted Warren returned to the air.

"We will bring you the rest of the President's statement later," the anchorman said, "after several special bulletins. We have just been informed that all 32 A.L.F. members of the House of Representatives have been placed under arrest, as well as two of the three A.L.F. Senators. S.U.U. national headquarters reports that Senator Jackson Edwards is still at large, and is currently being sought after."

Warren shuffled some papers. "We also have reports of scattered street-fighting in several cities between the S.U.U. and the Community Defenders. The fighting appears to be most intense in Chicago, where Special Urban forces have surrounded the national center of the A.L.F.'s paramilitary wing. We take you now to Ward Eméry, on the scene."

The image shifted. Emery was standing on the steps of the new Chicago Police Headquarters on South State Street. Every light in the building behind him burned brightly, and a steady stream of riot-equipped police was hurrying up and down the stairs.

"Not quite on the scene, Ted," he began. "Our crew was forcibly excluded from the area where the fighting is now in progress. We're here at Chicago Police Headquarters now, which you will recall was the focus of the battle during the 1985 riots. The local police and the Special Urban Units are doing their planning and coordinating from here."

Warren cut in with a voice-over. "What precisely has taken place?"

"Well," said Emery, "it started when a detachment of Special Urban Police arrived at Community Defender Central, as it's called, to arrest Mitchell Grinstein and several other organization leaders. I'm not sure who opened fire. But someone did, and there were several casualties. The Community Defenders have their headquarters heavily guarded, and they drove back the S.U.U. in the early skirmish that I witnessed. But things have changed since then. Although the local police have cordoned off a large portion of Chicago's South Side and excluded me and other reporters, I now understand that Grinstein and his Militiamen are holed up inside their building, which is under S.U.U. siege."

He looked around briefly. "As you can see, there's a lot of activity around here," he continued. "The local police are on overtime, and the Special Urban Units have mobilized their entire Chicago battalion. They're using their regular armored cars, plus some heavier weapons. And I've also heard reports that something new has been deployed by the S.U.U.—a light tank with street tires instead of treads, designed for city use."

"Are all the A.L.F. forces concentrated around Grinstein's headquarters?" Warren asked.

Emery shook his head. "No, not at all. The ghettos on the South and West sides are alive with activity. The local police have suffered several casualties, and there's been one case of a squad car being Molotov-cocktailed. Also, there are rumors of an impending A.L.F. counterattack on Police Headquarters. The building is symbolic to both sides, of course, since the renegade local Militiamen seized and razed the earlier building on this site during the 1985 fighting."

"I see," said Warren. "The A.L.F. is known to have active chapters on several college campuses in your area. Have you gotten any reports from them?"

"Some," Emery replied. "The police have been ignoring the campus chapters up to now, but we understand that a strong force of Liberty Troopers moved in on the University of Illinois' Chicago campus in an attempt to make citizens' arrests. Some fighting was reported, but resistance was only light. The students were mostly without arms while the Liberty Troopers, of course, are a paramilitary force."

"Thank you, Ward," Warren said, as the image suddenly shifted. "We'll be back to you later for an update. Now, we will continue with the rest of President Hartmann's most recent statement.

"For those who just flicked on, the President has just ordered the arrest of the A.L.F. leaders. This move was made with the support of the Vice-President, and thus presumably with the support of the Old Republicans, the President's partners in his coalition government. It's an important shift on the part of the Old Republicans. Last year, you will recall, Hartmann's efforts to pass his Subversive Registration Bill were thwarted when Vice-President Delaney and his followers refused to back the measure.

"Since the Liberty Alliance and the Old Republicans, between them, command a majority in both houses of Congress, Delaney's support of Hartmann guarantees Congressional approval of the President's actions tonight.

"And now, the rest of the presidential message . . ."

There were hills below, and dark forests in a shroud of night. And the only light was the sudden jagged brilliance of the lightning. But there were two thunders.

One was the thunder of the storm that churned above the forest. The other was the thunder of the jet, screaming between the stormclouds and the trees and laying down a trail of sonic booms across the landscape.

That was the Alfie. Reynolds watched it in his infrared scope, watched it play at Mach 1, slip back and forth over the barrier. And while he watched he gained on it.

He had stopped sweating, stopped thinking, stopped fearing. Now he only acted. Now he was part of the Vampyre.

He descended through the stormclouds, blind but for his instruments, lashed by the lightning. Everything that was human in him told him to pull up and let something else take the Alfie. But something else, some drive, some compulsion, told him that he must not hang back again.

So he descended.

The Alfie knew he was there. That was inevitable. It was simply holding its fire. As he was holding his missiles. He would save them until the last second, until the Alfie lasers were locked on him.

The Vampyre moved at half again the bomber's speed. Ripped through the last bank of clouds. Framed by the lightning. Fired its lasers.

The beams cut the night, touched the bomber, converged. Too far away. Hardly hot. But warming, warming. Every microsecond brought the sleek black interceptor closer, and the wand of light grew deadlier.

And then the other beam jumped upward from the bomber's tail. Swords of light crossed in the night. And the shrieking Vampyre impaled itself upon the glowing stake.

Reynolds was watching his infrared when it died. The mere touch of the enemy laser had been too much for the system's delicate opticals. But he didn't need it, now. He could see the bomber, ahead and below, outlined in the flashes.

There were alarms ringing, clamoring, slamming at his ears. He ignored them. It was too late now. Too late to pull away and up. Too late to shake the lasers.

Now there was only time to find a victim.

Reynolds' eyes were fixed on the bomber, and it grew larger by the microsecond. His hand was on the missile stud, waiting, waiting. The warheads were armed. The computers were locked, tracking.

The Alfie loomed large and larger in the eyeslit. And he saw its laser slicing through the dark. And around him, he could feel the Vampyre shake and shudder.

And he fired.

Four and five were flaming arrows in the night, climbing down at the Alfie. It seemed, almost, like they were sliding down the laser path that the Vampyre had burned.

Reynolds, briefly, saw his plane as the others must have seen it. Black and ominous, howling from the stormclouds down at them, lasers afire, draped in lightning, spitting missiles. Exhilaration! Glorydeath! He held the vision tightly.

The Alfie laser was off him, suddenly. Too late. The alarms still rang. His control was gone.

The Vampyre was burning, crippled. But from the flames the laser still licked out.

The bomber burned one missile from the sky. But the other was climbing up a jet. And the Vampyre's fangs now had a bite to them.

And then the night itself took flame.

Reynolds saw the fireball spread over the forest, and something like relief washed over him, and he shuddered. And then the sweat came back, in a rushing flood.

He watched the woods come up at him, and he thought briefly of ejecting. But he was too low and too fast and it was hopeless. He tried to capture his vision again. And he wondered if he'd get a medal.

But the vision was elusive, and the medal didn't seem to matter now.

Suddenly all he could think about was Anne. And his cheeks were wet. And it wasn't sweat.

He screamed.

And the Vampyre hit the trees at Mach 1.4.

There were circles under Warren's eyes, and an ache in his voice. But he continued to read.

". . . in Newark, New Jersey, local police are engaged in pitched street battles with the Special Urban Units. City officials in Newark, elected by the A.L.F., mobilized the police when the S.U.U. attempted to arrest them . . .

". . . latest announcement from S.U.U. headquarters says that Douglass Brown and six other leading A.L.F. figures died while attempting to escape from confinement. The attempted escape came during a surprise attack by Community Defense Militiamen on the jail where Brown and the others were imprisoned, the release says . . .

". . . both the Community Defense Militia and the Liberty Troopers have been mobilized from coast-to-coast by their leaders, and have taken to the streets. The Liberty Troopers are assisting the Special Urban Units in their campaign against the Community Defenders . . .

". . . President Hartmann has called out the National Guard . . .

". . . riots and looting reported in New York, Washington, Detroit, and numerous smaller cities . . .

". . . in Chicago is a smoldering ruin. Mitchell Grinstein is reported dead, as well as other top A.L.F. leaders. A firebombing has destroyed a wing of the new Police Headquarters . . . Loop reported in flames . . . bands of armed men moving from the ghetto sections into the Near North . . .

". . . Community Defenders in California charge that they had nothing to do with original attack . . . have demanded that the bodies be produced and identified . . . mass burial, already ordered . . .

". . . bombing of Governor's mansion in Sacramento . . .

". . . Liberty Alliance has called all citizens to take up arms, and wipe out the A.L.F. . . . that an attempted revolution is in progress . . . this was the plan all along, Alliance charges . . . California attack a signal . . .

". . . A.L.F. charges that California attack was Hartmann ploy . . . cites Reichstag fire . . .

". . . . Governor Horne of Michigan has been assassinated . . .

". . . national curfew imposed by S.U.U. . . . has called on all citizens to return to their homes . . . still out in one hour will be shot on sight . . .

". . . A.L.F. reports that Senator Jackson Edwards of New Jersey was dragged from his police sanctuary in Newark and shot by Liberty Troopers . . .

". . . martial law declared . . .

". . . reports that last bandit plane has been shot down . . .

". . . Army has been mobilized . . .

". . . Hartmann has declared death penalty for any who aid so-called revolutionaries . . .

". . . alleges . . .

". . . charges . . .

". . . reports . . ."

In Kentucky, a forest was burning. But no one came to put it out. There were bigger fires elsewhere.

IN THE WIND

Glen Cook

I

It's quiet up there, riding the ups and downs over Ginnunga Gap. Even in combat there's no slightest clamor, only a faint scratch and whoosh of strikers tapping igniters and rockets smoking away. The rest of the time, just a sleepy whisper of air caressing your canopy. On patrol it's hard to stay alert and wary.

If the aurora hadn't been so wild behind the hunched backs of the Harridans, painting glaciers and snowfields in ropes of varicolored fire, sequinning snow-catches in the weathered natural castles of the Gap with momentary reflections, I might have dozed at the stick the morning I became von Drachau's wingman. The windwhales were herding in the mountains, thinking migration, and we were flying five or six missions per day. The strain was almost unbearable.

But the auroral display kept me alert. It was the strongest I'd ever seen. A ferocious magnetic storm was developing. Lightning grumbled between the Harridans' copper peaks, sometimes even speared down and danced among the spires in the Gap. We'd all be grounded soon. The rising winds, cold but moisture-heavy, promised weather even whales couldn't ride.

Winter was about to break out of the north, furiously, a winter of a Great Migration. Planets, moons and sun were right, oracles and omens predicting imminent Armageddon. Twelve years had ticked into the ashcan of time. All the whale species again were herding. Soon the fighting would be hard and hopeless.

There are four species of windwhale on the planet Camelot, the most numerous being the Harkness whale, which migrates from its north arctic and north temperate feeding ranges to equatorial mating grounds every other year. Before beginning their migration they, as do all whales, form herds—which, because the beasts are total omnivores, utterly strip the earth in their passage south. The lesser species, in both size and numbers, are Okumura's First, which mates each three winters, Rosenberg's, mating every fourth, and the rare Okumura's Second, which travels only once every six years. Unfortunately . . .

It takes no mathematical genius to see the factors of twelve. And every twelve years the migrations do coincide. In the Great Migrations the massed whales leave tens of thousands of square kilometers of devastation in their wake, devastation from which, because of following lesser migrations, the routes barely recover before the next Great Migration. Erosion is phenomenal. The monsters, subject to no natural control other than that apparently exacted by creatures we called mantas, were destroying the continent on which our employers operated.

Ubichi Corporation had been on Camelot twenty-five years. The original exploitation force, though equipped to face the world's physical peculiarities, hadn't been prepared for whale migrations. They'd been lost to a man, whale supper, because the Corporation's pre-exploitation studies had been so cursory. Next Great Migration another team, though they'd dug in, hadn't fared much better. Ubichi still hadn't done its scientific investigation. In fact, its only action was a determination that the whales had to go.

Simple enough, viewed from a board room at Geneva. But practical implementation was a nightmare under Camelot's technically stifling conditions. And the mantas recomplicated everything.

My flight leader's wagging wings directed my attention south. From a hill a dozen kilometers down the cable came flashing light, Clonninger Station reporting safe arrival of a convoy from Derry. For the next few hours we'd have to be especially alert.

It would take the zeppelins that long to beat north against the wind, and all the while they would be vulnerable to mantas from over the Gap. Mantas, as far as we could see at the time, couldn't tell the difference between dirigibles and whales. More air cover should be coming up . . .

Von Drachau came to Jaeger Gruppe XIII (Corporation Armed Action Command's unsubtle title for our Hunter Wing, which they used as a dump for problem employees) with that convoy, reassigned from JG IV, a unit still engaged in an insane effort to annihilate the Sickle Islands whale herds by means of glider attacks carried out over forty-five kilometers of quiet seas. We'd all heard of him (most JG XIII personnel had come from the Sickle

Islands operation), the clumsiest, or luckiest incompetent, pilot flying for Ubichi. While scoring only four kills he'd been bolted down seven times—and had survived without a scratch. He was the son of Jupp von Drachau, the Confederation Navy officer who had directed the planet-busting strike against the Sangaree home-world, a brash, sometimes pompous, always self-important nine-teen year old who thought that the flame of his father's success should illuminate him equally—and yet resented even a mention of the man. He was a dilettante, come to Camelot only to fly. Unlike the rest of us, Old Earthers struggling to buy out of the poverty bequeathed us by prodigal ancestors, he had no driving need to give performance for pay.

An admonition immediately in order: I'm not here to praise von Drachau, but to bury him. To let him bury himself. Aerial combat fans, who have never seen Camelot, who have read only corporate propaganda, have made of him a contemporary "hero", a flying do-no-wrong competitor for the pewter crown already contested by such antiques as von Richtoffen, Hartmann and Galland. Yet these Archaicists can't, because they need one, make a platinum bar from a turd, nor a socio-psychological fulfillment from a scatterbrain kid . . . *

Most of the stories about him are apocryphal accretions generated to give him depth in his later, "heroic" aspect. Time and storytellers increase his stature, as they have that of Norse gods, who might've been people who lived in preliterate times. For those who knew him (and no one is closer than a wingman), though some of us might like to believe the legends, he was just a selfish, headstrong, tantrum-throwing manchild—albeit a fighter of supernatural ability. In the three months he spent with us, during the Great Migration, his peculiar talents and shortcom-ings made of him a creature larger than life. Unpleasant a person as he was, he became *the* phenom pilot.

*This paragraph is an editorial insertion from a private letter by Salvador del Gado. Dogfight believes it clarifies del Gado's personal feelings toward his former wingman. His tale, taken separately, while unsympathetic, strives for an objectivity free of his real jealousies. It is significant that he mentions Hartmann and Galland together with von Richtoffen; undoubtedly they, as he when compared with von Drachau, were flyers better than the Red Knight, yet they, and del Gado, lack the essential charisma of the flying immortals. Also, von Richtoffen and von Drachau died at the stick; Hartmann and Galland went on to more prosaic things, becoming administrators, commanders of the Luftwaffe. Indications are that del Gado's fate with Ubichi Corporation's Armed Action Command will be much the same.

—Dogfight

II

The signals from Clonninger came before dawn, while only two small moons and the aurora lighted the sky. But sunrise followed quickly. By the time the convoy neared Beadle Station (us), Camelot's erratic, blotchy-faced sun had cleared the eastern horizon. The reserve squadron began catapulting into the Gap's frenetic drafts. The four of us on close patrol descended toward the dirigibles.

The lightning in the Harridans had grown into a Ypres cannonade. A net of jagged blue laced together the tips of the copper towers in the Gap. An elephant stampede of angry clouds rumbled above the mountains. The winds approached the edge of being too vicious for flight.

Flashing light from ground control, searchlight fingers stabbing north and east, pulsating. Mantas sighted. We waggle-winged acknowledgment, turned for the Gap and updrafts. My eyes had been on the verge of rebellion, demanding sleep, but in the possibility of combat weariness temporarily faded.

Black specks were coming south low against the daytime verdigris of the Gap, a male-female pair in search of a whale. It was obvious how they'd been named. Anyone familiar with Old Earth's sea creatures could see a remarkable resemblance to the manta ray—though these had ten meter bodies, fifteen meter wingspans, and ten meter tails tipped by devil's spades of rudders. From a distance they appeared black, but at attack range could be seen as deep, uneven green on top and lighter, near olive beneath. They had ferocious habits.

More signals from the ground. Reserve ships would take the mantas. Again we turned, overflew the convoy.

It was the biggest ever sent north, fifteen dirigibles, one fifty meters and larger, dragging the line from Clonninger at half kilometer intervals, riding long reaches of running cable as their sailmen struggled to tack them into a facing wind. The tall glasteel pylons supporting the cable track were ruby towers linked by a single silver strand of spider silk running straight to Clonninger's hills.

We circled wide and slow at two thousand meters, gradually dropping lower. When we got down to five hundred we were replaced by a flight from the reserve squadron while we scooted to the Gap for an updraft. Below us ground crews pumped extra hydrogen to the barrage balloons, lifting Beadle's vast protective net another hundred meters so the convoy could slide beneath. Switchmen and winchmen hustled about with glass and plastic tools in a dance of confusion. We didn't have facilities for receiving more than a half dozen zeppelins—though these, fighting the wind, might come up slowly enough to be handled.

More signals. More manta activity over the Gap, the reserve squadron's squabble turning into a brawl. The rest of my squadron had come back from the Harridans at a run, a dozen mantas in pursuit. Later I learned our ships had found a small windwhale herd and while one flight busied their mantas the other had destroyed the whales. Then, ammunition gone, they ran for home, arriving just in time to complicate traffic problems.

I didn't get time to worry it. The mantas, incompletely fed, spotted the convoy. They don't distinguish between whale and balloon. They went for the zeppelins.

What followed becomes dulled in memory, so swiftly did it happen and so little attention did I have to spare. The air filled with mantas and lightning, gliders, smoking rockets, explosions. The brawl spread till every ship in the wing was involved. Armorers and catapult crews worked to exhaustion trying to keep everything up. Ground batteries seared one another with backblast keeping a rocket screen between the mantas and stalled convoy— which couldn't warp in while the entrance to the defense net was tied up by fighting craft (a problem unforeseen but later corrected by the addition of emergency entryways). They winched their running cables in to short stay and waited it out. Ground people managed to get barrage balloons with tangle tails out to make the mantas' flying difficult.

Several of the dirigibles fought back. Stupid, I thought. Their lifting gas was hydrogen, screamingly dangerous. To arm them seemed an exercise in self-destruction.

So it proved. Most of our casualties came when a ship loaded with ground troops blew up, leaking gas ignited by its own rockets. One hundred eighty-three men burned or fell to their deaths. Losses to mantas were six pilots and the twelve man crew of a freighter.

III

Von Drachau made his entry into JG XIII history just as I dropped from my sailship to the packed earth parking apron. His zepp was the first in and, having vented gas, had been towed to the apron to clear the docking winches. I'd done three sorties during the fighting, after the six of regular patrol. I'd seen my wingman crash into a dragline pylon, was exhausted, and possessed by an utterly foul mood. Von Drachau hit dirt long-haired, unkempt, and complaining, and I was there to greet him. "What do you want to be when you grow up, von Drachau?"

Not original, but it caught him off guard. He was used to criticism by administrators, but pilots avoid antagonism. One never knows when a past slight might mean hesitation at the trigger ring and failure to blow a manta off one's tail. Von Drachau's hatchet face opened and closed, goldfish-like, and one skeletal hand came up to an accusatory point, but he couldn't come back.

We'd had no real contact during the Sickle Islands campaign. Considering his self-involvement, I doubted he knew who I was—and didn't care if he did. I stepped past and greeted acquaintances from my old squadron, made promises to get together to reminisce, then retreated to barracks. If there were any justice at all, I'd get five or six hours for surviving the morning.

I managed four, a record for the week, then received a summons to the office of Commander McClennon, a retired Navy man exiled to command of JG XIII because he'd been so outspoken about Corporation policy.

(The policy that irked us all, and which was the root of countless difficulties, was Ubichi's secret purpose on Camelot. Ubichi deals in unique commodities. It was sure that Camelot operations were recovering one such, but fewer than a hundred of a half million employees knew what. The rest were there just to keep the windwhales from interfering. Even we mercenaries from Old Earth didn't like fighting for a total unknown.)

Commander McClennon's outer office was packed, old faces from the wing and new from the convoy. Shortly, McClennon appeared and announced that the wing had been assigned some gliders with new armaments, low velocity glass barrel gas pressure cannon, pod of four in the nose of a ship designed to carry the weapon system . . . immediate interest. Hitherto we'd flown sport gliders jury-rigged to carry crude rockets, the effectiveness of which lay in the cyanide shell surrounding the warhead. Reliability, poor; accuracy, erratic. A pilot was nearly as likely to kill himself as a whale.

But what could you do when you couldn't use the smallest scrap of metal? Even a silver filling could kill you there. The wildly oscillating and unpredictable magnetic ambience could induce sudden, violent electrical charges. The only metal risked inside Camelot's van Allens was that in the lighters running to and from the surface station at the south magnetic pole, where few lines of force were cut and magnetic weather was reasonably predictable.

Fifty thousand years ago the system passed through the warped space surrounding a black hole. Theory says that's the reason for its eccentricities, but I wonder. Maybe it explains why all bodies in the system have magnetic fields offset from the body centers, the distance off an apparent function of size, mass and rate of rotation, but it doesn't tell me why the fields exist (planetary magnetism is uncommon), nor why they pulsate randomly.

But I digress, and into areas where I have no competence. I should explain what physicists don't understand? We were in the Commander's office and he was selecting pilots for the new ships. Everyone wanted one. Chances for survival appeared that much better.

McClennon's assignments seemed indisputable, the best flyers to the new craft, four flights of four, though those left with old ships were disappointed.

I suffered disappointment myself. A blockbuster dropped at the end, after I'd resigned myself to continuing in an old craft.

"Von Drachau, Horst-Johann," said McClennon, peering at his roster through antique spectacles, one of his affectations, "attack pilot. Del Gado, Salvador Martin, wingman."

Me? With von Drachau? I'd thought the old man liked me, thought he had a good opinion of my ability . . . why'd he want to waste me? Von Drachau's wingman? Murder.

I was so stunned I could yell *let me out!*

"Familiarization begins this afternoon, on Strip Three. First flight checkouts in the morning." A few more words, tired exhortations to do our best, all that crap that's been poured on men at the front from day one, then dismissal. Puzzled and upset, I started for the door.

"Del Gado. Von Drachau." The executive officer. "Stay a minute. The Commander wants to talk to you."

IV

My puzzlement thickened as we entered McClennon's inner office, a Victorian-appointed, crowded yet comfortable room I hadn't seen since I'd paid my first day respects. There were bits of a stamp collection scattered, a desk beclutered, presentation holographs of Navy officers that seemed familiar, another of a woman of the pale thin martyr type, a model of a High Seiner spaceship looking like it'd been cobbled together from plastic tubing and children's blocks. McClennon had been the Naval officer responsible for bringing the Seiners into Confederation in time for the Three Races War. His retirement had been a protest against the way the annexation was handled. Upset as I was I had little attention for surroundings, nor cared what made the Old Man tick.

Once alone with us, he became a man who failed to fit my conception of a commanding officer. His face, which usually seemed about to slide off his skullbones with the weight of responsibility, spread a warm smile. "Johnny!" He thrust a wrinkled hand at von Drachau.

He knew the kid?

My new partner's reaction was a surprise, too. He seemed awed and deferential as he extended his own hand. "Uncle Tom."

McClennon turned. "I've known Johnny since the night he wet himself on my dress blacks just before the Grand Admiral's Ball. Good old days at Luna Command, before the last war." He chuckled. Von Drachau blushed. And I frowned in renewed surprise. I hadn't know von Drachau well, but had never seen or heard anything to suggest he was capable of being impressed by anyone but himself.

"His father and I were Academy classmates. Then served in the same ships before I went into intelligence. Later we worked together in operations against the Sangaree."

Von Drachau didn't sit down till invited. Even though McClennon, in those few minutes, exposed more of himself than anyone in the wing had hitherto seen, I was more interested in the kid. His respectful, almost cowed attitude was completely out of character.

"Johnny," said McClennon, leaning back behind his desk and slowly turning a drink in his hand, "you don't come with recommendations. Not positive, anyway. We going to go through that up here?"

Von Drachau stared at the carpet, shrugged, reminded me of myself as a seven year old called to explain some specially noxious misdeed to my creche-father. It became increasingly obvious that McClennon was a man with whom von Drachau was

nwilling to play games. I'd heard gruesome stories of his
ehavior with the CO JG IV.

"You've heard the lecture already, so I won't give it. I do
nderstand, a bit. Anyway, discipline here, compared to Derry or
he Islands, is almost nonexistent. Do your job and you won't have
: bad. But don't push. I won't let you endanger lives. Something
） think about. This morning's scrap left me with extra pilots. I
an ground people who irritate me. Could be a blow to a man who
）ved flying."

Von Drachau locked gazes with the Commander. Rebellion
tirred but he only nodded.

McClennon turned again. "You don't like this assignment."
Not a question. My face must've been a giveaway. "Suicidal,
ou think? You were in JG IV a while. Heard all about Johnny.
But you don't know him. I do, well enough to say he's got
›otential—if we can get him to realize aerial fighting's a team
,ame. By which I mean his first consideration must be bringing
imself, his wingman, and his ship home intact." Von Drachau
,rew red. He'd not only lost seven sailships during the Sickle
slands offensive, he'd lost three wingmen. Dead. "It's hard to
emember you're part of a team while attacking. You know that
ourself, del Gado. So be patient. Help me make something out of
ohnny."

I tried to control my face, failed.

"Why me, eh? Because you're the best flyer I've got. You can
tay with him if anyone can.

"I know, favoritism. I'm taking special care. And that's wrong.
You're correct, right down the line. But I can't help myself. Don't
hink you could either, in my position. Enough explanation.
That's the way it's going to be. If you can't handle it, let me know.
'll find someone who can, or I'll ground him. One thing I mean
o do: send him home alive."

Von Drachau vainly tried to conceal his embarrassment and
ınger. I felt for him. Wouldn't like being talked about that way
nyself—though McClennon was doing the right thing, putting his
notives on display, up front, so there'd be no surprises later on,
ınd establishing for von Drachau the parameters allowed him. The
Commander was an Old Earther himself, and on that battleground
ıad learned that honesty is a weapon as powerful as any in the
ırsenal of deceit.

"I'll try," I replied, though with silent reservations. I'd have to

do some handy self-examination before I bought the whole trick
bag.

"That's all I ask. You can go, then. Johnny and I have some
catching up to do."

I returned to the barracks in a daze. There I received condo-
lences from squadron mates motivated, I suppose, by relief at
having escaped the draft themselves.

Tired though I was, I couldn't sleep till I'd thought everything
through.

In the end, of course, I decided the Old Man had earned a favor.
(This's a digression from von Drachau's story except insofar as it
reflects the thoughts that led me to help bring into being the one
really outstanding story in Ubichi's Camelot operation.) McClennon was an almost archetypically remote, secretive, Odin/Christ
figure, an embastioned lion quietly licking private wounds in the
citadel of his office, sharing his pain and privation with no one.
But personal facts that had come flitting on the wings of rumor
made it certain he was a rare old gentleman who'd paid his
dues and asked little in return. He'd bought off for hundreds of
Old Earthers, usually by pulling wires to Service connections.
And, assuming the stories are true, the price he paid to bring
the Starfishers into Confederation, at a time when they held the
sole means by which the Three Races War could be won, was the
destruction of a deep relationship with the only woman he'd ever
loved, the pale Seiner girl whose holo portrait sat like an icon on
his desk. Treason and betrayal. Earthman who spoke with forked
tongue. She might've been the mother of the son he was trying to
find in Horst-Johann. But his Isaac never came back from the altar
of the needs of the race. Yes, he'd paid his dues, and at usurous
rates.

He had something coming. I'd give him the chance he wanted
for the boy . . . Somewhere during those hours my Old Earther's pragmatism lapsed. Old Number One, survival, took a
temporary vacation.

It felt good.

V

Getting along with von Drachau didn't prove as difficult as
expected. During the following week I was the cause of more
friction than he. I kept reacting to the image of the man rumor and
prejudice had built in my mind, not to the man in whose presence

I was. He was much less arrogant and abrasive than I'd heard—though gritty with the usual outworlder's contempt for the driving need to accomplish characteristic of Old Earthers. But I'd become accustomed to that, even understood. Outworlders had never endured the hopelessness and privation of life on the mother-world. They'd never understand what buying off really meant. Nor did any care to learn.

There're just two kinds of people on Old Earth, butchers and bovines. No one starves, no one freezes, but those are the only positives of life in the Social Insurance warrens. Twenty billion unemployed sardines. The high point of many lives is a visit to Confederation Zone (old Switzerland), where government and corporations maintain their on-planet offices and estates and allow small bands of citizens to come nose the candy store window and look at the lifestyle of the outworlds . . . then send them home with apathy overcome by renewed desperation.

All Old Earth is a slum/ghetto surrounding one small, stoutly defended bastion of wealth and privilege. That says it all, except that getting out is harder than from any historical ghetto.

It's not really what Old Earth outworlders think of when they dust off the racial warm heart and talk about the motherworld. What they're thinking of is Luna Command, Old Earth's moon and the seat of Confederation government. All they have for Old Earth itself is a little shame-faced under-the-table welfare money . . . bitter. The only resource left is human life, the cheapest of all. The outworlds have little use for Terrans save for work like that on Camelot. So bitter. I shouldn't be. I've bought off. Not my problem anymore.

Horst (his preference) and I got on well, quickly advanced to first names. After familiarizing ourselves with the new equipment, we returned to regular patrols. Horst scattered no grit in the machinery. He performed his tasks-within-mission with clockwork precision, never straying beyond the borders of discipline . . .

He confessed, as we paused at the lip of Ginnunga Gap one morning, while walking to the catapults for launch, that he feared being grounded more than losing individuality to military conformity. Flying was the only thing his father hadn't programmed for him (the Commander had gotten him started), and he'd become totally enamored of the sport. Signing on with Ubichi had been the only way to stick with it after his father had managed his appointment to Academy; he'd refused, and been banished from paternal grace. He *had* to fly. Without that he'd have nothing. The Commander, he added, had meant what he said.

I think that was the first time I realized a man could be raised outworld and still be deprived. We Old Earthers take a perverse, chauvinistic pride in our poverty and persecution—like, as the Commander once observed, Jews of Marrakech. (An allusion I spent months dredging; he'd read some obscure and ancient writers.) Our goals are so wholly materialistic that we can scarcely comprehend poverty of the spirit. That von Drachau, with wealth and social position, could feel he had less than I, was a stunning notion.

For him flying was an end, for me a means. Though I enjoyed it, each time I sat at catapult head credit signs danced in my head; so much base, plus per mission and per kill. If I did well I'd salvage some family, too. Horst's pay meant nothing. He wasted it fast as it came—I think to show contempt for the wealth from which he sprang. Though that had been honest money, prize and coup money from his father's successes against the Sangaree.

Steam pressure drove a glasteel piston along forty meters of glasteel cylinder; twenty seconds behind von Drachau I catapulted into the ink of the Gap and began feeling for the ups. For brief instants I could see him outlined against the aurora, flashing in and out of vision as he searched and circled. I spied him climbing, immediately turned to catch the same riser. Behind me came the rest of the squadron. Up we went in a spiral like moths playing tag in the night while reaching for the moons. Von Drachau found altitude and slipped from the up. I followed. At three thousand meters, with moonlight and aurora, it wasn't hard to see him. The four craft of my flight circled at ninety degree points while the rest of the squadron went north across the Gap. We'd slowly drop a thousand meters, then catch another up to the top. We'd stay in the air two hours (or we ran out of ammunition), then go down for an hour break. Five missions minimum.

First launch came an hour before dawn, long before the night fighters went down. Mornings were crowded. But by sunrise we seemed terribly alone while we circled down or climbed, watched the Gap for whales leaving the Harridans or the mantas that'd grown so numerous.

Daytimes almost every ship concentrated on keeping the whales north of the Gap. That grew more difficult as the density of their population neared the migratory. It'd be a while yet, maybe a month, but number and instinct would eventually overcome the

ear our weapons had instilled. I couldn't believe we'd be able to
top them. The smaller herds of the 'tween years, yes, but not the
emming rivers that would come with winter. A Corporation
mbued with any human charity would've been busy sealing mines
nd evacuating personnel. But Ubichi had none. In terms of
nancial costs, equipment losses, it was cheaper to fight, sacri-
cing inexpensive lives to salvage material made almost priceless
y interstellar shipment.

VI

ignals from the ground, a searchlight fingering the earth and
ashing three times rapidly. Rim sentries had spotted a whale in
e direction the finger pointed. Von Drachau and I were front. We
egan circling down.

We'd dropped just five hundred meters when he wag-winged
isual contact. I saw nothing but the darkness that almost always
logged the canyon. As wide as Old Earth's Grand Canyon and
ree times as deep, it was well lighted only around noon.

That was the first time I noticed his phenomenal vision. In
ollowing months he was to amaze me repeatedly. I honestly
elieve I was the better pilot, capable of outflying any manta, but
is ability to find targets made him the better combat flyer.

The moment I wagged back he broke circle and dove. I'd've
ircled lower. If the whale was down in the Gap itself that might
ean a three thousand meter fall. Pulling out would overstrain
ne's wings. Sailplanes, even the jackboot jobs we flew, are
ragile machines never intended for stunt flying.

But I was wingman, responsible for protecting the attack pilot's
ear. I winged over and followed, maintaining a constant five
undred meters between us. Light and shadow from clouds and
nountains played over his ship, alternately lighting and darkening
ne personal devices he'd painted on. A death's-head grinned and
vinked . . .

I spied the whale. It was working directly toward Beadle. Size
nd coloring of the gasbag (oblate spheroid sixty meters long,
atched in shades from pink to scarlet and spotted with odd other
olors at organ sites) indicated a juvenile of the Harkness species,
nat with the greatest potential for destruction. Triangular vanes
rotruding ten meters from muscle rings on the bag twitched and
uivered as the monster strove to maintain a steady course. Atop
t in a thin Mohawk swath swayed a copse of treelike organs

believed to serve both plantlike and animal digestive and meta bolic functions. Some may have been sensory. Beneath it sensory tentacles trailed, stirring fretfully like dreaming snakes on the head of Medusa. If any found food (and anything organic was provender for a Harkness), it'd anchor itself immediately. Hundreds more tentacles would descend and begin lifting edibles to mouths in a tiny head-body tight against the underside of the gasbag. There'd be a drizzling organic rainfall as the monster dumped ballast/waste. Migrating whale herds could devastate great swaths of countryside. Fortunately for Ubichi's operations, the mating seasons were infrequent.

The Harkness swelled ahead. Horst would be fingering his trigger ring, worrying his sights. I stopped watching for mantas and adjusted my dive so Horst wouldn't be in line when I fired . . .

Flashing lights, hasty, almost panicky. I read, then glanced out right and up, spied the manta pair. From high above the Harridans they arrowed toward the whale, tips and trailing edges of their wings rippling as they adjusted dive to each vagary of canyon air. But they were a kilometer above and would be no worry till we'd completed our pass. And the other two ships of our flight would be after them, to engage while Horst and I completed the primary mission.

The relationship between mantas and whales had never, to that time, been clearly defined. The mantas seemed to feed among the growths on whale backs, to attach themselves in mated pairs to particular adults, which they fiercely defended, and upon which they were apparently dependent. But nothing seemed to come the other way. The whales utterly ignored them, even as food. Whales ignored everything in the air, though, enduring our attacks as if they weren't happening. If not for the mantas, the extermination program would've been a cakewalk.

But mantas fought at every encounter, almost as if they knew what we were doing. A year earlier they'd been little problem. Then we'd been sending single flights after lone wandering whales, but as migratory pressures built the manta population had increased till we were forced to fight three or four battles to each whale attack—of which maybe one in twenty resulted in a confirmed kill. Frustrating business, especially since self-defense distracted so from our primary mission.

Luckily, the mantas had only one inefficient, if spectacular, weapon, the lightning they hurled.

That fool von Drachau dropped flaps to give himself more firing time. Because I began overtaking him, I had to follow suit. My glider shuddered, groaned, and an ominous snap came from my right wing. But nothing fell apart.

Fog formed before Horst's craft, whipped back. He'd begun firing. His shells painted a tight bright pattern in the forest on the whale's back. Stupidly, I shifted aim to the same target. Von Drachau pulled out, flaps suddenly up, used his momentum to hurl himself up toward the diving manta pair, putting them in a pincer.

A jagged bit of lightning flashed toward von Drachau. I cursed. We'd plunged into a trap. Mantas had been feeding in the shelter of the whale's back organs. They were coming up to fight.

I'd begun firing an instant before the flash, putting my shells in behind Horst's. Before the water vapor from my cannon gas fogged my canopy I saw explosions digging into the gasbag. I started to stick back and fire at the mantas, but saw telltale ripples of blue fire beneath the yellow of my shells. The bag was going to blow.

When the hydrogen went there'd be one hell of an explosion. Following Horst meant suicide.

The prime purpose of the explosives was to drive cyanide fragments into whale flesh, but sometimes, as then, a too tight pattern breached the main bag—and hydrogen is as dangerous on Camelot as elsewhere.

I took my only option, dove. With luck the whale's mass would shadow me from the initial blast.

It did. But the tip of my right wing, that'd made such a grim noise earlier, brushed one of the monster's sensory tentacles. The jerk snapped it at the root. I found myself spinning down.

I rode it a while, both because I was stunned (I'd never been downed before, accidentally or otherwise) and because I wanted the craft to protect me from downblast.

The sun had risen sufficiently to illuminate the tips of the spires in the Gap. They wheeled, jerked, reached up like angry claws, drawing rapidly closer. Despite the ongoing explosion, already shaking me, blistering the paint on my fuselage, I had to get out.

Canopy cooperated. In the old gliders they'd been notoriously sticky, costing many lives. This popped easily. I closed my eyes and jumped, jerking my ripcord as I did. Heat didn't both me. My remaining wing took a cut at me, a last effort of fate to erase my life-tape, then the chute jerked my shoulders. I began to sway.

It was cold and lonely up there, and there was nothing I could do. I was no longer master of my fate. You would have to be an Old Earther near buying off to really feel the impact of that. Panicky, I peered up at the southern rim of the Gap—and saw what I'd hoped to see, the rescue balloon already on its way. It was a hot air job that rode safety lines payed out from winches at the edge. If I could be salvaged, it'd be managed. I patted my chest pockets to make sure I had my flares.

Only then did I rock my chute away so I could see what'd happened to von Drachau.

He was into it with three mantas, one badly wounded (the survivor of the pair from the Harkness—the other had died in the explosion). He got the wounded one and did a flap trick to turn inside the others. His shells went into the belly of one. It folded and fell. Then the rest of our flight was pursuing the survivor toward the Harridans.

I worried as burning pieces of whale fell past. Suppose one hit my chute?

But none did. I landed in snow deep in the Gap, after a cruel slide down an almost vertical rock face, then set out my first flare. While I tried to stay warm, I thought about von Drachau.

I'd gone along with his attack because I'd had neither choice, nor time to think, nor any way to caution him. But that precipitous assault had been the sort that'd earned him his reputation. And it'd cost again. Me.

Didn't make me feel any better to realize I'd been as stupid in my target selection.

A rational, unimpetuous attack would've gone in level with the whale, from behind, running along its side. Thus Horst could've stayed out of sight of the mantas riding it, and I could've avoided the explosion resulting from a tight fire pattern in the thin flesh of the back. Shells laid along the whale's flanks would've spread enough cyanide to insure a kill.

Part my fault, but when the rescue balloon arrived I was so mad at Horst I couldn't talk.

VII

Von Drachau met the rescue balloon, more concerned and contrite than I'd've credited. I piled out steaming, with every intention of denting his head, but he ran to me like a happy puppy, bubbling apologies, saying he'd never had a chance at a whale . . .

righteous outrage became grumpiness. He was only nineteen, emotionally ten.

There were reports to be filed but I was in no mood. I headed for barracks and something alcoholic.

Von Drachau followed. "Sal," he said with beer in his mustache, "I mean it. I'm sorry. Wish I could look at it like you. Like this's just a job . . ."

"Uhm." I made a grudging peace. "So can it." But he kept on. Something was biting him, something he wanted coaxed out.

"The mantas," he said. "What do we know about them?"

"They get in the way."

"Why? Territorial imperative? Sal, I been thinking. Was today a set-up? If people was working the other side, they couldn't've set a better trap. In the old ships both of us would've gone down."

"Watch your imagination, kid. Things're different in the Islands, but not that different. We've run into feeding mantas before. You just attacked from the wrong angle." I tossed off my third double. The Gap bottom cold began leaking from my bones. I felt a bit more charitable. But not enough to discuss idiot theories of manta intelligence.

We already knew many odd forms of intelligence. Outworlders have a curious sensitivity to it, a near reverence puzzling to Old Earthers. They go around looking for it, especially in adversity. Like savages imputing powers to storms and stones, they can't accept disasters at face value. There has to be a malignant mover.

"I guess you're right," he said. But his doubt was plain. He *wanted* to believe we were fighting a war, not exterminating noxious animals.

Got me thinking, though. Curious how persistent the rumor was, even though there was no evidence to support it. But a lot of young people (sic!—I was twenty-eight) are credulous. A pilot, dogfighting a manta pair, might come away with the notion. They're foxy. But intelligence, to me, means communication and cooperation. Mantas managed a little of each, but only among mates. When several pairs got involved in a squabble with us, we often won by maneuvering pairs into interfering with one another.

The matter dropped and, after a few more drinks, was forgotten. And banished utterly when we were summoned to the Commander's office.

The interview was predictable. McClennon was determined to ground von Drachau. I don't know why I defended him. Labor united against management, maybe . . .

Guess Horst wasn't used to having a friend at court. When we left he thanked me, but seemed puzzled, seemed to be wrestling something inside.

Never did find out what, for sure—Old Earthers are tight-lipped, but von Drachau had the best of us beaten—but there was a marked improvement in his attitude. By the end of the month he was on speaking terms with everyone, even men he'd grossly alienated at JG IV.

That month I witnessed a dramatic improvement in Horst's shooting. His kills in the Sickle Islands had been almost acciden-tal. Changing from rockets to cannons seemed to bring out his talent. He scored kill after kill, attacking with a reckless abandon (but always with a care to keep me well positioned). He'd scream in on a manta, drop flaps suddenly, put himself into a stall just beyond the range of the manta's bolt, then flaps up and fall beneath the monster when he'd drawn it, nose up and trigger a burst into its belly. Meanwhile, I would fend off the other till he was free. My kill score mounted, too.

His was astonishing. Our first four weeks together he downed thirty-six mantas. I downed fourteen, and two whales. I'd had fifty-seven and twelve for four years' work when he arrived, best in the wing. It was obvious that, if he stayed alive, he'd soon pass not only me but Aultmann Zeisler, the CO JG I, a ten year veteran with ninety-one manta kills.

Horst did have an advantage we older pilots hadn't. Target availability. Before, except during the lesser migrations, the wing had been lucky to make a dozen sightings per month. Now we piled kills at an incredible rate.

Piled, but the tilt of the mountain remained against us. Already stations farther south were reporting sightings of small herds that had gotten past us.

It was coming to the point where we were kept busy by mantas. Opportunities to strike against whales grew rare. When the main migratory wave broke we'd be swamped.

Everyone knew it. But Derry, despite sending reinforcements, seemed oblivious to the gravity of the situation. Or didn't care. A sour tale began the rounds. The Corporation had written us off. The whales would remove us from the debit ledger. That facilities of Clonninger and stations farther down the cable were being expanded to handle our withdrawal didn't dent the rumors. We Old Earthers always look on the bleak side.

In early winter, after a severe snowstorm, as we were digging out, we encountered a frightening phenomenon. Cooperation among large numbers of mantas.

VIII

It came with sunrise. Horst and I were in the air, among two dozen new fighters. The wing had been reinforced to triple strength, one hundred fifty gliders and a dozen armed zeppelins, but those of us up were all the ground personnel had been able to dig out and launch.

Signals from ground. Against the aurora and white of the Harridans I had no trouble spotting the Harkness whales, full adults, leaving a branch canyon opposite Beadle. Close to a hundred, I guessed, the biggest lot yet to assault the Gap. We went to met them, one squadron circling down. My own squadron, now made up of men who'd shown exceptional skill against mantas, stayed high to cover. We no longer bothered with whales, served only as cover for the other squadron.

I watched for mantas. Had no trouble finding them. They came boiling 'round the flank of an ivory mountain, cloud of black on cliff of white, a mob like bats leaving a cave at sunset. Hundreds of them.

My heart sank. It'd be thick, grim, and there was no point even thinking about attack formations. All a man could do was keep away and grab a shot at opportunity. But we'd take losses. One couldn't watch every way at once.

A few mantas peeled off and dove for the ships attacking the whales. The bulk came on, following a line that'd cross the base.

We met. There were gliders, mantas, shells and lightning bolts thicker than I'd ever seen. Time stood still. Mantas passed before me, I pulled trigger rings. Horst's death's-head devices whipped across my vision. Sometimes parts of gliders or mantas went tumbling by. Lower and lower we dropped, both sides trading altitude for speed.

Nose up. Manta belly before me, meters away. Jerk the rings. Fog across the canopy face, but no explosions against dark flesh. We struggled to avoid collision, passed so close we staggered one another with our slipstreams. For a moment I stared into two of the four eyes mounted round the thing's bullet head. They seemed to drive an electric line of hatred deep into my brain. For an instant I believed the intelligence hypothesis. Then shuddered as I sticked down and began a rabbit run for home, to replace my ammunition.

A dozen mantas came after me. Horst, alone, went after them.

I later learned that, throwing his craft about with complete abandon, he knocked nine of those twelve down before his own ammunition ran out. It was an almost implausible performance though one that need not be dwelt upon. It's one of the mainstays of his legend, his first ten-kill day, and every student of the fighting on Camelot knows of it.

The runway still had a half meter of snow on it. The three mantas followed me in, ignoring the counterfire of our ground batteries. I was so worried about evading their bolts that I went in poorly, one wing down, and ended up spinning into a deep drift. As a consequence I spent two hours grounded.

What I missed was sheer hell. The mantas, as if according to some plan, clamped down on our landing and launching gates, taking their toll while our craft were at their most vulnerable. In the early going some tried to blast through the overhead netting. That only cost them lives. Our ground batteries ate them up. Then they tried the barrage balloons, to no better effect.

Then the whales arrived. We'd been able to do nothing to stop them, so busy had the mantas kept us. They, sensing food beneath the net, began trying to break in. Our ground batteries fired into the dangling forests of their tentacles, wrecking those but doing little damage to the beasts themselves. Gigantic creaks and groans came from the net anchor points.

For pilots and ground crews there was little to do but prepare for a launch when circumstances permitted. I got my ship out, rearmed, and dragged to catapult head. Then for a time I stood observer, using binoculars to watch those of our craft still up.

In all, the deaths of a hundred fourteen mantas (four mine, ten Horst's) and twenty-two whales were confirmed for the first two hours of fighting. But we would've gone under without help from down the cable.

When the desperation of our position became obvious the Commander signalled Clonninger. Its sailcraft came north, jumped the mantas from above. They broke siege. We launched, cats hurling ships into the Gap as fast as steam could be built. Horst and I went in the first wave.

Help had come just in time. The whales had managed several small breaches in the netting and were pushing tentacles through after our ground people.

Even with help the situation remained desperate. I didn't think it'd take long for the mantas, of which more had come across, to clamp down again. When they did it'd only be a matter of time till

e whales wrecked the net. I pictured the base destroyed, littered
ith bones.

Before we launched, the Commander, ancient with the strain,
poke with each pilot. Don't know what he said to the others, but
imagine it was much what he told me: if I judged the battle lost,
) run south rather than return here. The sailcraft had to be
alvaged for future fighting. If we were overrun the fighting would
iove to Clonninger.

And in my ear a few words about taking care of von Drachau.
said I would.

But we survived. I won't say we won because even though we
ianaged to break the attack, we ourselves were decimated. JG
(III's effectiveness was ruined for the next week. For days we
ould barely manage regular patrols. Had we been hit again
e'd've been obliterated.

That week McClennon three times requested permission to
vacuate nonessential ground troops, received three refusals. Still,
  seemed pointless for us to stay when our blocking screen had
een riddled. Small herds were passing daily. Clonninger was
nder as much pressure as we and had more trouble handling it.
heir defenses weren't meant to stand against whales. Their
ailplanes often had to flee. Ground personnel crouched in deep
unkers and prayed the whales weren't so hungry they'd dig them
ut.

Whale numbers north of the Harridans were estimated at ten
housand and mantas at ten to twenty. Not vast, but overwhelming
1 concentration. Populations for the whole continent were about
ouble those, with the only other concentrations in the Sickle
slands. By the end of that week our experts believed a third of the
larridan whales had slipped past us. We'd downed about ten
ercent of those trying and about twenty-five percent of the
iantas.

IX

 fog of despair enveloped Beadle. Derry had informed McClen-
on that there'd be no more reinforcements. They were needed
urther south. Permission to withdraw? Denied again. We had
nly one hundred twelve effective sailcraft. Ammunition was
hort. And the main blow was yet to fall.

It's hard to capture the dulled sense of doom that clung so thick.
t wasn't a verbal or a visible thing, though faces steadily
ngthened. There was no defeatist talk. The men kept their

thoughts to themselves—but couldn't help expressing them through actions, by digging deeper shelters, in a lack of crisp efficiency. Things less definable. Most hadn't looked for desperate stand when they signed on. And Camelot hadn't prepared them to face one. Till recently they'd experienced only a lazy, vacation sort of action, loafing and laughter with a faint bouquet of battle.

One evening Horst and I stood watching lightning shoot among the near pure copper peaks of the Harridans. "D'you ever look one in the eye?" he asked.

Memory of the manta I'd missed. I shuddered, nodded.

"And you don't believe they're intelligent?"

"I don't care. A burst in the guts is all that matters. That's cash money, genius or retard."

"Your conscience doesn't bother you?"

Something was bothering him, though I couldn't understand why. He wouldn't worry bending human beings, so why aliens? Especially when the pay's right and you're the son of a man who'd become rich by doing the same? But his reluctance wasn't unique. So many people consider alien intelligence sacred—without any rational basis. It's a crippling emotional weakness that has wormed its way into Confederation law. You can't exploit a world with intelligent natives . . .

But conscience may've had nothing to do with it. Seems, in hindsight, his reluctance might've been a rationalized facet of his revolt against his father and authority.

Understandably, Ubichi was sensitive to speculations about manta intelligence. Severe fines were laid on men caught discussing the possibility—which, human nature being what it is, made the talk more persistent. Several pilots, Horst included, had appealed to McClennon. He'd been sympathetic, but what could he have done?

And I kept wondering why anyone cared. I agreed with the Corporation. That may have been a defect in me.*

*If this thought truly occurred to del Gado at the time, it clearly made no lasting moral impression. News buffs will remember that he was one of several Ubichi mercenaries named in Confederation genocide indictments stemming from illegal exploitation on Bonaventure, though he was not convicted.

—Dogfight

As soon as we recovered from attack, for morale purposes we launched our last offensive, a pre-emptive strike against a developing manta concentration. Everything, including armed zeppelins, went. The mission was partially successful. Kept another attack from hitting Beadle for a week, but it cost. None of the airships returned. Morale sagged instead of rising. We'd planned to use the zepps in our withdrawal—if ever authorized.

In line of seniority I took command of my squadron after a manta made the position available. But I remained von Drachau's wingman. That made him less impetuous. Still addicted to the flying, he avoided offending a man who could ground him. I was tempted. His eye was still deadly, but his concern over the intelligence of mantas had begun affecting his performance.

At first it was a barely noticeable hesitance in attack that more than once left blistered paint on his ship. With his timing a hair off he sometimes stalled close enough for a manta's bolt to caress his craft. My admonitions had little effect. His flying continued to deteriorate.

And still I couldn't understand.

X

His performance improved dramatically six days after our strike into the Harridans, a day when he had no time to think, when the wing's survival was on the line and maximum effort was a must. (He always performed best under pressure. He never could explain how he'd brushed those nine mantas off me that day. He'd torn through them with the cold efficiency of a military robot, but later couldn't remember. It was as if another personality had taken control. I saw him go through three such possessions and he couldn't remember after any.) It was a battle in which we all flew inspired—and earned a Pyrrhic victory . . . the back of the wing was broken, but again Beadle survived.

The mantas came at dawn, as before, and brought a whale herd with them. There'd been snow, but this time a hard night's work had cleared the catapults and sailships. We were up and waiting. They walked—or flew—into it. And kept coming. And kept coming.

And by weight of numbers drove us to ground. And once we'd lost the air the whales moved in.

McClennon again called for aid from Clonninger. It came. We broke out. And soon were forced to ground again. The mantas refused to be dismayed. A river came across the Gap to replace losses.

Clonninger signalled us for help. From Beadle we watched endless columns of whales, varicolored as species mixed, move down the dragline south. We could do nothing. Clonninger was on its own.

McClennon order a hot air balloon loaded with phosphorous bombs, sent it out and blew it amidst the mantas crowding our launch gate. Horst and I jumped into their smoke. The entire mission we ignored mantas and concentrated on the whales, who seemed likely to destroy the net. Before ammunition ran out we forced them to rejoin the migration. But the mantas didn't leave till dark.

Our ground batteries ran out of rockets. Half our ships were destroyed or permanently grounded. From frostbite as much as manta action (the day's high was -23° C.), a third of our people became casualties. Fourteen pilots found permanent homes in the bottom of Ginnunga Gap. Rescue balloons couldn't go after them.

Paradoxically, permission to withdraw came just before we lost contact with Clonninger.

We began our wound-licking retreat at midnight, scabby remnants of squadrons launching into the ink of the Gap, grabbing the ups, then slanting down toward Clonninger. Balloons began dragging the line.

Clonninger was what we'd feared for Beadle: churned earth and bones ethereally grim by dawn light. The whales had broken its defenses without difficulty. Appetites whetted, they'd moved on. From three thousand meters the borders of the earth-brown river of devastation seemed to sweep the horizons. The silvery drag cable sketched a bright centerline for that death-path.

We were patrolling when the first airships came south. The skies were utterly empty, the ground naked, silence total. Once snow covered the route only memory would mark recent events . . .

Days passed. The Clonninger story repeated itself down the cable, station after station, though occasionally we found salvage-able survivors or equipment. Operations seemed ended for our ground units. But for us pilots it went on. We followed the line till we overtook straggler whales, returned to work.

As the migration approached Derry corporate defenses stiff-ened. Though we'd lost contact, it seemed our function at the Gap had been to buy time. True, as I later learned. A string of Beadle-like fortress-bases were thrown across the northern and

Sickle Islands routes. But even they weren't strong enough. As the mantas learned (even I found myself accepting the intelligence proposition), they became more proficient at besieging and destroying bases. The whales grew less fearful, more driven by their mating urge. Mantas would herd them to a base; they'd wreck it despite the most furious defense. Both whales and mantas abandoned fear, ignored their own losses.

JG XIII was out of the main action, of course, but we persevered—if only because we knew we'd never get off planet if Derry fell. But we flew with little enthusiasm. Each additional destroyed base or mine (whatever Ubichi was after had to be unearthed) reassured us of the inevitability of failure.

When a man goes mercenary in hopes of buying off, he undergoes special training. Most have a paramilitary orientation. (I use "mercenary" loosely.) Historical studies puzzled me. Why had men so often fought on when defeat was inevitable? Why had they in fact given more of themselves in a hopeless cause? I was living it then and still didn't understand. JG XIII performed miracles with what it had, slaughtered whales and mantas by the hundreds, and that after everyone had abandoned hope . . .

Horst reached the one fifty mark. I reached one hundred twenty. Almost every surviving pilot surpassed fifty kills. There was just thirty-three of us left.

XI

On the spur of the moment one day, based on two considerations, I made my first command decision: good winds during patrol and a grave shortage of supplies. For a month the wing had been living and fighting off the remnants of stations destroyed by migrating whales. Rations were a single pale meal each day. Our remaining ammunition was all with us on patrol.

When I began this I meant to tell about myself and Horst-Johann von Drachau. Glancing back, I see I've sketched a story of myself and JG XIII. Still, it's almost impossible to extricate the forms—especially since there's so little concrete to say about the man. My attempts to characterize him fail, so robotlike was he even with me. Mostly I've speculated, drawn on rumor and used what I learned from Commander McClennon. The few times Horst opened at all he didn't reveal much, usually only expressing an increasing concern about the mantas. Without my speculations he'd read like an excerpt from a service file.

The above is an admonition to myself: don't digress into the heroism and privation of the month the wing operated independently. That wasn't a story about von Drachau. He endured it without comment. Yet sleeping in crude wooden shelters and eating downed manta without complaining might say something about the man behind the facade, or something about changes that had occurred there. Hard to say. He may've ignored privation simply because it didn't impinge on his personal problems.

We were in the air, making the last patrol we could reasonably mount. I had command. In a wild moment, inspired by good ups and winds, I decided to try breaking through to Derry territory. Without knowing how far it'd be to the nearest extant station—we hadn't seen outsiders since borrowing the Clonninger squadrons. That Derry still held I could guess only from the fact that we were still to its north and in contact with mantas and whales.

The inspiration hit, I wag-winged *follow me* and went into a long shallow glide. Derry itself lay over two hundred kilometers away, a long fly possible only if we flitted from up to up. Much longer flights had been made—though not against opposition.

It took twelve hours and cost eight sailcraft, but we made it. It was an ace day for everyone. There seemed to be a Horst-like despair about the mantas that left them sluggish in action. We littered the barren earth with their corpses. Horst, with seven kills, had our lowest score. Because I was behind him all the while I noticed he wasn't trying, shot only when a pilot was endangered. This had been growing during the month. He was as sluggish as the mantas.

Our appearance at Derry generated mixed reactions. Employees got a big lift, perhaps because our survival presented an example. But management seemed unsettled, especially by our kill claims, our complaints, and the fact that there were survivors they were obligated to rescue. All they wanted was to hold on and keep the mines working. But aid to JG XIII became an instant *cause célèbre*. It was obvious there'd be employee rebellion if our survivors were written off.

I spent days being grilled, the price of arrogating command. The others were supposed to remain quarantined for debriefing, but evaded their watchers. They did the public relations job. Someone spread the tales that were the base for von Drachau's legend.

I tried to stop that, but to do so was beating my head against a wall. Those people in the shrinking Derry holding needed a hero—even if they had to make him up, to fill in, pad, chop off rough corners so he'd meet their needs. It developed quickly. I wonder how Horst would've reacted had he been around for deep exposure. I think it might've broken his shell, but would've gone to his head too. Well, no matter now.

Myself, I'd nominate Commander McClennon as the real hero of JG XIII. His was the determination and spirit that brought us through. But he was an administrator.

Much could be told about our stay at Derry, which lasted through winter and spring, till long after the manta processes of intellection ponderously ground to the conclusion that we humans couldn't be smashed and eaten this time. The fighting, of course, continued, and would till Confederation intervened, but it stayed at a modest level. They stopped coming to us. Morale soared. Yet things were really no better. The mating whales still cut us off from the south polar spaceport.

But the tale is dedicated to Horst-Johann von Drachau. It lasts only another week.

XII

Once free of interrogation, I began preparing the wing to return to action. For years I'd been geared to fighting; administration wasn't easy. I grew short-tempered, began hunting excuses to evade responsibility. Cursed myself for making the decision that'd brought me inside—even though that'd meant volunteer crews taking zepps north with stores.

An early official action was an interview with Horst. He came to my cubby-office sullen and dispirited, but cheered up when I said, "I'm taking you off attack. You'll be my wingman."

"Good."

"It means that much?"

"What?"

"This stuff about manta intelligence."

"Yeah. But you wouldn't understand, Sal. Nobody does."

I began my "what difference does it make?" speech. He interrupted.

"You know I can't explain. It's something like this: we're not fighting a war. In war you try to demonstrate superiority of arms, to convince the other side it's cheaper to submit. We're trying for extermination here. Like with the Sangaree."

The Sangaree. The race his father had destroyed. "No big loss."

"Wrong. They were nasty, but posed no real threat. They could've been handled with a treaty. We had the power."

"No tears were shed . . ."

"Wrong again. But the gut reaction isn't over. You wait. When men like my father and Admiral Beckhart and Commander McClennon and the other militarists who control Luna Command fade away, you'll start seeing a reaction . . . a whole race, Sal, a whole culture, independently evolved, with all it might've taught us . . ."

It had to be rationalization, something he'd built for himself to mask a deeper unhappiness. "McClennon? You don't approve of him?"

"Well, yeah, he's all right. I guess. But even when he disagreed, he went along. In fact, my father never could've found the Sangaree homeworld without him. If he'd revolted then, instead of later when his actions turned and bit back . . . well, the Sangaree would be alive and he'd be off starfishing with Amy."

I couldn't get through. Neither could he. The speeches on the table were masks for deeper things. There's no way to talk about one thing and communicate something else. "Going along," I said. "What've you been doing? How about the kid who squawks but goes along because he wants to fly? That's what we're all doing here, Horst. Think I'd be here if I could buy off any other way? Life is compromise. No exceptions. And you're old enough to know it."*

Shouldn't've said that. But I was irritable, unconcerned about what he'd think. He stared a moment, then stalked out, considering his own compromises.

Two days later my ships were ordered up for the first time since our arrival. Command had had trouble deciding what to do with us. I think we weren't employed because the brass were afraid we were as good as we claimed, which meant (by the same illogical process that built legends around Horst and the wing) that our survival wasn't just a miracle, that we'd really been written off but had refused to die. Such accusations were going around and Command was sensitive to them.

We went up as air cover for the rescue convoy bringing our survivors in from up the cable. We wouldn't've been used if another unit had been available. But the mantas had a big push on, their last major and only night offensive.

Del Gado may indeed have said something of the sort at the time, and have felt it, but again, once the pressure was off, he forgot. He has been bought off for years, yet remains with Ubichi's Armed Action Command. He must enjoy his work.
                                                                                      —Dogfight

Winds at Derry are sluggish, the ups are weak, and that night there was an overcast masking the moons. The aurora is insignificant that far south. Seeing was by lightning, a rough way to go.

We launched shortly after nightfall, spent almost an hour creeping to altitude, then clawed north above the cable. Flares were out to mark it, but those failed us when we passed the last outpost. After that it was twenty-five ships navigating by guesswork, maintaining contact by staying headache-making alert during lightning flashes.

But it was also relaxing. I was doing something I understood. The whisper of air over my canopy lulled me, washed the week's aggravations away.

Occasionally I checked my mirrors. Horst maintained perfect position on my right quarter. The others spread around in ragged formation, yielding compactness and precision to safety. The night threatened collisions.

We found the convoy one hundred twenty kilometers up the line, past midnight, running slowly into the breeze and flashing signals so we'd locate them. I dropped down, signalled back with a bioluminescent lantern, then clawed some altitude, put the men into wide patrol patterns. Everything went well through the night. The mantas weren't up in that sector.

Dawn brought them, about fifty in a flying circus they'd adopted from us. We condensed formation and began slugging it out.

They'd learned. They still operated in pairs, but no longer got in one another's way. And they strove to break our pairs to take advantage of numbers. But when a pair latched onto a sailplane it became their entire universe. We, however, shot at anything, whether or not it was a manta against which we were directly engaged.

They'd overadopted our tactics. I learned that within minutes. When someone got half a pair, the other would slide out of action and stay out till it found a single manta of opposite sex. Curious. (Shortly I'll comment on the findings of the government investigators, who dug far deeper than Ubichi's exobiologists. But one notion then current, just rumor as the sentience hypothesis became accepted, was that manta intelligence changed cyclically, as a function of the mating cycle.)

We held our own. All of us were alive because we were good. Dodging bolts was instinctual, getting shells into manta guts second nature. We lost only two craft, total. One pilot. Two thirds of the mantas went down.

Horst and I flew as if attached to ends of a metal bar. Book perfect. But the mantas forced us away from the main fray, as many as twenty concentrating on us. (I think they recognized our devices and decided to destroy us. If it were possible for humans to be known to mantas, they'd've been Horst and I.) I went into a robotlike mood like Horst's on his high-kill days. Manta after manta tumbled away. My shooting was flawless. Brief bursts, maybe a dozen shells, were all I used. I seldom missed.

As sometimes happened in such a brawl, Horst and I found our stations reversed. A savage maneuver that left my glider creaking put me in the wingman slot. During it Horst scored his hundred fifty-eighth kill, clearing a manta off my back. Far as I know that was the only time he fired.

The arrangement was fine with me. He was the better shot; let him clear the mess while I protected his back. We'd resume proper positions when a break in the fighting came.

A moment later Horst was in firing position beneath a female who'd expended her bolt (it then took several minutes to build a charge). He bored in, passed so close their wings nearly brushed. But he didn't fire. I took her out as I came up behind.

The eyes. Again I saw them closely. Puzzlement and pain(?) as she folded and fell . . .

Three times that scene repeated itself. Horst wouldn't shoot. Behind him I cursed, threatened, promised, feared. Tried to get shells into his targets, but missed. He maneuvered so I was in poor position on each pass.

Then the mantas broke. They'd lost. The rest of the squadron pursued, losing ground because the monsters were better equipped to grab altitude.

Horst went high. At first I didn't understand, just continued cursing. Then I saw a manta, an old male circling alone, and thought he'd gotten back in track, was going after a kill.

He wasn't. He circled in close and for a seeming eternity they flew wingtip to wingtip, eyeballing one another. Two creatures alone, unable to communicate. But something passed between them. Nobody believes me (since it doesn't fit the von Drachau legend), but I think they made a suicide pact.

Flash. Bolt. Horst's ship staggered, began smoking. The death's-head had disappeared from his fuselage. He started down.

I put everything in my magazines into that old male. The explosions tore him to shreds.

I caught Horst a thousand meters down, pulled up wingtip to wingtip. He still had control, but poorly. Smoke filled his cockpit. Little flames peeped out where his emblem had been. The canvas was ripping from his airframe. By hand signals I tried to get him to bail out.

He signalled he couldn't, that his canopy was stuck. Maybe it was, but when McClennon and I returned a month later, after the migration had passed south, I had no trouble lifting it away.

Maybe he wanted to die.

Or maybe it was because of his legs. When we collected his remains we found that the manta bolt had jagged through his cockpit and cooked his legs below the knees. There'd've been no saving him.

Yet he kept control most of the way down, losing it only in the last five hundred meters. He stalled, spun, dove. Then he recovered and managed a low angle crash. He rolled nose over tail, then burned. Finis. No more Horst-Johann.

I still don't understand.*

*"Hawkins, you keep harping on the 'meaning' of Horst's death. Christ, man, that's my point: it had no meaning. In my terms. By those he utterly wasted his life; his voluntary termination didn't alter the military situation one iota. Even in terms your readers understand it had little meaning. They're vicarious fighters; their outlooks aren't much different than mine—except they want my skin for taking a bite from their sacred cow. Horst was a self-appointed Christ-figure. Only in martyr's terms does his death have meaning, and then only to those who believe any intelligence is holy, to be cherished, defended, and allowed to follow its own course utterly free of external influence. What he and his ilk fail to understand is that it's right down deep-streamed fundamental to the nature of our intelligence to interfere, overpower,

*exploit and obliterate. We did it to one another before First
Expansion; we've done it to Toke, Ulanonid and Sangaree;
we'll continue doing it.*

*"In terms of accomplishment, yes, he bought something with
his life. An injunction against Ubichi's operations on Camelot. There's your meaning, but one that makes sense only in
an ethical framework most people won't comprehend. Believe me, I've tried. But I'm incapable of seeing the universe
and its contents in other than tool-cattle terms. Now have the
balls to tell me I'm in the minority."*

From a private letter by Salvador del Gado.

—Dogfight

XIII

According to the latest, the relationship between manta and whale
is far more complex than anyone at Ubichi ever guessed.
(Guessed—Ubichi never cared. Irked even me that at the height
of Corporate operations, Ubichi had only one exobiologist on
planet—a virologist-bacteriologist charged with finding some
disease with which to infect the whales. Even I could appreciate
the possible advantages in accumulation of knowledge.) At best,
we thought, when the intelligence theory had gained common
currency, the whales served as cattle for the mantas . . .

Not so, say Confederation's researchers. The mantas only
appear to herd and control the whales. The whales are the true
masters. The mantas are their equivalent of dogs, fleet-winged
servants for the ponderous and poorly maneuverable. Their very
slow growth of ability to cope with our aerial tactics wasn't a
function of a cyclic increase in intelligence, it was a reflection of
the difficulty the whales had projecting their defensive needs into
our much faster and more maneuverable frame of reference. By
means of severely limited control.

At the time it seemed a perfectly logical assumption that the
mantas were upset with us because we were destroying their food
sources. (They live on a mouse-sized parasite common amongst
the forest of organs on a whale's back.) It seemed much more
unlikely, even unreasonable, that the whales themselves were the
ones upset and were sending mantas against us, because those
were better able to cope, if a little too dull to do it well.
The whales always carried out the attacks on our ground facilities,
but we missed the hint there.

It seems the manta was originally domesticated to defend whales from a pterodactyl-like flying predator, one which mantas and whales had hunted almost to extinction by the time Ubichi arrived on Camelot. As humans and dogs once did with wolves. Until the government report we were only vaguely aware of the creatures. They never bothered us, so we didn't bother them.

The relationship between whales and mantas is an ancient one, one which domestication doesn't adequately describe. Nor does symbiosis, effectively. Evolution has forced upon both an incredibly complex and clumsy reproductive process that leaves them inextricably bound together.

In order to go into esterus the female manta must be exposed to prolonged equatorial temperatures. She mates in the air, in a dance as complex and strange as that of earthly bees, but only with her chosen mate. Somewhat like Terran marsupials, she soon gives birth to unformed young. But now it gets weird. The marsupial pouch (if such I may call it for argument's sake) is a specially developed semi-womb atop the back of a *male* whale. While instinct compels her to deposit her young there, the male whale envelopes the she-manta in a clutch of frondlike organs, which caress her body and leave a whitish dust—his "sperm". Once her young have been transferred, the female manta goes into a kind of travel-frenzy, like a bee flitting from flower to flower visiting all nearby whales. Any receptive female she visits will, with organs not unlike those of the male, stroke the "sperm" from her body.

Incredibly complicated and clumsy. And unromantic. But it works.

We never would've learned of it but for Horst—who, I think, had nothing of the sort in mind when he let that old manta bolt him down.

And that's about all there is to say. It's a puzzle story. Why did von Drachau do it? I don't know—or don't want to know—but I work under severe handicaps. I'm an Old Earther. I never had a father to play push-me pull-you with my life. I never learned to care much about anything outside myself. A meager loyalty to companions in action is the best I've ever mustered. But enough of excuses.

The fighting with mantas continued four years after Horst's death, through several lesser migrations that never reached the mating grounds. Then a government inquiry board finally stepped in—after Commander McClennon and Fleet Admiral von Drachau had spent three years knocking on doors at Luna Command

(Ubichi's wealth has its power to blind). Their investigations still aren't complete, but it seems they'll rule Camelot permanently off limits. So Horst did buy something with his life. Had he not died, I doubt the Commander would've gotten angry enough to act.

That he did so doesn't entirely please me, of course. I inherited his position. Though I pulled down a handsome income as JG XIII's wing leader and on-going top killer, I loathed the administrative donkey work. Still, I admire the courage he showed.

I also admire Horst, despite his shortcomings, despite myself. But he wasn't a hero, no matter what people want to hear me say. He was a snot-nosed kid used to getting his own way who threw a suicidal tantrum when he saw there was no other way to achieve his ends . . .

And that's it, the rolling down of the socks to expose the feet of clay. Believe the stories or believe his wingman. It's all the same to me. I've got mine in and don't need your approval.*

*Not true, in your editor's opinion. Especially in his private communications, del Gado seems very much interested in finding approval of things he has done. Perhaps he has a conscience after all. He certainly seems desperate to find justification for his life.

—Dogfight

THE NUPTIAL FLIGHT OF WARBIRDS

Algis Budrys

The woman gasped slightly as he began to see her. Dusty Haverman smiled comfortably, extending his lean arm in its brocaded scarlet sleeve, white lace frothing at his wrist. He tilted the decanter over the crystal stem glass shimmering in the stainless air of the afternoon, and rosy clarity swirled within the fragile bell. "You'll enjoy that," he said to her. "It doesn't ordinarily travel well."

She was very pale, with dark, made-up eyes and lips drawn a startling red. A lavender print scarf was bound around her neck-length smoke-black hair, and she wore a lavender voile dress with a full calf-length skirt and a bellboy collar. Below the collar, the front of the dress was open to the waist in a loose slit.

She sat straight in her chair. Her plum-colored nails gripped the ends of the decoratively carved wooden arms. The breeze, whispering over the coarse grass that grew in odd-shaped meadows between the lengths of sandy concrete, stirred her hair. She looked around her at the sideboard, the silver chafing dishes of hot hors d'oeuvres, the Fragonard and the large Boucher hung on ornate wooden racks, the distant structures and the marker lights thrusting up here and there from the edges of the grass. She watched Haverman carefully as he sank back into his own chair, crossed his knees, and raised his own glass. "To our close acquaintanceship," he was saying in his slightly husky voice, a distinguished-looking man with slightly waving silver hair worn a little long over the tops of the ears, and a thin-ish, carefully trimmed silver mustache hovering at the rim of the rose cordial. He wore a white silk ascot.

The woman, who had only a very few signs of latter twentyishness about the skin of her face and the carriage of her body, raised one sooty eyebrow. "Where are we?" she asked. "Who are you?"

Haverman smiled. "We are at the juncture of runways twenty-eight Left and forty-two Right at O'Hare International Airport. My name is Austin Gelvarry."

The woman looked around again, more quickly. Her silk-clad knee bumped the low mahogany table between them, and Haverman had to reach deftly to save her glass. She settled back slowly. "It certainly isn't Cannes," she agreed. She reached for the wine, keeping one hand spread-fingered over the front of her bosom as she leaned. Her eyes did not leave Haverman's face. "How did you do this?"

Gelvarry smiled. "How could I not do it, Miss Montez? Ah, ah, no, don't do that! Don't press so hard against your mouth. *Sip*, Miss Montez, please! Withdraw the glass a slight distance. Now draw the upper lip together just a suggestion, and *delicately* impress its undercurve upon the swell of edging. Sip, Miss Montez. As if at a blossom, my dear. As if at a chalice." He smiled. "You will get to like me. I was in the Royal Flying Corps, you know."

Just at first light, the mechanics would have the early patrol craft lined up on the cinders beside the scarred turf of the runway. They would waken Gelvarry with the sound of the propellers being pulled through. He would lie-up in his cot, his eyes very wide in the dim, listening to the *whup, whup, whup!*

The mechanics ran in three-man teams, one team for each of the three planes in the flight. One would be just letting go the lower tip of the wooden airscrew and jumping a little sideward to turn and double back. One would be doubling back, arms pumping for balance, head cocked to watch the third man, who would be just jumping into the air, arms out, hands slightly cupped to catch the tip of the upper blade as it started down.

They ran in perfect rhythm, and they would do this a dozen times before they attempted to start the aircraft. They said it was necessary to do this with the Trompe L'Oiel engine, which was a French design.

Sergeant-Major MacBanion had instituted this drill. If it were not performed precisely, the cylinder walls would not be evenly lubricated when the engines were started. The cylinder walls would score, and very likely seize up a piston, and all you fine young gentlemen would be dropping your arses, beg pardon (with a wink) all over the perishing map of bleeding Belgium. Then he knocked the dottle out of his pipe, scratched the ribs of the little gray monkey he liked to carry, and turned his shaved neck to shout something to an Other Rank.

Sar'n-Major Mac's speaking voice was sharp and confident, and his manner assertive, in dealing with matters of management. In speaking to Gelvarry and the other flying personnel, however, he was more avuncular, and it seemed to Gelvarry that he saw more than he sometimes let on.

Gelvarry, who was hoping for assignment soon to the high squadron, reckoned that Sergeant-Major MacBanion might have more to do with that than his rank augured for. Nominally, he was only in charge of instruction for transitioning to high squadron aircraft, but since Major Harding never emerged from his hut, it was difficult to believe he was not dependent on Sergeant-Major MacBanion for personnel recommendations.

Gelvarry swung his legs over the side of the cot, taking an involuntary breath of the Nissen hut's interior. Gelvarry's feet had frosted a bit on a long flight the previous week and were quite tender. He limped across the hut, arranging his clothes, and went over to the washstand.

Gelvarry felt there was no better high squadron candidate in the area at the present time. Barton Fisher of XIV Recon Wing had more flight time, but everyone knew Armed Chase flew harder, and Gelvarry had been in Armed Chase for the past year, now being definitely senior man at this aerodrome and senior flying personnel in the entire MC Armed Chase Wing. "I should like very much to apply for assignment to the high squadron, Sir," he rehearsed as he brushed his teeth. But since he had no idea what Major Harding looked like, the face in the mottled fragment of pier glass remained entirely his own.

He spat into the waste bucket and peered at the results. His gums were evidently still bleeding freely. Squinting into the mirror, he lathered his face and began shaving with a razor that had been most indifferently honed by Parkins, the batman Gelvarry shared with the remainder of his flight in the low squadron. Parkins had been reduced from Engine Artificer by Sar'n-Major Mac, and quite right. "Give 'im a drum of oil and a stolen typewriter," Gelvarry grumbled as he scraped at the gingery stubble on his pale cheeks. "He'll jump his bicycle and flog 'em in the village for a litre of Vouvray."

He rubbed his face with a damp gray towel full of threads and bent to stare out the end window. The weather was expectable; mist just rising, still snagging a little in the tops of the poplars; eastern sky giving some promise of rose; and the windsock pointing mendaciously inward. By the time they'd completed their sweep, low on petrol and ready for luncheon and a heartfelt sigh, it would have shifted straight toward Hunland and God help the poor sod who attempted the feat of gliding home on an engine stopped by fuel shortage or, better yet, enemy action also involving injury to flying personnel. All up then, my lad, and into the *Lagerkorps* at the point of some *gefreiter's* bayonet, to spend the remainder of the war laying railroad lines or embanking canals, *Gott Mit Uns* and *Hoch der Fuehrer!* for the Thousand Year Empire, God grant it mischief.

In fact, Gelvarry thought, going out of the hut and running along the duckboards with his shoulders hunched and his hands in his pockets, the only good thing about the day to this point was that his headache was nowhere near as bad as it deserved to be. Perhaps there was truth in the rumor that Issue mess brandy had resumed being shipped from England. It had lately been purchased direct under plausible labels from blue-chinned peasant gentlemen who cut prices in deference to the bravery of their gallant allies.

"Get out of my way, you creature," he puffed to Islingden, John Peter, Flying Officer, otherwise third Duke of Landsdowne, who was standing on the boards with a folded *Gazette* under his arm, studying the sky. "If you're done in there, show some consideration." They danced around each other, arms out for balance, "Nigger Jack" Islingden clutching the *Gazette* like a baton, his large teeth flashing whitely against his olive-hued Landsdowne complexion, introduced via a Spanish countess by the first Duke, neither of them wishing to step off the slats into the spring mud, their boot toes clattering, until Gelvarry at last gained entrance to the officers' latrine.

The dampness rising from the ground was all through his bones. Gelvarry shivered without cease as he sprinted along the cinder track toward his SE-5, beating his arms across his chest. He paused just long enough to scribble a receipt for the aircraft and return the clipboard to the Chief Fitter, found the reinforced plate at the root of the lower plane, stepped up on it and dropped into the cockpit, his hands smearing the droplets of dew on the leather edging of the rim. He felt himself shaking thoroughly now, proceeding with the business of handsignalling the other two pilots—Landsdowne and a sergeant pilot named O'Sullivan—and ensuring they were ready. He signalled Chocks Out, and the ground personnel yanked sharply at the lines, clearing his wheels and dropping flat to let his lower planes pass over.

As soon as he jassed the throttle to smooth his plugs and build takeoff power, a cascade of water blew back into his face from the top of the mainplane, and he stopped shivering. He glanced left and right, raised his arm, flung his hand forward, and advanced the throttle. The trim little Bristol, responsive as a filly, leapt forward. For a few moments, she sprang and rebounded to every inequality of the turf, while her flying wires sang into harmony with the increasing vibration of the engine and airscrew. The droplets on the doped fabric turned instantly into streaks over the smoke-colored oil smears from the engine. Then there was suddenly the smooth buzzing under his feet of the wheels rotating freely on their axles, all weight off, and the SE-5 climbed spiritedly into the dawn, trailing a momentary train of spray that glistened for an instant in the sunlight above the mist. Soon enough, the remaining condensation turned white and opaque, forming little flowers where the panes of his windscreen were jointed into their frames. Gelvarry held the stick between his knees and smoothed his gloves tighter over his hands, which retained little trace of their former trembling.

Up around Paschendaele they were dodging nimbly among some clouds when Gelvarry suddenly plucked his Very pistol from its metal clip in the cockpit and fired a green flare. Nigger and O'Sullivan jerked their courses around into exact conformity with his as they, too, now saw the *staffel* of Albatros falling upon them. They pointed their noses up at a steep angle toward the *Boche,* giving the engines more throttle to prevent stalling, and briefly testing the firing linkages of their twin Vickers guns. Tracer bullets left little spirals of white smoke in the air beyond Gelvarry's engine, to be sucked up immediately as he nibbled in behind them. He glanced at Landsdowne and Paddy, raising one thumb. They clenched their fists and shook them, once, twice, toward the foe who, mottled with garish camouflage, dropped down with flame winking at the muzzles of the Spandau *maschingewehren* behind the gleaming arcs of their propellers.

Gelvarry felt they were firing too soon. Nevertheless, there was an abrupt drumming upon his left upper plane, and then a ripping. He saw a wire suddenly vibrate its middle portion into invisibility as a slug glanced from it. There was no damage of consequence. He held his course and refrained from firing, only thinking of how the entire aircraft had quivered to the drumming, and of how when the fabric split it was as if something swift and hot had seared across the backs of his hands. It was Gelvarry's professional opinion that such moments must be fully met and studied within the mind, so that they lose their power of surprise.

There were eight Albatros in the diving formation, he saw, and therefore there might be as many as four more stooging about in the clouds waiting to down stragglers.

The stench of overheated castor oil came back from his engine and coated his lips and tongue. He pushed his goggles up onto his forehead, hunched his face down into the full lee of the windscreen, and now, when it might count, began firing purposeful short bursts.

The Albatros is a difficult aircraft to attack head-on because it has a metal propeller fairing and an in-line engine, so that many possible hits are deflected and the target area is not large. On the other hand, the Albatros is not really a good diver, having a tendency to shed its wings at steeper angles. Gelvarry had long ago reasoned out that even an apparently sound Albatros main-plane is under considerable stress in a dive, and so he fired a little above the engine, hoping to damage the struts or even the main spar, but noting that as an inevitable consequence there might also be direct or deflected hits on the windscreen. He did not wish to be known as a deliberate shooter of pilots, but there it was.

The *staffel* passed through the flight of SE-5s with seven survivors, one of which, however was turning for home with smoke issuing from its oil cooler. The three British aircraft, necessarily throttling back to save their engines, began to mush out of their climbing attitude. Three Albatros which had been waiting their turn now launched a horizontal attack.

His head swivelling while he half-stood in the cockpit, searching, Gelvarry saw the three fresh Albatros emerge from the clouds. Below him, six of the original assault were looping up to rejoin. On his right, Paddy's aircraft displayed miscellaneous splinters and punctures of the empennage, and was trailing a few streamers of fabric, but appeared to be structurally sound. O'Sullivan, however, was beating at the breechblock of one of his guns with a wooden mallet, one hand wrapped around an

nterplane strut to hold him forward over the windscreen, the other
usy with its hammering as it tried to pop out the overexpanded
hell casing. His aircraft was wallowing as he inadvertently
udged the stick back and forth with his legs.

On the left, Nigger was nosedown, his airscrew windmilling,
opy smoke and pink fire blowing back over the cockpit. For a
noment, the SE-5's ailerons quickly flapped into a new configu-
ation, and the rudder and elevators came over as Landsdowne
ried to sideslip the burning. But they were, in any case, at 7000
eet and at this height there was really no point to the maneuver.
.andsdowne stood up in the cockpit as the aircraft came level
gain, saluted Gelvarry, and jumped, his collar and helmet thickly
railing soot.

"So long, Nig," Gelvarry murmured. He glanced up. A mile
bove them, the silvery flash of sunlight upon the *Ticonderoga*'s
lanks dazzled the eye; nevertheless, he thought he could make out
he attendant cloud of dark midges who were the high squadron.
Ie looked to his right and saw that O'Sullivan was being hit
epeatedly in the torso by gunfire, white phophorus tracer spirals
merging from the plucked leather of his coat.

Gelvarry took in a deep breath. He pushed his aircraft into a
alling right bank, kicked right rudder, and passed between two of
he oncoming Nazis. He converted the bank into the shallow
living roll, and so went down through the climbing group of
Albatros at an angle which made it useless for either side to fire.
Ie had also placed all his enemies in such a relationship to him
hat they would have had to turn and dive at suicidal inclinations
n order to overtake him as he darted homeward.

He flew above the remains of villages that look like old bones
awash in brown soup, and over the lines that were like a river on
he moon, its margins festooned with wire to prevent careless
Selenites from stumbling in. A high squadron aircraft dropped
lown and flew beside him for a while, as he had heard they
ometimes did lately.

He glanced over at the glossy stagger-wing biplane, its color
lack except for the white-lettered unit markings, a red-and-white
norizontally striped rudder panel, and the American cocardes with
he five-pointed white star and orange ball in the center. The pilot
vas looking at him. He wore a pale yellow helmet, goggles that
lashed in the sun, and a very clean white scarf. He raised a hand
nd waved reservedly, as one might across a tier of boxes at the
:oncert hall. Then he pulled back on his stick and the black

aircraft climbed away precipitously, so swiftly that Gelvarry half-expected a crackling of displaced air, but instead heard, very faintly over his own engine, the smooth roar of the other's exhaust. He found that his own right hand was still elevated, and took it down.

He came in over the poplars, and found that he was going to land cross-wind. Ground personnel raised their heads as if they had been grazing at the margins of the runway. He put it down anyhow, swung it about, and taxied toward the hangar, blipping the engine to keep the cylinder heads from sooting up, and finally cut his switch near where Sergeant-Major MacBanion was standing waiting with the little gray monkey perched on his right shoulder. As the engine stopped, the cold once again settled into Gelvarry's bones.

"All right, Sir?" Sar'n-Major Mac asked, looking up at him. The monkey, too, raised its little Capuchin face, the small lobstery eyes peering from under the brim of a miniature *kepi*.

Gelvarry put his hands on the cockpit rim, placed his heels carefully on the transverse brace below the rudder bar, and pushed himself back and up. Then he was able to slip down the side of the fuselage. He stood slapping his hands against his biceps.

Sergeant-Major MacBanion put a hand gently on his shoulder. "And the remainder of the flight, Sir?"

Gelvarry shrugged. He pulled off his helmet and goggles and stuffed them into a pocket of his coat. He stamped his feet, despite the hurt. Then as the cold began to leave him, he merely stood running his hands up and down his arms, and hunching his back.

"Never mind, Sir," Sar'n-Major Mac said softly. "I've come to tell you we've had an urgent message. You're posted to high squadron immediately, Sir."

Gelvarry found himself weeping silently.

"Follow me to Major Harding's hut, please, Sir," Sergeant-Major MacBanion said quietly and gravely. "Don't concern yourself about the aircraft—we'll see to it."

"Thank you," Gelvarry whispered. He walked behind the spare, erect figure to the Major's hut, watching the monkey gently waving the swagger stick. Then he waited outside, rubbing his hands over his cheeks, feeling the moisture trapped between his palm and the oil film on his skin. He hated the coating in his nostrils and on the roof of his mouth, and habitually scraped it off his lips between his teeth.

Sergeant-Major MacBanion came out of the dark hut, shut the door positively, said, "That's all right, then, Sir," turned his face slightly and shouted: "Private Parkins on the double if you please!"

Parkins came running up with a thud of boots on damp cinders and saluted energetically. "Yes, Sar'n-Major?"

"Parkins, I want you to list three reserve flying personnel with appropriate aircraft for this afternoon's sweep. Make it the three senior men. What flying personnel will that leave at this station during the afternoon hours?"

"Two, Sar'n-Major, in addition to this officer." Parkins nodded slightly toward Gelvarry without taking his eyes off Sergeant-Major MacBanion's steady gaze.

"Don't concern yourself with this officer, Parkins; Chaplain and I'll be taking care of him."

Parkins brought out the sapient manner he had been withholding. "Right, Sar'n-Major. I'll just have Major Harding send them other two officers over to Wing in the Rolls to sign for some engine spares, and that'll clear the premises nicely. I'll take the time to sort through this officer's kit for shipping home, then, as well, shall I?"

"I think not, Parkins," Sergeant-Major MacBanion said meaningly, and Parkins could be seen to bob his Adam's apple. "That is Major Harding's duty. That's what commanding officers are for." The thick, neatly clipped brows drew into a speculating frown. "You're slipping very badly, aren't you, Parkins? I wonder what a rummage through your duffel might turn up; I can't say I care for the smell of your breath."

"Hit's mouthwash, Sar'n-Major!" Parkins exclaimed. "A bit of a soother for me sore bicuspid, like!"

"I'll give you sore, Private Parkins, I surely will," Sergeant-Major Mac declared. "Pull yourself together long enough to attend to your own tasks. You're to telephone Wing for three replacement flying personnel to join here tonight, correct? And there's the lorry and the working party to organize; I want this officer's aircraft crashed *and* burning, no doubt about it, *in* No Man's Land, *be*fore teatime, and *if* that's all quite sufficiently clear to you, my man, you *will* see to it forth*with*!"

Parkins saluted, about-faced, and trotted off, sweating. The Sergeant-Major smiled thinly after him, then turned to Gelvarry. "This way, then, please, Sir," he said, and stepped onto the footpath worn through the scrub beside Major Harding's hut.

Following him, Gelvarry was startled to note the neatly cultivated domestic vegetable plot behind the rusty corrugated sheet iron of the Major's dwelling. There were seed packets up on little stakes at the ends of rows, and string stretched in a zigzag web for runnerbeans. Lettuce and carrots were poking up tentatively along one side, and most of the rows were showing early evidence of shooting. A spade with an officer's cap dangling over the handle was thrust into a dirt-encrusted pile of industrial furnace clinkers that had apparently been extracted from the soil.

"Padre!" Sergeant-Major MacBanion called ahead. "Here's an officer to see you!"

Father Collins thrust his head around the fly of his dwelling tent, which was situated beyond the shrubs screening Major Harding's hut from this far end of the aerodrome. He was a round-faced man of kindly appearance whom Gelvarry had occasionally seen in the mess, fussing with the Sparklets machine and otherwise making himself useful and approved of. He came and moved a little distance toward them along the path, and then waited for them to come up. He put out his hand to shake Gelvarry's. "Always here to be of help," he said.

Sergeant-Major MacBanion cleared his throat. "This'll be a high squadron posting, Padre."

Father Collins nodded a little crossly. "One gathers these things, Sergeant-Major MacBanion. Well, young fellah, let's get to it, then, shall we?" His expression softened and he studied Gelvarry's face carefully. "No need prolonging matters, then, is there? Not a decision to be taken lightly, but, once made, to be followed expeditiously, eh?" He put an arm around Gelvarry's shoulders. Gelvarry found himself grateful for the animal warmth; the cold had been at his ribs again. He went along up the path with Father Collins and Sar'n-Major Mac, and when they reached the little overgrown rise where Father Collins's tent was situated, he stopped. He found he was looking down at a revetment where the transition aircraft was kept.

He walked around and around, a slight smile on his lips, ducking under the planes and squeezing by the end of the rudder where it was nearly right up against the rear embankment. He ran his fingertips lightly over the impeccably doped fabric and admired the workmanship of the rudder and elevator hinges, the delicately shaped brass standoffs that gave extra purchase to the control

ables. Everything was new; the smell of the aircraft had the tang
f a fitter's storage locker.

He stopped and faced it from outside the revetment. The slim
lack aircraft pointed its rounded nose well up over his head; it
vas much larger than he'd expected from seeing one in the air;
e'd thought perhaps the pilot was slightly built.

It rested gracefully upon its two fully spatted tires, with a
eardrop-shaped auxiliary fuel tank nestled up between the fully
aired landing gear struts. Its rest position on its tailskid set it on
n angle such that the purposefully sturdy wings grasped muscu-
arly at the air. A glycol radiator slung at the point of the cowling's
aw promised to sieve with jubilation through the stream hurled
ackward by the three-bladed metal airscrew.

There were very few wires; the struts appeared to be quite thin
rontally, but were faired back for lateral strength. It would, yes it
vould, burgeon upward through the air with every ounce of power
vailable from that promising engine hidden behind the lovingly
haped panels, and it would stoop like a bird of prey. It would not
reak or whip in the air; its fuselage panels would not drum and
ipple; the dope of its upper surfaces would not star and flake off
nder the compression of warping wings in a battle maneuver, and
ne would not find, after twenty or thirty hours, that the planes
nd the stabilizer had been permanently shaken out of alignment
vith each other.

This aircraft had the same markings as the one that had flown
lown briefly, except for the actual numerals. In addition to the
ational cocardes, it also bore a unit insigne—a long-barreled
lintlock rifle crossed upon a powderhorn.

Gelvarry felt a prickling pass along the short hairs of his
orearms as he thought of flying under that banner. A great-great-
ancle was reputed in his family to have been among that company
vanished in search of Providence Plantations, as others had done
n attempting to find Oglethorpe's Colony or the fabled inland
cities of Virginia Dare's children. North America was a continent
of endless forest and dark rumor. And yet something, it seemed—
ome seed possessed of patience—had been germinating *Ticond-
rogas* and aircraft construction works all the while, and within
each of Mr. Churchill's remarkable winnow.

"This is the Curtis P6E 'Hawk,' " Sar'n-Major Mack said at his
lbow. "This model is the ultimate development of what will
e considered the most versatile armed chase single-place biplane
ver designed. The original airframe will be introduced in the

mid-1920s. As you see it here, it is fitted with United States Army
Air Corps–specified inline liquid-cooled four-stroke engine devel
oping 450 horsepower, and two fixed quick-firing thirty-calibre
machine guns geared to shoot through the airscrew. The U.S
Navy version, known as the 'Goshawk,' will use the Wrigh
'Whirlwind' radial air-cooled engine. Both basic versions are very
highly thought of, will remain in service in the U.S. until the
mid-1930s, and a few 'Hawk' versions will be used by the
Republican air forces in the Spanish Civil War, should tha
occur."

Father Collins had been up at the cockpit, leaning in to polish
the instrument glass with a soft white cloth. He came down now
pausing to wipe the step into the fuselage and the place on the
wing root where he had rested his other foot.

"All quite ready now," he said, carefully folding the cloth and
putting it away in his open-mouthed black leather case. He rested
his hand on Gelvarry's shoulder. "We've kept her in prime
condition for you, lad—no one's ever flown her before; Sar'n
Major and I just ticked her over now and then, kept her clean and
taut; the usual drill."

Gelvarry was nodding. As the moment drew near, he found
himself breathing with greater difficulty. Tears were gathering in
his eyes. He turned his face away awkwardly.

"Now, as for the hooking on," Sergeant-Major MacBanion was
saying briskly, "I'm certain you'll manage that part of it quite
well, Sir." He was pointing up at the trapeze hook fixed to the
center of the mainplane like the hanger of a Christmas tree ball,
and Gelvarry perforce had to look at him attentively.

"Pity there's no way to rehearse the necessary maneuver, Sir,'
Sar'n-Major Mac went on, "but they say it comes to one. Only a
matter of matching courses and speeds, after all, and then just
easing up in there."

Gelvarry nodded. He still could not speak.

"Well, Sir," the Sergeant-Major concluded. "Care to try a few
circuits and bumps around the old place before taking her to your
new posting? Get the feel of her? Some prefer that. Many just
climb right in and go off. What'll it be, Sir?"

Gelvarry found himself profoundly disturbed. Something was
rising in his chest. Father Collins looked at him narrowly and
raised his free hand toward MacBanion. "Perhaps we're rushing
our fences, Sergeant-Major. Just verify the cockpit appurtenances
there and give us a moment meanwhile, will you?" He turned

Gelvarry away from the aircraft and sauntered beside him casually, his arm around Gelvarry's shoulders again.

"Troubles you, does it?"

Gelvarry glanced at him.

"But there was no doubt in your mind when you spoke to
MacBanion about this, was there?"

Gelvarry blinked, then shook his head slowly.

"It's good sense, you know. You'd be leaving us the other way,
shortly, if it weren't for this. Bound to." He dug in his pocket for
his pipe and blew through it sharply to clear the stem. "Sergeant-
Major's been discussing it for weeks. Thin as a charity widow,
he's been calling you, and twice as pale, except for the Hennessey
roses in your cheeks, beggin' all flyin' officers' pardon, Sir. He's
been wanting to do something about it."

Gelvarry gave a high, short laugh.

Father Collins chuckled tolerantly. "Ah, no, no, Lad, hoping
we'd make the choice for you is not the same. We always wait till
the man requests it. Have to, eh? Suppose a man were posted on
our say-so; liable to resent it, wouldn't he be, don't you think?
Might kick up a fuss. Word of high squadron might reach Home.
And we can't have that, now, can we?"

Gelvarry shook his head, walking along with his lips between
his teeth, his lustrous eyes on his aimless feet.

"Mothers' marches on Whitehall, questions in Parliament—If
they're alive, put 'em back on duty or bring 'em home to the
shellshock ward—that sort of thing. Be an unholy row, wouldn't
you think? And so much grief renewed among the loved ones, to
say nothing of the confusion; it would be cruel. Or what would
they say at the Admiralty if officers and gentlemen began
discussing another Mr. Churchill, he cruising about the skies like
the Angels of Mons, furthermore? For that matter, I imagine *their*
Mr. Churchill would have quite a bit to say about it, and none of
it pleasant to the tender ear, eh?"

Gelvarry smiled as well as he was able. He had never laid eyes
on or heard the young Mr. Churchill; he imagined him a plump,
shrill, prematurely balding fellow in loosely tailored clothing,
gesturing with a pair of spectacles.

Father Collins gently turned Gelvarry back toward the aircraft.
"We'll miss you, too, you know," he said quietly. "But we must
move along now. It's best if other flying personnel can't be certain
who's in high squadron and who's left us in the old stager's way,
don't you agree? Gives everyone a bit of something to look

forward to as the string shortens. MacBanion's a genius at clearing the field, but time *is* passing. Don't worry, Boy—Major Harding does a lovely job of seeing to it nothing's sent home as shouldn't be, and of course I'll be conveying the tidings by my own hand." They were back beside the P6E. Sergeant-Major MacBanion was standing stiffly attentive, the monkey in the crook of his arm with one small hand curled around the butt of the swagger stick.

"I believe I'll try taking her straight out, Sergeant-Major," Gelvarry said.

"Right, Sir. That's the way! Just a few things to remember about the controls, Sir, and you'll find she goes along quite nicely."

"And thank you very much, Father. I appreciate your concern."

"Nonsense, my boy. Only natural. Just keep it in mind we're all still hitting the Bavarian Corporal where he hurts; high or low makes little difference. Bit more comfortable up where you'll be, I shouldn't wonder, but I'm sure you've earned it. Tenfold. Easily tenfold."

"Let my family down as easily as you can, will you, Father?" Gelvarry said.

"Ah, yes, yes, of course."

Gelvarry climbed up into the cockpit. He sat getting the feeling of how it fit him. He waggled the stick and nudged the rudder—there were pedals for his feet, rather than a pivoted bar, but the principle was the same.

Sar'n-Major Mac got up the lower plane root and leaned into the cockpit over him. "Here's your magneto switch, and that's your throttle, of course; some of these instruments you can just ignore—can't imagine why a real aviator'd want them, tell the truth—and this is a wireless telegraphy device, but you don't need *that*—can you imagine, from the way the seat's designed when Padre and I take 'em out of the shipping crate, I'd say you were intended to be sitting on a parachute, of all things; get yourself mistaken for a ruddy civilian, next thing—but this, here's, your supercharger cut-in."

"Supercharger?"

"Oh, right, right, yes, Sir, no telling how high you might find *Ticonderoga*; things could be a bit thin. And in that vein, Sir, you'll note this metal bottle with petcock and flexible tubing. That's your oxygen supply; simply place the end of the tube in your mouth, open the petcock as required, and suck on it from time to time at altitudes above 12,000 feet, or lower if feeling a bit winded. Got all that, Sir?"

"Yes, thank you, Sar'n-Major."

"Very good! Well, then, Sir, Padre'll be wanting another brief word with you, and then anytime after that, we'll just get her started, shall we? I understand the Navy type has a crank thing called an inertia starter, but the old familiar way's for us. After that, I'd suggest a little taxiing for the feel of the controls and throttle, and then just head her into the wind, full throttle, and pleasure serving with you, Sir, if I do say so. You'll find she favors her nose a little, so keep throttle down a bit until you bring her nearer to level; I imagine she stalls something ferocious. But there'll be no trouble; never had any trouble yet. Just head west and look about; you'll see your new post up there somewhere. Can't really miss it, after all—large enough. Anything else, Sir?"

"No. No, thank you, Ma—Sergeant-Major MacBanion."

MacBanion's right eyebrow had been rising. It dropped back into place. He patted Gelvarry manfully atop the shoulder. "That's the way, Sir. Have a good trip, and think of us grubbing away down here, once in a while, will you?" He jumped from the lower plane and Father Collins came up, holding the bag. "Might be a longish flight, Son," he said. "You've had nothing to eat or drink since midnight, I believe. So you'll be wanting some of this." He opened the bag and handed Gelvarry a small flask and a piece of bread. "And there's windburn at those altitudes." He put ointment on Gelvarry's forehead and eyelids. "Have a safe flight," he said.

Gelvarry nodded. "Thank you again." When Father Collins jumped down, Gelvarry ducked his head below the level of the cockpit coaming and wiped his face. He put his arm straight up in the air and rotated his hand. Sergeant-Major MacBanion and he began the starting procedure.

The aircraft handled very well. He did a long figure eight over the aerodrome at low altitude after he'd gotten the feel of it. The ground personnel of course were busy at their various tasks. An unfamiliar figure leaning with one foot on a garden spade waved up casually from behind Major Harding's hut. The monkey was perched on a new pineboard crate Father Collins and Sergeant-Major MacBanion were manhandling down into the revetment from the back of an open lorry. As Gelvarry flew over, the little creature scrambled up to the apex of the tilting box, grinned at him, and raised its kepi.

Past the field, Gelvarry did a creditable Immelmann turn, gained altitude, settled himself a little more comfortably on the cushion made from a gunnysack stuffed with rags, and flew toward the afternoon sun, looking upward.

The aircraft *was* a joy, he gradually realized. He probed tentatively at the pedals and stick, at first, hardly recognizing he was doing so because he was under the impression his mind was full of confusions and sorrows. But as he held steadily west, his back and his arse heavy in the seat, his mind began to develop a certain wire-hard incised detachment which he recognized from his evenings with the brandy. In fact, as he gained more and more altitude, and began to rock the wings jauntily and even to give it a little rudder so that he set up a slight fishtail, he could almost hear the messroom piano, as it was every day after nightfall, all snug around the stove, grinning at each other if they could, and roaring out: "Warbirds, Warbirds, ripping through the air/Warbirds, Warbirds, fighting everywhere/Any age, any place, any foreign clime/Warbirds of Time!"

Catching himself, Haverman slipped the oxygen tube into his mouth and opened the valve on the bottle. As the dry gas slid palpably into his mouth and down his throat, the squadron theme faded from the forefront of his mind, and he began to fly the aircraft rather than play with it. He reached out, his bared wrist numbingly exposed for a moment between glove and cuff, and cut in the supercharger. There was a thump up forward of the firewall, and the engine note steadied. There was a faint, somewhat reassuring new whine in its note.

He began to feel quite himself again, encased within the indurate fuselage, his dark wings spread stiffly over the crystal-clear air below, the gleaming fabric inviolate as it hissed almost hotly through the wind of its passage. He took another pull on the oxygen. He gazed over the side of the cockpit. Down there, little aircraft were dodging and tumbling, their mainplanes reflecting sunlight in a sort of passionate Morse. He knew that message, and he drew his head back inside the cockpit. He resumed searching the deepened blue of the sky above him. And in a little bit, he saw a silver glint northwest of the sun. He turned slightly to aim straight for it, and flew steadily.

After a while, Gelvarry noticed that his throat was being dessicated by the steady flow of the oxygen. He shut the valve and spat out the tube. Pulling the Padre's chased silver flask from the

bosom of his tunic, he drank from it. He also ate the cold dry
bread. He did not feel particularly sustained by the snack, but the
flask was quite nice as a present.

As he went, the distant speck took on breadth as well as length,
and then details, size, and a gradual dulling down as the silvered
cloth covering began to reveal some panels fresher than others,
and the effect of varying hands at the brushwork of the doping. It
now looked much as it did on those occasions when it hovered
above the aerodrome and Mr. Churchill came down in his wicker
car at the end of a cable, as he had done in addressing the squadron
several times during Gelvarry's posting.

Ticonderoga in flight upon the same level as the tropopausal
winds, however, was even larger, somehow, and the light fell
altogether differently upon it, now that he looked at it again.
Boring purposefully onward, its great airscrews turning invisibly
but for cyclic reflections, it filled the very world with a monster
throbbing that Gelvarry could not hear as sound over the catlike
snarlings of his own engine, but to which every surface of his
aircraft, and in fact of his mouth and of the faceted goggles over
his eyes, vibrated as if being struck by driving wet snow.

Ticonderoga suspended a dozen double-banked radial engines
in teardrop pods abaft its main gondola; they seemed to float just
below its belly like subsidiary craft of its own kind. Gelvarry, who
had seen one or two zeppelin warcraft, was struck by the major
differences—*Ticonderoga*'s smoothly tapered rather than bluntly
rounded tail and bow; its almost fishlike control surfaces, with
ventral and dorsal vertical stabilizers, and matching symmetrical
horizontal planes, rather than the kitelike box-sections of the
Fuehrer's designs; the many glassed compartments and blisters
along the hull, and the smoothly faired main and after gondolas,
rather than a single rope-slung control car. But the main thing was
the size, of course. He resumed taking oxygen.

As he drew nearer, tucking himself into its shadow as if under
a great living cloud, *Ticonderoga* began blinking a red light at him
from a ventral turret just abaft the great open bay in its belly
amidships. Then three aircraft launched from that yawning hangar, dropping one, two, three like a stick of bombs but immediately gaining flying speed and wheeling into formation around
him. He saw their unit numbers were in sequence with his. He
waved, and their three pilots waved back.

Gelvarry watched them, fascinated. They flew with mesmerizing
precision, carving smooth arcs in the air as if on wires, showing

no reaction at all to the turbulence back along *Ticonderoga*'s hull. They circled him effortlessly; they in fact created the effect of turning about him while really flying flat spirals along the dirigible's flight path. Gelvarry waved again to show his appreciation of their skill, barely remembering to breathe. His gauntleted hands touched lightly at his own stick and throttle, not so much to make changes as to remind himself that he was flying, too.

One of the P6Es had a commander's broad bright stripe belting its fuselage. As soon as it was clear Gelvarry understood enough to hold while they maneuvered, the flight leader could be seen bringing his wireless microphone to his lips and speaking to *Ticonderoga*. The landing trapeze came lowering steadily down out of the bay, and hung motionless, a horizontal bar streaming along across the line of flight at the end of its complicated-looking latching tether.

The leader looked across at Gelvarry, light shining on his goggles, and pointed to one of the other Hawks, which immediately moved out of formation and approached the trapeze. Gelvarry nodded so the leader could see it; they were teaching him. Then he watched the landing aircraft intently.

The hook rising out of the center of the mainplane was designed very much like a standard snap-hook. Once it had been pushed hard against the trapeze bar, it would open to hook around it, and then would snap shut. The trick, Gelvarry thought as he watched his squadronmate sway from side to side, was to center the hook on the bar at exactly the right height. Otherwise, the P6E's nose would be forced to one side or the other of the ideal flight line, and there might be embarrassing consequences.

But the pilot brought it off nicely, apparently unconcerned about tipping his airscrew into the tether or slashing his mainplane fabric with the trapeze. He sideslipped once to bring himself into perfect alignment, and put the hook around the bar with a slight throttle-blip that put one little puff of blue smoke out the end of his exhaust pipe. Then he cut throttle, the trapeze folded around the hook to make assurance double sure, and he was drawn up into the hangar bay, *allez-oop!* in one almost continuous movement.

In a moment, the trapeze came down again, and the second pilot did essentially the same thing. The other half of the trick was not to create significant differences between the forward speeds of the dirigible and the aircraft along their identical flight lines, and Gelvarry lightly touched his throttle again, without moving it just

et. But when he glanced across at the leader, he was being
estured forward and up, and the trapeze was once more waiting.
he leader drifted down and to the side, where he could watch.

Gelvarry took in a good breath from the bottle and came up into
he turbulence, well back of the trapeze but at about the right
eight. He took another breath, and his mind crisped. He touched
he throttle with delicate purposefulness, and came inching up on
he bar, which was rocking rhythmically from side to side until he
ut his knees to either side of the stick and rocked his body from
ide to side. Thus rocking the ailerons to compensate, thus
evealing that the bar had been quite steady all along, and that he
vas now reasonably steady with it. He was coming in an inch or
wo off center. He gulped again at the tube. What can happen? he
hought dispassionately, and twitched the throttle between thumb
nd forefinger, a left-handed pinball player's move. With a clash
nd a bang, the hook snapped over and the trapeze folded. He
losed throttle and cut the magneto instantaneously, *slip-slap*, and
e was already inside the shadow of the hangar, swaying sicken-
ngly at the end of the tether, but already being swung over toward
he landing stage, with a whine of gears from the tether crane,
vhose spidery latticework arm overhead blended into the shad-
wy, endlessly repeated lattice girders that formed frame after
dentical frame, a gaunt cathedral whose groins and mullions
etreated into diminishing distances fore and aft, housing the great
ulks of the helium bags, interlaced by crew catwalks and ladders,
potted here and there by worklights but illuminated in the main
y the featureless old-ivory glow through the translucent hull
naterial.

Suddenly there was no sound immediately upon his ears, except
or the pinging of his exhaust pipes and cylinder heads. The great
oaring of passage pierced into the air was gone. What was
eft instead was a distant buzz, and the sighing rush of air rubbing
over the great fabric.

The P6E's tailskid, and then its tires, touched down on the
anding stage. A coveralled man wearing a hood over his mouth
nd a bottle on his back stepped up on the lower plane, then
eached to the mainplane and disengaged the hook from the
rapeze, which was swung away instantly. Other aircraft handlers
tood looking impatiently at Gelvarry, who lifted himself up out of
he cockpit and down to the jouncy perforated-aluminum deck.
down past his feet, he could see the structures of the lower hull,

and the countryside idling backward below the open bay before
the leader's Hawk nosed blackly forward toward the trapeze.

He could see almost everywhere within the dirigible. Here and
there, there were housed structures behind solid dural sheets
or stretched canvas screens. Machinery—winches, generators,
pumps—and stores of various kinds might interrupt a line of sight
to some extent, but not significantly. Even the helium bags were
not totally opaque. (Nor rigid, either; he could see them breathing,
pale, and creased at the tops and bottoms, and he could hear their
casings and their tethers creaking.) He felt he could shout from
one end of *Ticonderoga* to the other; might also spring into the air
toward that stanchion, swing to that brace, go hand over hand
along the rail of that catwalk, scramble up that ladder, swing by
that cable to that inspection platform, slip down that catenary,
rebound from the side of that bag, land lightly over there on the
other side of the bay and present himself, grinning, to his fellow
pilots standing there watching him now, all standing at ease, their
booted feet spread exactly the same distance apart, their hands
clasped behind their backs, their cavalry breeches identically
spotless, their dark tunics and Sam Browne belts all in a row
above beltlines all at essentially the same height, their helmets on
and their goggles down over their eyes.

He licked his lips. He glanced up guiltily toward the catwalk
higher up in the structure, where a row of naked gray monkeys the
size of large children was standing, paws along the railing,
motionless, studying things. Gelvarry glanced aside.

The flight leader's plane was swung in and then rolled back to
join the dozen others lashed down along the hangar deck. The man
had jumped down out of the cockpit; he strode toward Gelvarry
now. As he approached, Gelvarry saw his features were nonde-
script.

"You're to report to Mr. Churchill's cabin for a conference at
once," he said to Gelvarry. He pointed. "Follow that walkway.
You'll find a hatch forward of the main helium cells, there. It
opens on the midships gondola. Mr. Churchill is waiting."

Gelvarry stopped himself in midsalute. "Aren't you going to
take me there?"

The flight leader shook his head. "No. I can't stand the place.
Full of the monkeys."

"Ah."

"Good luck," the officer said. "We shan't be seeing more of

each other, I'm afraid. Pity. I'd been looking forward to serving with you."

Gelvarry shrugged uncomfortably. "So it goes," he said for lack of something precise to say, and turned away.

He followed directions toward the gondola. As he moved along, the monkeys flowed limb-over-limb above him among the higher levels of the structural bracing, keeping pace. As they traveled, they conducted incidental business, chattering, gesticulating, knotting up momentarily in clumps of two and three individuals in the grip of passion or anger that left one or two scurrying away cowed or indignant, the level of their cries rising or falling. The whole group, however, maintained the general movement with Gelvarry.

He was fairly certain he remembered what they were, and he did what he could to ignore them.

He came to the gondola hatch, which was an engine-turned duraluminum panel opening on a ladder leading down into a long, windowed corridor lined with crank-operated chest-high machines, at each of which crouched and cranked a monkey somewhat smaller than Gelvarry. As he set foot on the ladder, several of the larger monkeys from the hull spaces suddenly shoved past him, all bristles and smell, forcing their way into the corridor. They were met with immediate, shrieking violence from the nearest machine monkeys, and Gelvarry swung himself partway off the ladder, his eyes wide, maintaining his purchase with one boot toe and one gloved hand while he peered back over his shoulder at the screams and wrestlings within the confined space.

Bloodied intruder monkeys with their pelts torn began to flee back toward safety past him, voiceless and panting, their expressions desperate. The attempted invasion was becoming a fiasco at the deft hands of the machine monkeys, who fought with ear-ripping indignation, uttering howls of outrage while viciously handling the much more naive newcomers. Out of the corner of his eye, Gelvarry saw exactly one of the intruders—who had shrewdly chosen a graying and instinctively diffident machine monkey several positions away from the hatch—pay no heed to the tumult and close its teeth undramatically and inflexibly in its target's throat. In a moment, the object of the maneuver was a limp and yielding bundle on the deck. While all its fellows streamed up past Gelvarry and took, dripping, to the safety of the hull braces, the one victorious new monkey bent over the dispossessed machine and began turning the crank. No attention was paid to it as things within the gondola corridor returned to normal.

Gelvarry closed and secured the hatch while monkeys returned to their machines. The wounded ones ignored their hurts cleverly. Neither neighbor of the successful invader paid any overt attention to matters as they now stood, but Gelvarry noticed that as they bobbed and weaved at their machines, with the new monkey between them and with the dead cranker supine at his feet, they unobtrusively extended their limbs and tails to nudge lightly at the body, until they had almost inadvertently kicked it out of sight behind the machines.

Each of the machines displayed a three-dimensional scene within a small circular platform atop the device. Aircraft could be seen moving in combat among miniature clouds over distant background landscapes. Doped wings glistened in the sunlight, turning, turning, reflecting flashes. Dot dot dot. Dash dash dash. Dot. Dot. Dot. Gelvarry brushed forward between the busy animals and moved toward the farther hatch at the other end of the corridor. Atop the nearest machine, he saw a Fokker *dreidekker* painted red, whipping through three fast barrel rolls before resuming level flight above the floundering remains of a broken Nieuport. Dot dot dot dash.

The monkey at that machine frowned and cranked the handle backwards. The Baron's triplane suddenly reversed its actions. Dash dot dot dot. The Nieuport reassembled. Stork insignia could be seen painted on its fuselage. The crank turned forward again. The swastika-marked red wings corkscrewed into their victory roll again above the disintegrating Frenchman.

The monkey at the machine was crooning and bouncing on the balls of its feet, rubbing its free hand over his lips. It moved several knobs at the front of the viewing machine, and the angle changed, so that the point of view was directly from the cockpit of the Fokker, and pieces of the Nieuport flew past the wing struts to either side. The monkey jabbed its neighbors with its elbows and nodded toward the action. It searched the face on either side for reaction. One of them, turning away from a scene of Messerschmitt 262 tactical jet fighters rocketing a column of red-starred T-34 tanks on the ice of Lake Ladoga, glanced over impatiently and pushed back at the Fokker monkey's shoulder, resuming its attention to its own concerns. But the other neighboring monkey was kinder. Despite the fact that its flight of three Boeing P-26s was closing fast on a terrified Kawanishi flying boat over the Golden Gate Bridge, it paused long enough to glance at the Baron's victory, pat its neighbor reassuringly on the back, and utter a chirp of approbation. Pleased, the first monkey was immediately rapt in rerunning the new version of the scene. The kind monkey stole a glance over again, shrugged, and resumed cranking its own machine.

Gelvarry continued pushing between the monkeys to either side. The flooring was solid, but springy underfoot. The ceiling was convex, and wider than the floor, so that the duraluminum walls tapered inward. They were pierced for skylights above the long banks of machines, but *Ticonderoga* was apparently passing through clouds. There were rapid alterations of light at the ports, but only slight suggestions of any detail. Over the spasmodic grinding of the cranks, and the constant slight vocalizations of the monkeys, the sound of air washing over the walls and floor could be made out if one paused and listened ruminatively.

Gelvarry reached Mr. Churchill's compartment door. He knocked, and the reassuring voice replied: "Come!" He quickly entered and closed the sheet-metal panel securely behind him.

The compartment was large for his expectations. Its deck was parqueted and dressed in oriental carpets. Armchairs and taborets were placed here and there, with many low reading lamps, and opaque drapes swayed over the portholes. Mr. Churchill sat heavily in a Turkish upholstered chair at the other end of the room, facing him, wearing his pinstriped blue suit with the heavy watchchain across the rounded vest. He gripped a freshly lighted Uppman cigar between his knuckles. The famous face was drawn up into its wet baby scowl, and Gelvarry at once felt the impact of the man's presence.

"Ah," Mr. Churchill said. "None too soon. Come and sit by me. We have only a moment or two, and then they shall all be here." His mouth quirked sideward. "Rabble," he growled. "Counterjumpers."

Gelvarry moved forward toward the chair facing the Prime Minister. "Am I a unique case, Sir?" he said, sitting down with a trace of uneasiness. "I was told high squadron posting was voluntary only."

Mr. Churchill raised his eyebrows and turned to the taboret beside him. He punched a bronze pushbell screwed to the top. "Unique? Of course you're unique, man! You're the principal, after all." A doorway somewhere behind him opened, and a young woman with soot-black hair and bee-stung lips entered wearing a French maid's costume. She brought a silver tray on which rested two crystal tumblers and a bottle of the familiar Hennessey *Rx Official*. "Very good! Very good!" Mr. Churchill said, pouring. "Mr. Dunstan Haverman, I'm introducing Giselle Montez," he said, giving her name the Gallic pronunciation. "It is very possible that you shall"—he shrugged—"meet again." Gelvarry tried not to appear much out of countenance as Miss Montez brought the salver and stood gracefully silent, her eyes downcast, while he took his tumbler. "Charmed," he said softly.

"Thank you," she murmured, turned, and retreated through her doorway. She had left the bottle with Mr. Churchill.

Gelvarry sipped. Mr. Churchill raised his glass. "Here's to reality."

Haverman shuddered. "No," he said, drinking more deeply anyway, "I was beginning to depend on it too much. Sam, what's going wrong?"

Sam grunted as the amber liquid hit his own esophagus. He was normally a self-contained, always pleasant-spoken individual— the typical golf or tennis pro at the best club in the county—who in Haverman's long experience of him had once frowned when a drunk at a business luncheon had pawed a waitress. And then calmly tipped a glass of icewater into the man's lap, costing himself a thirty-nine-week deal.

"Sam?" Haverman peered through the Hennessey effect at his grimacing old acquaintance.

"Take a look." The leaner, longer-legged, short-haired man sitting in the chrome-and-leather captain's chair turned toward the hard-edged cabinet standing beside him. The pushbell atop it seemed incongruous. Sam flipped up a panel and punched a number on the keyboard behind it. He closed the panel and nodded toward a cleared area of the panelled, indirectly lighted room. Haverman immediately recognized it as a holo focus, of course, even before he remembered what an inlaid circle in the flooring signified. It was a large one—half again the size of normally sold commercial receivers—as befitted the offices of a major industry figure.

Laurent Michaelmas appeared; urbane, dark-suited, scarlet flower in his lapel. "Good day," he said. "I have the news." He paused, one eyebrow cocked, hands slightly spread, waiting for feedback.

Sam raised his voice slightly above normal conversational level. "Just give us the broadcast industry top story, please," he said, and the Michaelmas projection flicked almost imperceptibly into a slightly new stance, then bowed and said:

"The top broadcast story is also still the top general story, sir. Now here it is:" He relaxed and stepped aside so that he was at the exact edge of the circle, visually related to the room floor level, while the remainder of the holo sphere went to an angled overhead view of Lower Manhattan.

"Well, today is October 25, 1992, in New York City, where the impact of the latest FCC ruling is still being assessed by programming departments of all major media." The scene-camera point of view became a circling pan around Wall Street Alley, picking up the corporate logos atop the various buildings: RCA, CBS, ABC, GTV, Blair, Neilsen. In a nice touch, the POV zoomed smoothly on an upper-story window, showing what appeared to be a conference room with three or four gesticulating figures somewhat visible through the sun-repelling glass. It was excellent piloting, too—the camera copter was being handled smoothly enough in the notorious off-bay cross-currents so that the holo scanner's limited compensatory circuits were able to take all the jiggle and drift out of the shot. Here was a flyer, Haverman thought, who wouldn't be a disgrace at the trapeze. Then he winced and took another nibble at the Hennessey.

"While viewers reaped an unexpected bonanza," Michaelmas said, and the background cut to an interior of a typical dwelling and a young man and woman watching Laurent Michaelmas with expressions of pleasant surprise, "industry spokesmen publicly lauded the FCC's Reception Release Order." The cut this time was to a pleasant-looking fellow in a casual suit, leaning against a holo cabinet. He smiled and said: "Folks, it's got to be the greatest thing since free tickets to the circus." He patted the cabinet. "Imagine! From now on, you can receive *every* and *any* channel right where you are, no matter *what* type of receiver you own! Yes, it's true—for only a few pennies, we'll bring you and install one of the new Rutledge-Karmann adapter units, with the best coherer circuit possible, that'll transform any receiver into an *all-channel* receiver! Now, how about that? Remember, the government says we have to use top-quality components, and we have to sell to you at *our cost*! So—" He grinned boyishly. "Even if we wanted to screw you, we can't."

"Others, however," Michaelmas said, "were not so sanguine. Even in public."

The holo went to Fingers Smart in the elevator lobby of what was recognizably the New York FCC building. He was striding out red-faced, followed by several figures Haverman could recognize as GTV attorneys and GTV's favorite consulting lawyer. "When interviewed, GTV Board Chairman Ancel B. Smart had this to say at 1:15 P.M. today:"

Now it was a two-shot of Smart being faced by an interested, smiling Laurent Michaelmas, while the lawyers milled around and tried to get a word in edgewise. Nobody ever effectively got between that friendly-uncle manner of Michaelmas's and whoever he was after.

"That's exactly right, Larry," Smart was saying. "We built the holovision industry the way it is because the FCC wanted it that way then. Now it wants it another way, and that's it. Public interest. Well, damn it, we're part of the public, too!" Smart's other industry nickname was Notso.

"Are you going to continue fighting the ruling?"

A belated widening of Smart's eyes now occurred. "Who says we're fighting it? We were here getting clarification of a few minor points. You know GTV operates in the public interest."

Sam chuckled, unamused, while Haverman peered and thought. GTV controlled eighty-seven entertainment channels that operated twenty-four hours a day. There were six GTV-owned channels leased to religious and political lobbies. There was also, of course, GTV's ten percent share of the public network subsidy. Paid off in programs given to PTV from the summer Student Creative internship plan.

That was how the dice had fallen when the Congress legislated cheap 3-D TV. The existing broadcast companies were trapped in their old established images with heavy emphasis on sports or news, women's daytime, musical variety, feature documentary anthologies, and the like. That had left an obvious vacuum which GTV had filled promptly.

All-channel receivers at an affordable price had been out of the question. As usual, Congress had been straining technology to its practical limits, and compromises had had to be made in the end. A good half of the receivers sold, Haverman remembered, were entertainment only. Now, apparently, because of something very cheap called the Harmon-Cutlass or something, he wouldn't have to remember it any longer.

"Oh!" he said, raising his eyes to Sam's nod.

Michaelmas cocked his head at Smart. "Just one or two more questions, please. Are you saying you haven't already cut your ratings guarantees to your advertisers? I believe your loss this quarter has just been projected at nearly twenty percent of last year's profits."

Smart glanced aside to his legal staff. But he was impaled on Michaelmas's smile. He tried one of his own; it worked beautifully at the annual entertainment programming awards dinner. "Come on, Larry—you know I'm no bean-counter. GTV's going to continue to offer the same top-drawer—"

"Well, one would assume that," Michaelmas said urbanely. "You have most of the season's product still on the shelf, unshown. No one would expect you to just dump a capital investment of that scope. What is your plan for after that? Or don't you expect to be the responsible executive six months from now?"

"Ouch!" Haverman said.

"I don't think I have to answer that here," Smart said quickly. He frowned at Michaelmas as he moved to step around him. "Come to think of it, you're in competition with us now, aren't you?" He actually laid a hand on Michaelmas's arm and pushed him a little aside, or would have, if Michaelmas didn't have a dancer's grace. "No further comment," Smart said, and strode off.

Michaelmas turned toward the point of view, while the background faded out behind him and left him free-standing. He shrugged expressively. "These little tiffs sometimes occur within the fellowship of broadcasting," he said with a smile. "But most observers would agree that competition is always in the public interest." There was the faintest of flicks to a stock tape; computer editing was instantaneous in real time, smooth, and due to become smoother. Even now, only an eye expecting it could detect it. "And that's how it is today," flick, "in broadcasting," flick, "and in the top story at this hour." He bowed and was gone.

Haverman rolled his eyes. "What happened?" he said. "I thought Hans Smart had a lock on Congress."

Sam grinned crookedly and grimly. "He's dead, poor chap. His liver gave out two weeks ago, and there went Notso's brains."

"Physiology got to the wrong brother."

"Yeah. It wouldn't have been as bad as it was, but three days before he went, NBC sprang a prime-time documentary. It was about this new little engineering company in Palo Alto that could pick up all channels on your $87.50 Sony portable. He wasn't cold in the ground before a dozen senators were on the all-channel bandwagon. The House delegation from California began lobbying as a bloc, New York City, and then Nassau and Dutchess counties jumped in, and the next you know Calart-Hummer or whatever it is, is the law of the land. Hans Smart could handle legislators with the best of 'em, but I don't think it was the booze that killed him; it was that friggin' feature."

Sam grinned more genuinely. "It was a beaut. NBC sent out engraved invitations, on paper, messenger-delivered to every member of Congress and anybody else they figured could swing a little. About six months ago, they had bought excerpt rights to about a dozen old *Warbirds* things. Newsfeature use only; you know how that goes, I guess. Well, it all turned up in that show. Michaelmas walking around narrating over it. Only that scaled it down behind him, so he was just stepping around over the battlefields and the planes were buzzing around him while he just smiled and talked. King damned Kong in a pinstripe suit. You wouldn't have believed it. Show it to you sometime; everybody in the business must have made a copy of it. Scare hell out of you. Even if you weren't personally involved, I mean."

Haverman sucked a little more Hennessey carefully between his lips and across the edges of his tongue. "What's been happening to the *Warbirds* ratings, Sam?"

Ticonderoga Studios produced other things besides *Warbirds*, but *Warbirds* was what it was known for in the industry, the *Warbirds* was GTV's top-rated show. GTV's contract was what kept Ticonderoga flying.

"Well, Dusty, we're having to be ingenious." Sam looked down at the stick between his fingers, then broke it open and inhaled in a controlled manner. "These things are pretty good," he remarked. "I think they'll catch on."

Haverman settled himself carefully in his chair. "Isn't this thing bound to settle out? I mean, it's a new toy. Notso may flail around for a while—"

Sam nodded, but not encouragingly. "He's gone. He knows it. But he's telling himself he can make it unhappen if he just yells and shits loud enough. Flailing around isn't the phrase you need. But he's gone. I've got some GTV stock; want it?"

"It'll work its way back up again, Sam," Haverman said carefully. "Especially if Smart gets kicked out by the Board and they hire a new president." Haverman suddenly sat up straighter. "Hey, Sam, why couldn't that be you?"

"I've thought about that."

"Right! It's perfect for them—a top gun from outside, but not too far outside. An experienced new broom. The PR is made for it, friend!"

"I don't want it."

Haverman looked at him watchfully. "Oh?"

Sam shook his head. "Too soon. I'm staying right where I am and building a record. Some other poor son of a bitch can have the next couple of years to get ulcerated in."

Haverman pursed his lips thoughtfully. "It's going to be that bad." He had one hundred percent respect for Sam's judgment. "I guess I'm being a little slow. If our audience can switch away to other channels, can't their people switch to GTV?"

"All of them can and some of them will. But they're hardcore generalists; they'll take a little of us, and a little of CBS, and a little of NBC, and a little of Funkbeobachter, and a little Shimbun, and some ABC, and God knows what else when the new relay sets go in. No, these are the kind of people that're used to a little of everything, no matter what network they're from. Any of 'em that hankered for a little side action from GTV or anyplace else could afford additional sets long ago. But *our* viewers, you know—" He held his hand out, palm up, and slowly turned it over.

Haverman said reluctantly: "That's not how we talk at the awards dinners."

"I don't see any chicken and peas around here right now," Sam said. "There's no way I would have pulled you out of your milieu if I didn't think we were in trouble."

"We can counterprogram," Haverman said emphatically. "We've got the skills and the facilities."

"Yes, I have."

"O.K. We can do news and sports stuff like the other people. That's the way it's going to go anyhow—back to the way it was in flat-V time, when everybody had a little of everything."

"Yeah, but not now," Sam said. "Later. Meanwhile, how do we get the National League to break its contract with ABC? Where do you think CBS's legal department would be if we started talking option-breakers to Mandy Carolina? Two years from now, Michaelmas's contract is up for renewal at NBC. There's talk he's thinking of going freelance. *That*'ll start a trend. Give me enough bucks, and I'll build you a top-rated action news show. *Then*.

Then, Dusty," he said gently. "Not now. And now is when
Fingers Smart and old Sam the Ticonderoga are fighting for their
lives, you know?" He inhaled deeply on the stick and threw the
exhausted pieces to the floor.

"I can't start another league to compete with what ABC can
show my people. There aren't that many big jocks in the world.
And I can't find another talk show hostess; only God can make a
mouth. I can't get Michaelmas, I can't get Melvin Watson. I *can*
get the guy who's sick of being Skip Jacobson's Sunday-night
backup, and so what. What I've got is actors. I can get actors. I
can get enough actors to fill eighty times twenty-four hours of
programming every week, if I have to." Sam sighed. "I can make
actors. So can anybody else; it's no secret how you do almost two
thousand different shows a week, thirty-nine weeks a year. So you
know what I've got left?" Sam leaned forward.

"Me," Sam said. "I've got me, and what's in me here." He
tapped his head and patted his crotch. "And we're gonna find out
how many years it's good for."

The silence had persisted palpably. "And me, Sam," Haverman
said finally.

"Uh-huh," Sam said. He poured another shot into Haverman's
glass. "Here," he said, and sipped his own to knock off the stick
effect. "Have a snort. Now, listen. You're my guy, and don't
forget it. You were one of the first people to sign on with me, and
you've been the principal of *Warbirds* ever since almost the
beginning."

Haverman nodded emphatically. There had been a Rex something or other. But that was long ago. "I have a following," he
said confirmingly, as if that was what he thought mattered to Sam
about him. And of course it was one of the things that did matter.
It must. Sam was not a creative for his health.

"That's right," Sam said gently. "And I'm going to protect you,
and you're going to help me."

"I'm not going back into *Warbirds*."

"Something like *Warbirds*. Something recognizably like it, and
you're going to have the same character name."

Haverman cocked his head. "But there *are* going to be
changes."

"Oh, yes. Got to have those, so it can be new and different. But
not too many, really—got to save something so they can identify
with the familiar. It'll have airplanes and things."

"Ah," Haverman said warily.

"A new show. All your own. Name over the title. We're going to promo hell out of it—'Haverman Moves!' Maybe 'Dusty Moves!' I don't know. Hell with it. Think of something better. Not the point. We'll get every one of the *Warbirds* audience, and with that kind of promo, we'll get plenty of new looks. Once they've looked, we'll have 'em. Guarantee it."

"Well, certainly, if it's one of your ideas—"

"Hell, yes, it's one of mine. More important, it's the one whose time has come. What the hell—eighty-odd channels of our own for a looker to choose from, and God knows how many more coming from all kinds of places. It's got to happen; I can hit the FCC with First Amendment and Right of Free Choice at the same time. It'll be years before they beat me. And you know something, Duster?" he said in a suddenly calm voice, "I don't think they're ever going to beat me. I think we really can make it stick."

"Oh?" Haverman felt the skin prickle sharply at the backs of his hands. He had never seen Sam like this; only heard of such moments, when the conviction of having thought and done exactly right transformed his good friend's face. The triumphant force of having created a truth came blazing from his eyes. And when he said "I think we can make it stick," his voice reharmonized itself so that though it never rose in volume, it might have been played by solo viola. Haverman could only say again: "Oh."

Sam was grinning. Grinning. "It's beautiful, Duster," he said. "Once we've beaten the test case, we can do another thing—open up a whole channel to the genre. Maybe more than one. And you shoot the whole thing on one set, with a couple of pieces of furniture and just a handful of props, and a holoprojected background. There's no long shot, and damned little tracking, so you do it with two cameras. One, if you're willing to settle. But I wouldn't. Or at least I'd want a damn good optical reflector to back me up. A whole new show, and then a whole channel full of new shows, for a third—maybe a fourth—of what anything else costs."

"And I'm going to do the first one," Haverman said. "Smart'll go for it. He has to. What kind of show is it, exactly, Sam?"

When Sam explained it to him further, he sat shaking his head. "Oh, no, Sam, no, I'm not sure I could do that."

But Sam said: "Sure you can."

• • •

Haverman sat uncertainly through the beginning of the conference. First the door to the office corridor was opened, and the senior technical staff came in, Hal, the most senior, carried a model of an aircraft carrier and a model of a silvery biplane, both of which he set down on Sam's white table. Sam turned them over in his hands, and nodded and winked at Hal, who smiled and sat down in the nearest of the informally grouped chairs. Dusty sat back along the wall, in a comfortable alcove next to Miss Montez's door, waiting.

Sam looked around at his people. "Everybody ready? O.K., let's give the great man a call," he said, and apparently punched up Ancel Smart's phone number, because Smart, after a little work with a secretary, appeared in the holo circle. He sat in a chair with his own people around him, and said heavily: "Shoot."

"Right," Sam said. "Anse, you know Hal and the rest of the boys, here. Now, we're proposing as follows—"

And it continued from there, with Smart nodding from time to time, or interposing a question, and changing his POV to watch whoever on the Ticonderoga staff was giving him the data. Then he'd turn back to Sam. Occasionally, one of Smart's people would address Sam. But it was Smart and Sam one-on-one, as it ought to be, Dusty saw, beginning to feel better as his friend clearly established dominance over the meeting. Smart was inclined to cough and play with his chin. Sam sat slim and upright, his hands, spread-fingered, molding premises in the air above the white tabletop where the models waited. Dusty began to feel better as Sam grew.

"All right, I promise you this show'll grab 'em and won't let go. I've taken a closer look at the tentative figures we discussed earlier, and I'll stand behind 'em." Sam named an in-the-can cost half of what it might have been. "And no concept fee, absolutely nothing in front. I get it back on reruns; we go to full rate on those, but, what the hell, if we ever *see* reruns, you're golden and you don't care, right? O.K., so that's Part One of what Ticonderoga's prepared to do. What do you do, Anse?"

Smart nodded. "Like I said. If it packages up the way you described, GTV'll help with the Feds. We've still got an office in Washington, after all, and my brother left a well-trained staff."

"Specifically, you're agreeing to hold Ticonderoga harmless in the event of criminal penalties or monetary losses caused by legal or regulatory action. Is that correct?"

One of Smart's legal staff suddenly leaned forward and began to whisper urgently in his ear. Smart waved him off impatiently. "That's right. I haven't changed my mind."

"On the record, and on behalf of GTV?" Sam pointed toward his own lawyer, who held up a sealed recorder.

"If we buy the program at all, GTV defends," Smart confirmed.

"O.K.," Sam said. "Now I'm gonna tell you who's in it."

"Ah."

"According to the formula we discussed," Sam said, turning to his holo box, talking aside, "we're going for a total ego-spectrum across four archetypical blocs. Now, each block embodies several potent identification features. We go young woman, young but experienced man, older and ego-stable woman, fully sophisticated man at the top end of middle age. We go soft, wiry, tight, sinewy; dark, reddish, blondy, silver. Sometimes we vary a little; there's room to do it; you get different overlaps, but you still cover it all the way across your maximized consumer ideals. We anchor at each end with an identifiable regular, but we can vary in he middle. Right so far?"

Smart nodded. "Acceptable." His and Sam's lawyers nodded.

"All right." Sam was still turned toward the control cabinet and speaking along his shoulder at Smart. He began to slowly raise one arm toward the top of the box. It was a good move; Haverman could see the tension building in Smart, and the distraction that was mirrored in the flickering of his eyes. More and more, Haverman felt the welling of admiration for Sam, and the comfort of being one of his people. "Now, you buy the concept of guest celebrities?"

"As long as they fit the formula."

"As long as they fit the formula defined above," Sam corroborated. "Are you worried about our being able to create authenticity?"

"With your makeup and research departments? Never. You guarantee audience believability, and I'll take your word for it right now."

"So guaranteed. Done." Sam nodded. "All right, we work from now on the assumption that the celebrity pair on each show will cover the two middle blocs, and Ticonderoga has discretion there as long as the portrayals remain convincing. To whom? Do you want to designate an audience-reaction service, Ancel?" His hand was poised above the holo controls now.

Smart shrugged. "We've been using TeleWinner all along. Let's give 'em this, too. Split the cost, right?" He chuckled. "What the hell, you know the reason GTV buys *Warbirds* is because I'm hooked on it. I'm my own symbol-bloc survey; they just make it official."

Sam smiled faintly. Audience size was what made it official.

"And, what the hell," Smart said, "you're keeping the alternate time tracks premise for the new show, aren't you? So if somebody says Rocky Marciano wasn't left-handed or Sonja Henie didn't roller-skate, well, hell, that was *then* but this is *elsewhen*, right? But it has to *look* right; that we've got to have."

"Absolutely." Even if there'd been no other public source of visual data, there was GTV's own Channel 29, steadily programming out reprocessed old movie and newsreel footage for all the WWII war babies who'd just missed it. The reprocessing was done by TStudiolab, Inc., one of Sam's subsidiaries.

"Okay, so we've got all that out of the way," Smart said. "Now let's see the goods."

"Of course." Sam smiled. His hand moved unexpectedly, and rang the little pushbell. "Let me introduce our talented newcomer. The next big word in viewer households, known to you and me as the young bloc archetype and all that implies, but professionally known as Giselle Montez—"

On her cue, Miss Montez came through her door in a high squadron pilot's uniform, the leather of her boots and Sam Browne belt glistening. She swept off her aluminized goggles and her helmet with one deft swirl of the hand that released her cloud of hair, and stood holding them on her hip, while her other hand rested its fingertips at the first button in the vee of her tunic. Ancel Smart leaned forward sharply in his chair. His mouth formed a loose o.

"Thank you, Miss Montez," Sam said, and she about-faced and walked out quickly; the door closed behind her with one darting flip of her fingertips. "And at the other end of the spectrum, the fine silver of sophisticated experience." Sam touched the cabinet controls. A sketch materialized in the air, facing Smart. It was a deceptively loose artist's rendering, life size, of a whipcordy-slim man with delicate limbs and waving, glossy white hair struck with contrasting pewter-colored low-lights. The expression of the aristocratic face suggested certain things.

Smart nodded reservedly. "Yes. All right. Looks all right. Who's going to play it? Something familiar about him. Who was your artist using for a model? Dusty Haverman?" Smart grinned.

Sam did not. He simply kept looking steadily at Smart, whose eyes first narrowed, then enlarged. "You're kidding! You're— How do we do *Warbirds* without him?—Jesus—" He slapped his thigh. "Perfect! It's perfect! It's a stroke, Sam, a fuckin' stroke!"

"Sure," Sam said.

The back of the meeting was broken. It was all a big long happy glide thereafter. Sar'n-Major Mac would come to the fore as the real manager of low squadron, and Private Parkins would play up raffishly. Major Harding's part would be padded a little, and Father Collins would listen to his troubles as he thrashed about trying to assert himself and spoil MacBanion's schemes. At its own expense, as an additional contribution to the relief of the crisis, Ticonderoga Studios would go back into the existing unshown episodes and re-edit to the new slant, so the Gelvarry character would be free to Go West, grow up, and change shows immediately. Sam had some experimental footage, it seemed, which might fit some of that.

In return, GTV would guarantee renewal next year. About next year—Sam's latest idea was to move on to dirigible-launched P6E's against Fiat CR32 biplanes; he held up the glittering model of the 220-mph Italian fighter, which had not gone out of use until 1938. They would be launched from the *Graf Zeppelin,* which had been Nazi Germany's sole aircraft carrier. Named for the man who pioneered practical lighter-than-air flight.

Smart considered the possibilities and the twists. "Cute," he admitted. "I like it." He shook his head. "I don't know where you get your ideas, Sam. Christ. Planes that sound like cars comin' off a ship that sounds like a dirigible, and what do they run up against? Damn! Yeah—let me see some footage pretty soon, will you?"

Sam had some, it seemed, which would fit some of that. They'd be able to show a rough cut in about a week.

"How about the new show? How soon can I have that?"

Well, it took a little while to get the actors into the milieu. Smart could understand that.

Yes, he could. But—

Oh, they'd push it. Tell you what; how about a progress report in ten days?

Well, if that meant they were close to delivery on the pilot episode.

Right. The *pilot* episode.

Everybody suddenly laughed, and Sam promised to send the little models over to Smart's office right away, for the shelves over the bar.

Smart punched off, and everybody in Sam's conference room began to grin and make enthusiastic quips. They were a high-morale outfit. It almost reminded Haverman of— Well, it should, shouldn't it? Art mirrors life.

Haverman got up from his inconspicuous seat and went over to Sam. "I thought it went very well."

Hal raised an eyebrow. "Well, hello!" he said.

Sam smiled reassuringly. "You heard the man, Duster," he said. "GTV's buying it, and they'll protect us. So it's all right." His eyes said: *I told you I'd take care of you.*

"I'm sure of that," Haverman said with conviction. "It's a Ticonderoga production," and everyone within earshot smiled.

"Why don't we get started?" Sam said and, putting an arm around his shoulders, walked with him out through the door to the technical spaces, which in this area were half-partitioned work-rooms and offices grouped-up to either side of the long central aisle that ran back toward the sound stages. Overhead were the whitewashed skylights and the zigzag trusses of the broad, arching roof, and to either side of them were the sounds of word-processing machines and footage splicers. They walked along to a side aisle, and there Sam had to leave him, after opening and holding open for him the heavy wood-grained door marked ACTORS AND MEDICAL PERSONNEL ONLY.

A bright-looking young medical person leafed through his print-out. "Dusty Haverman," he said wonderingly. "I never knew you'd been an accounting student."

"Isn't Doctor Virag going to do me? Doctor Virag and I know each other very well," he said, sitting stiffly in his chair.

The medical person did his best to smile disarmingly. "Doctor Virag is no longer with us, I'm afraid. Time passes, you know. I'm Doctor Harcourt; I think you'll find me competent. Sam personally asked me to take you."

"Oh. Well, I didn't mean to imply—"

"That's all right, Mr. Haverman. Now, if you'll just relax, Miss Tauchnitz will begin removing that hairpiece and so forth." Harcourt's fingers danced over keys, and he peered at the screen beside his chair. "Let me just refresh myself on this—yes, well, I think you may find it a relief to wear your own hair, for one thing; we'll just bleach it up a little bit. And we'll tan you. That'll be better than that tarty pinky-cheeks tinting, don't you think? Other than that, there's just a *tiny* bit of incising to do . . . a touch of a lift to one eyebrow, and that'll have the desired effect, I'm sure. Oh, yes, the cosmetology here is minimal, minimal. Which is just as well, since we do have a rather thick book of response-adjustments to perform, but, then, none of us is perfect for our role in life, really. Or is it 'are perfect'? Would you happen to know which it is, Miss Tauchnitz?"

When they had that done, they walked him down the corridors, past the rows of costume mannequins, and to the processing room, which was hung in soft black nonreflecting fabric, and where they had symphonic control of the lighting. They put him in the chair with the trick armrests and the neck brace.

"This is wine, Mr. Haverman," and he peered aside at the rollaway table with the clear decanter of rosy clarity, and the goblet. As long as he moved his arm smoothly and no more quickly than was gracious he could reach out and take it, and sip. "That's right. Have some more," the pleasant voice behind him said, and when he had had some more, they showed him a holo of Miss Montez and stimulated an electrode.

"Ah! Ah-ah-ah!"

"A little more wine, Mr. Haverman." And again the Montez and the incredible sensation beside which all past experience paled.

To see her come fully lighted out of the featureless soft warm darkness, and to feel what he could feel when she did that, he had only to reach out and take more wine. There was no thought in him of a spastic attempt to pluck something from his skull.

"Shouldn't you be feeding me oysters or Vitamin E? Perhaps some Tiger's Milk?" he jested once after they had stopped the wine and given him some Hennessey to refresh him. The pleasant voice murmured a throaty chuckle behind him.

When there was no further response to his gambit, he said: "Ah, well, I've really always been a steak and potatoes man, actually," and carelessly reached around to circle his hand into the unknown space behind him, but the pleasant voice said: "More wine, Mr. Gelvarry," and an unnoticeable hand put the goblet into his fingers. "Good enough," Gelvarry said. "Ah! Yes, yes, good enough, I say."

• • •

They showed him a slim, freckled woman with prominent front teeth, dressed in a calf-length skirt and a cardigan sweater over a cotton blouse. She wore soft leather street boots over dark lisle stockings, and moved like something wary in a strange part of the forest. They wiped, and went to a reprocessed, tinted, computer-animated photo of a famous person this was supposed to represent, and when he sipped the wine, they gave him the pleasure effect. Soon enough in the process he found it difficult to distinguish between the photo and the actress in her costume, no matter how the costume changed per reveal, for they always had a fresh photo after each wipe-and-switch, and the costume had clearly been cued by something in the photo, as much as chiffon can be patterned to remind one of gingham. In truth, in a while, he could not distinguish at all, and he found that although after a while they didn't wipe the actress, he had to concentrate very hard to make her out behind the features he now saw for her. So they gave him more wine, and the idea of concentrating was, to his relief, lost.

They did roughly the same thing with the identity of the purposeful young man with the angelic eyes.

And it was done.

"It's good, Sam," Haverman said, sitting in the office with the Hennessey.

"Sure," Sam said.

"I feel it. I feel absolutely certain." He ran a hand along the silvery waves at the side of his head, and touched one finger to his pencil mustache. His hand was lean and browned by the suns of expensive resorts. A chased gold ring set with a ruby glittered on his little finger. "The way you can make me see the guests, instead of the actors playing them—"

"Yeah, well, they aren't actually playing them, you know. We've got this computer tied into the cameras, and when those people move around, the image data gets put through and modified by this fancy program I had the fellows work up. It's pretty good; probably gets better. As long as the players don't do anything grossly out of character, the computer can edit the image to fit the model character. That's what goes on the air."

"But how do I see it, playing with them?"

"Well, you can't, Duster, that's why we do that hocus-pocus in the dark room. One of the hocus-pocuses." Sam patted him lightly at the neck. "Saves you having to act, you know, old Duster." He was sitting beside him on the couch, and leaned forward to cap the Hennessey.

"I think I could act it," Haverman said very softly.

Sam sighed. "Well, perhaps you could. But you see, this way it all goes smoothly and very naturally, don't you see? No lines to remember, no breaks for lunch—But those are all technical details, Dus, and there's absolutely no need for you to learn them."

"Still and all," Haverman said. "Still and all." Sam was uncapping the wine now. "I think you're very inventive," Haverman hastened. "That was always true of you. Do you know what I think? I think your next computer program will make it completely unnecessary to have anyone walking around for the cameras to focus on. Sam, that's true, isn't it? That's what you'd really, really like, isn't it?"

"Why, that's not true at all," Sam almost said; Haverman strained to hear him say that, and it seemed to him he was saying it, just outside the range of human hearing. He peered, and he craned his neck. But Sam was saying: "It's almost studio time, Dus. Have some wine," in his pleasant voice.

Haverman sighed. "Oh, all right, if that's the best you can do."

"My name is Austin Gelvarry," he repeated to Miss Montez, who was probably staring over his shoulder at the glistening, intricately decorated brass bed. "I have the power to call up whatever pleases me." He sipped from his glass, as she was doing. A nice light was developing in her eyes.

"I—seem to remember something different—"

"Have some more wine. It does no harm. It's strong drink that is raging," Gelvarry said, preoccupied, watching the little monkey plucking fruit from the bowl on the sideboard. The monkey caught his eye and winked.

"Listen," Miss Montez said. "It's just you can't find a secretary job anywhere anymore," but she was sipping.

Gelvarry smiled. Beyond her a Lockheed Electra was just touching down, crabbing a little in the wind as one might very well expect of so small an aircraft, even if it were an all-metal cabin twin. She settled in nicely, with just a spurt of blue smoke at the tires, and began to run out. He watched the pilot swing the Electra around deftly, and begin taxiing toward them.

"Do I please you, Austin?" Miss Montez said over the rim of

her glass, looking at him through her lashes. She seemed quite nicely settled in now.

"Ah," Gelvarry said. "Ah." The Electra came to a halt and the cabin door popped open. A slim figure jumped down and waved, and began running toward them. "Here's Amelia!" Gelvarry exclaimed gladly.

A Ryan high-wing monoplane, lacking the reflection of sun on windscreen glass, came over low, light glittering at its engine-turned cowling. A figure waved down from a side window, and then the *Spirit of St. Louis* banked away to line up upwind, flaring out for its landing, its prominent wheels seeming to reach down for the ground against the red outline of the evening sun. Gelvarry and Miss Montez both half-rose with pleasure. "And here's Lucky Lindy now!"

TIME OF WAR

Mack Reynolds

There was a light flashing red.

Alex hit the release button with the heel of his hand, flicked his eyes to the dial in question.

Animal heat.

He dropped both the speed and altitude levers, banked steeply and dove. His eyes went to the screen, he reached up and increased magnification tenfold. His fingers danced over buttons, searching out the appropriate chart. It flashed onto the map-screen.

Damn. The beetle was above that poorly mapped, all but unknown Balkan area where the Thrace of Greece and the Macedonia of Yugoslavia met Bulgaria. The nearest cities of any size would have been Yugoslavian Skopje, Greek Salonika, Bulgarian Plovdiv, but he was far from the ruins of any of them.

As the ground came up, his eyes shot to the dial again. Quite a bit of animal heat. Probably a man.

A man in this area? Alex pursed his lips. Possible, but not probable.

He was less than two miles in altitude, now. He increased magnification again. The vicinity was highly wooded.

He adjusted his metallic sensors, fossil fuel sensors, nuclear power sensors. For all he knew, this was a Comic trap and they were trying to suck his beetle in. Seemed unlikely, though. He hadn't spotted a Comic in this area for a goodly time.

When he was within a mile of the surface, he cut propulsion completely and hovered. His eyes went back to the chart and he enlarged it to ultimate. It still didn't give him much. The area had been fought over, ravaged, destroyed and rebuilt since the days of Philip and Alexander but it had never really been charted in the modern sense. There were the remains of a small farming town to the south; however, he couldn't make out if it might be Rodopolis in what had once been Greece, or Novo Selo in Macedonia.

He scowled at the dial. There was more heat radiation than was called for by one person. Perhaps there were two or three. It was possible, no matter how unlikely. The human animal is gregarious; given any opportunity at all he will seek out his fellows, even though it might increase his chances of destruction.

He flicked his eyes over to the cocking handles of the minirockets, though he knew he had checked them out before take-off. Given life below, Alex was in a position to start snuffing it out like candles.

The trouble was, exactly where was he, over Comic territory or their own?

He had made that mistake with the fishing boat, off the coast of Cuba. He had thought, of course, that the two terrified occupants had been enemy civilians. It had been sickening to find his mistake later.

He zeroed-in on the source of body heat, brought the beetle up to a slow, careful speed. It might still be a Comic trap, but he could find no signs of the presence of mechanical equipment in the vicinity. He dropped lower, tense now. He was getting awfully close. He kept his right hand very near the trigger of one of the minirockets.

Suppose it was some peasant, miraculously saved from the holocaust. How was he to know, in this area, if the man was Greek, Macedonian or Bulgar? As he recalled, the nationalities blended into each other at this point to such a degree that even borders made precious little difference.

All of a sudden, he brought the beetle to a halt and began to chuckle. There in a small meadow, clearing would be the better term, browsed a woebegone cow.

It had been a long time since he had seen a cow. Alex looked at it for a long moment, ruefully. In his youth, he had spent some time on a farm and had loved every minute. It had been fate that had put him into an educational bracket which had wound him up as the pilot of a beetle.

He shook his head, even as he reached for the altitude lever. Had he become a farmer, he would now, without question, have been dead. And even though family, relatives, friends, sweetheart were now all passed away, life is to be lived.

He shot into patrol pattern again, resetting his sensors. His chronometer told him he had only a few more moments to go.

When his time had elapsed, he put the beetle into orbit, threw the automatic control switch, then stood up, yawning. He stretched greatly, then massaged the back of his neck. He had a tendency to tighten up when on patrol.

Alex turned and threw the cogs on the metal door behind him. He stepped into the corridor beyond and headed for the executive officer's office.

Nick was on the desk. He said, "How did it go?"

Alex yawned again. "Nothing. I begin to suspect that there's nobody left at all in my area. The fallout must have got those that survived."

Nick grunted. "The Comics would like it, if they knew we thought so. Don't underestimate the human animal, Alex. He survives under some of the most impossible circumstances. Peter ran into a whole island of Eskimo in the northern Pacific."

Alex was surprised. "What did he do?"

"Blasted them, of course. They were Comics."

Alex wondered, inwardly. Eskimo. Possibly they didn't have the vaguest knowledge of the war, nor why it was they were being killed. But Nick was right. Man had a fantastic ability to survive.

Nick said, "You left your beetle in orbit?"

"That's right," Alex said wearily. "It isn't due for a check-out yet." He turned to go, but then recalled the animal he had seen.

He said, "You know what I saw today? A cow. I thought I was getting a heat indication of at least one man, but it was a cow. Wonder how it ever survived."

Nick said, "The last time I was on patrol, I saw four deer."

"Oh? What did you do?"

"What could I do? I was over Comic territory. I blasted them."

"Blasted them! Well, *why*?" Alex felt a sinking sensation. With so precious little major life left at all on Earth, who could wish to butcher deer?

Nick was irritated. "I told you. It was Comic territory. Had there been any human life hiding out, surviving somehow or other, the deer would have been potential food. I killed them. In the same way as if you saw a house standing, you'd blast it, so that it couldn't be used for shelter." He hesitated for a moment, then said, "Was she being milked?"

The other's mind had been on the deer. He said, "How do you mean?"

"The cow. Was she being milked?"

"How would I know?"

"The udder, you ninny. If it was full, she was being milked, which would mean, in turn, that there's somebody doing the milking."

"I didn't get any indication of further animal heat."

"Could be in some sort of dugout. It's surprising how quickly some of the survivors have adapted to protecting themselves against us. Not that they're any smarter than our people. They've worked out a dozen ways of perserving themselves against those buzz-fighters the Comics use."

Alex grunted. He had long been of the opinion that the higher-ups would do better to spend more effort protecting their civilians who had survived, rather than continuing to seek out the pitiful remnant of the Comics who were still alive. However, he didn't say anything. Nick had a mono-rail mind, when it came to official position. *Anything* the brass decided was gospel to Nick.

Alex said, "I'll take another look at the cow, tomorrow, if I can find it again. Even if it is being milked, I'm not sure it's in what was formerly our own territory, of theirs."

Nick said, "Well, you know what the general said, when in doubt."

Alex repressed a shudder, as he headed back for his sleeping quarters. The general had never jockeyed a beetle in his life. Had never had to blast a noncombatant. Perhaps he wouldn't be quite so devout a retaliationist, had he to follow his own orders.

In the morning, going by the twenty-four hour Earth Clock, Alex came awake slowly. There had been a time, when he had been an ambitious young officer, that he had tried to discipline himself away from this practice. Now he had given up. In truth, the half hour or so that he allowed to lapse between first stirrings of consciousness and full awakening was the happiest of his day. Happiest wasn't quite the word. There was no such reality as happiness in the life now led. But at least his semi-dream state was the most nearly satisfying.

In half control of his dream-thinking, he could steer his thoughts in what direction he would. Back over yesteryear when there had been ambitions, appetites, goals. When there had been arts to appreciate, crafts to study, entertainments to enjoy.

There had been Anna to love. And what was Anna now? A cinder. If not a cinder, a terrified, under-fed, under-clothed, under-sheltered fugitive from the Comic buzz-fighter who patrolled, even as Alex patrolled, seeking out the last remnants of life.

He had allowed his thoughts to go where he would rather they not stray. He came fully awake and swung his legs out over the edge of the bunk.

He went through the usual routine of getting cleaned up and dressed, the never ending sameness of it all, and made his way to the mess.

As he ate the food of the hydroponic beds, the yeast cellars, he scanned the freshly printed day's bulletin.

An inspiration editorial by the general. The day would soon come when, the Comics utterly defeated, the personnel of moon-base would return to Earth and begin the task of reconstruction.

Alex grunted. He sometimes suspected that the general had fed his ideas into one of the typer-computors with standing orders that for each issue of the bulletin a new editorial be turned out, saying the same thing over and over again in a slightly altered version.

The fact was that there was precious little chance that the Comics would ever be utterly defeated. Their super-Sputnik, as the junior officers had dubbed it, was as impregnable to attack as was the moon-base. And this truth had long since been accepted. The efforts to eliminate their mutual bases had been so costly that neither side any longer attempted it. Such fighting as took place between them, were the rare meetings above the surface of Earth, when beetle met buzz-fighter, usually through inadvertence, and fought it out.

If the truth were known, the general didn't even encourage that. The two fighting craft were so equally matched that one side's losses balanced the other's, and they were running short on the beetles they needed to prosecute the retaliation.

Which brought him to another item in the bulletin. A sneak landing had been made hurriedly in the antarctic and a sizeable amount of supplies loaded upon one of the freighter-craft. The supplies had been left over from the days when the nations had in considerable cooperation been exploring that remote continent.

Alex grunted. So that's where so many of the beetles had been, protecting the scavenging raid. It was a minor victory. In fact, more than balanced by the Comic Raid earlier when they had dispatched an equivalent space freighter to one of the Pacific islands where they had managed to locate a supply of fuel.

He wondered at the need of secrecy here on the moon-base. It was hard to believe that any Comic agents might be among them. And even if there was, how in the world could such an agent ever get a message to the enemy? No, Alex suspected that their rigid security measures were nonsense, left-over methods of an earlier period. The military mind was slow to change, even in the age of space war.

And here was the story of Peter's successful attack upon the Eskimo. Evidently there had been at least a score of them. Alex shook his head. How could it possibly have been known that they were from Comic territory, originally? The Eskimo were nomadic. Food supply, such as it was, would dictate that they move as much as a hundred miles in a week.

It was the same problem he had faced on the patrol yesterday.

Even had he spotted a survivor of the world debacle, how could he know whether the person was originally a resident of Comic territory? In desperate search of food and shelter, and protection from the ruthless attacks of beetles and buzz-fighters, such a refugee might travel many a mile from his place of origin.

The speaker called his name.

He was to report for immediate patrol.

That was only mildly surprising. The men who had covered the antarctic sneak landing had probably been on duty for long hours beyond the usual. They would need rest. He was comparatively fresh.

He came to his feet, adjusted his tunic on the off chance that he might meet one of the brass hats in the corridors and be dressed down for sloppy appearance, and started for the cubicle which he usually occupied when piloting a remote-control beetle.

At this hour he met only one other person. One of the women scientists. He saluted her, as regulations called for, but she ignored him and bustled on.

It came to Alex, sourly, even as he continued, that this horse-faced, cow-figured specimen was probably one of the few remaining females of his species who might survive to help replenish the Earth. If any at all survived. Briefly, he wondered if the high-ups had decided upon a program of breeding. If they had, it should best get underway even whilst they were still here on

Luna. Most of these women scientists were by no means young-sters. Some must already be past the menopause.

He reached the executive officer's preserve, reported, got his assignment, which was identical to yesterday's, saluted, and continued to his cubicle. He wondered how many beetles were out today. He hadn't seen any of the other fellows in the corridors, or in the mess. Probably everybody who could be spared was on patrol. The Comics were probably in a tizzy over the Antarctic raid, and would be speeding up their retaliation.

He hung his jacket up and seated himself at the control chair, before the screens, the panels, the dials, switches, triggers, gauges and all the rest of it. And even as he went through the standard routine of taking over the beetle, now in fast orbit, his memory went back to the long studies that had been involved in learning this business of eliminating every unit of human life in the lands of the enemy. At the time of his training, he had never expected it to ever come to this. But, then, he doubted if anyone else had, either.

At the very last, he threw the docking handles of the mini-rockets, threw off the automatic control, and accepted the piloting of the vicious little beetle.

It was a full hour later, an hour of carefully scanning over a large area of southern Europe, when he came to the vicinity where he had spotted the cow the day before.

He had little doubt that he could find the animal again. And yes, there it was. The indicator flashed animal heat.

He increased the magnification of his viewing screen, and sent the beetle darting toward the little meadow the cow had been grazing in the day before.

For the moment, engrossed in his object, he had failed to keep a constant eye on his other screens and scanning devices. Thus it was that his first warning of attack was a flashing ball of fire which, he realized, must have missed the miniature craft he was piloting from afar, by a scant half mile.

Automatically he upped the speed lever, and pulled the direc-tional stick backward, slamming for altitude. He banged open all screens, darted his head around, seeking the source of the attack. The unclear power sensor was flashing green warning, the alarm siren was whining. Impatiently, he brushed them both to inoper-ation. He decreased magnification on all screens, desperately seeking the foe over the broadcast area, even as he took standard evasive action.

Wherever and whoever his enemy, the Comic wasn't the man he might be. Alex's beetle should have been crisped by now. As it was, he hadn't even been nicked.

And, yes, there it was! A one man buzz-fighter, of course.

It was their one big advantage over the Comics. The enemy craft contained a living pilot who died in defeat. The beetles, piloted remotely from the moon-base, could be destroyed surely enough, but it was impossible for a pilot to be lost. War in air and space had come a long way since the Fokkers and Spads of World War One fought it out over the Western Front.

The buzz-fighters, comparatively large and cumbersome, must needs come down from their artificial satellite base before taking over their retaliation patrols. It was a time consuming, man consuming matter and Alex had a secret admiration for the stamina involved.

Even as they began their jockeying of death, roaring about the sky in great screaming of agonized machinery, great roaring of rockets and jets, he realized that the other must have spotted Alex's beetle toward the end of a patrol, and comparatively was physically exhausted.

Only that would account for the fact that the foe's reactions were obviously slow. Ordinarily, a buzz-fighter gave as much as it took. Indeed, it had some advantages over the tiny beetle. For one thing, it mounted a heavier firepower, a greater supply of bolts. The beetle's sole armament were the two minirockets, nuclear charged and capable of blasting a fairly good-sized town. Alex didn't know how many bolts the buzz-fighter boasted, but he knew it was considerably more than two.

He dropped sharply in a feint, came up roaring from below.

He had blisters of cold sweat on his forehead, could feel his shirt sticking to this back. He inevitably perspired in action. Safe, hundreds of thousands of miles away from the combat he might be, but in action you largely forgot that. Not completely though. At least in your subconscious you knew you were untouchable. But how about that enemy pilot? If his craft took a bolt, then all was over. At most, Alex would get a reprimand for being inept.

For the briefest of split seconds, the buzz-fighter was in his sighter screen, past the cross hairs, but in it. He slashed his fist out at the trigger button and his screen blurred momentarily as the beetle's weight dropped suddenly with the release of the minirocket.

Then there was glare!

A near hit? Had the missile's sensors caught enough of the enemy's heat to detonate?

Or was it another fluke blast? The minirockets Armament was turning out these days weren't up to original standards. Which wasn't surprising in view of the improvising they had to do, what with limited materials.

He came around in a roar—a roar tens upon tens of thousands of miles from his ear—and banged the screens to increased magnification.

And stared.

He had never seen before a buzz-fighter merely crippled. On all other occasions when he had come against the enemy fighters, they had flared up like magnesium upon being hit. Flared up from the atomic attack in such wise that there could be no question of survival on the part of the Comic pilot.

But now this one was fluttering to earth, like a wounded air-borne bird.

He kicked controls around and headed for it.

He had a double problem. He had exactly one minirocket left and couldn't waste it. The enemy pilot must be destroyed beyond any doubt. There were a limited number of Comic pilots left, and each one departed hastened the day when the war could be considered over and the general's oft proclaimed return to Earth became a reality.

But there was also the chance that the enemy was still in condition to mount a counter-attack on his diminutive enemy. Alex had no way of knowing whether or not the other was still conscious, but he must assume that he was. The buzz-fighter had caught only the edge of the minirocket blast, and had evidently had delicate equipment so smashed that it was no longer fully operative.

He came in with care. With so much care, that the buzz-fighter managed to sink to a landing, by coincidence, in the same meadow in which Alex had spotted the cow the previous day.

He banked around quickly, and dropped the beetle's speed. Perhaps the other was dead. In which case, the thing was to make every effort to get a full size combat unit down there with a freighter-craft and try to capture the buzz-fighter intact, before the lads on the super-Sputnik caught on and fired a real flattener to blast this whole section of the Balkans. The technicians and scientists there at moon-base had never had the opportunity to take apart a buzz-fighter. Given such a chance, it might lead to some discovery that would make a decisive difference in the prosecuting of the war.

But no. Even as he maneuvered his diminutive fighter into the clearing, a figure broke from the side of the enemy craft and dashed for the woods. At the same split second, the buzz-fighter began to glow in heat, and rapidly crumbled into a mass of flaming nothingness.

The Comic had sabotaged his craft. Alex swore, but his obscenities broke off in the middle.

The other was garbed in shorts and halter, and blonde hair was streaming behind even as she ran for what little protection the trees might offer.

Meaninglessly, as he darted his beetle after her, the thought came to his mind, was the briefness of clothing due to heat in the buzz-fighter, or was it a matter of saving weight?

There was something strangely familiar in her desperate flight and then it came to him. She ran as Anna ran. As Anna had once run. Her figure, too, was Anna's. Youthful, firm, but all rounded woman. This enemy pilot could be no more than in her mid-twenties.

He had heard that the Comics used women as well as men in the war in space and air, but he had secretly thought it propaganda, as he thought most of the atrocity stories. Evidently, it was true enough. Comic manpower was evidently as short as his own side's.

She was nearly to the edge of the clearing, running desperately hard, her firm, shapely legs pumping.

She must have known, as he so well knew, that her flight was meaningless. A bolt from his beetle would blast everything in an area the diameter of a mile, reducing it to nothing. But life is so much to be lived, even the last ultimate minute.

Suddenly he pulled back the control stick and, pointing the beetle skyward, hit at the same moment both the remaining minirocket trigger and the speed lever. The bolt went arching off into the depths of space, and the beetle headed home.

He threw it into automatic and came to his feet, rubbing the back of his neck as hard as he could press fingers into the flesh.

He went out into the corridor and headed toward the exec's office. Nick was on the desk, as he had been the day before.

Nick looked up. "Thought you were on patrol over the Balkans."

"I was. I fired both my bolts. I've got the beetle on automatic coming in for fresh minirockets."

Nick looked at him. "Two bolts to finish off a cow?"

"A buzz-fighter jumped me, while I was going in to blast the animal. I managed to hit it."

Nick was immediately doubly alert. "Wonderful!" He reached for a report pad. "Absolutely sure of destruction?"

"Yes," Alex said. "It burnt to a crisp."

"Wonderful!" Nick crowed, writing rapidly. "You'll get another citation."

Alex said wearily, "I feel pooped. I think I'll take a nap."

Before he turned to leave, Alex said slowly, "Nick, why do we call them Comics?"

"Eh?" The other continued writing the report.

"The enemy, over in that super-Sputnik of theirs, the artificial satellite."

Nick thought about it, finally shrugged his shoulders. "I don't know. I suppose it's derived from the fact that in the old days we used to ridicule them by saying their young people, their students, spent more time reading cartoon books, comic books, you know, than they did studying the sciences."

"Oh," Alex mused. "I wonder what they call us?"

Nick said stiffly, "I would hardly know, but probably something unworthy of our admitted idealistic goals."

Alex made his way to his quarters and slumped down on his bed. His face worked as he stared up at the ceiling. Somehow, he thought that she would survive. The cow was there.

Lieutenant Alex Moiseyevich Menzhinsky knew he was a traitor. The thing was—she ran so very much like Anna had run, back when there was an Anna, back when they'd both been youngsters on the collective.

AGAINST THE LAFAYETTE
ESCADRILLE

Gene Wolfe

I have built a perfect replica of a Fokker triplane,
except for the flammable dope. It is five meters,
seventy-seven centimeters long and has a wing span of seven
meters, nineteen centimeters, just like the original. The engine is
an authentic copy of an Oberursel UR II. I have a lathe and a
milling machine and I made most of the parts for the engine
myself, but some had to be farmed out to a company in Cleveland,
and most of the electrical parts were done in Louisville, Kentucky.

In the beginning I had hoped to get an original engine, and I
wrote my first letters to Germany with that in mind, but it just
wasn't possible; there are only a very few left, and as nearly as I
could find out none in private hands. The Oberursel Worke is no
longer in existence. I was able to secure plans though, through the
cooperation of some German hobbyists. I redrew them myself
translating the German when they had to be sent to Cleveland. A
man from the newspaper came to take pictures when the Fokker
was nearly ready to fly, and I estimated then that I had put more
than three thousand hours into building it. I did all the airframe
and the fabric work myself, and carved the propeller.

Throughout the project I have tried to keep everything as
realistic as possible, and I even have two 7.92 mm Maxim
"Spandau" machine-guns mounted just ahead of the cockpit. They
are not loaded of course, but they are coupled to the engine with
the Fokker Zentralsteuerung interrupter gear.

The question of dope came up because of a man in Oregon I
used to correspond with who flies a Nieuport Scout. The authentic
dope, as you're probably aware, was extremely flammable. He
wanted to know if I'd used it, and when I told him I had not he

became critical. As I said then, I love the Fokker too much to want to see it burn authentically, and if Antony Fokker and Reinhold Platz had had fireproof dope they would have used it. This didn't satisfy the Oregon man and he finally became so abusive I stopped replying to his letters. I still believe what I did was correct, and if I had it to do over my decision would be the same.

I have had a trailer specially built to move the Fokker, and I traded my car in on a truck to tow it and carry parts and extra gear, but mostly I leave it at a small field near here where I have rented hangar space, and move it as little as possible on the roads. When I do because of the wide load I have to drive very slowly and only use certain roads. People always stop to look when we pass, and sometimes I can hear them on their front porches calling to others inside to come and see. I think the three wings of the Fokker interest them particularly, and once in a rare while a veteran of the war will see it—almost always a man who smokes a pipe and has a cane. If I can hear what they say it is often pretty foolish, but a light comes into their eyes that I enjoy.

Mostly the Fokker is just in its hangar out at the field and you wouldn't know me from anyone else as I drive out to fly. There is a black cross painted on the door of my truck, but it wouldn't mean anything to you. I suppose it wouldn't have meant anything even if you had seen me on my way out the day I saw the balloon.

It was one of the earliest days of spring, with a very fresh, really indescribable feeling in the air. Three days before I had gone up for the first time that year, coming after work and flying in weather that was a little too bad with not quite enough light left; winter flying, really. Now it was Saturday and everything was changed. I remember how my scarf streamed out while I was just standing on the field talking to the mechanic.

The wind was good, coming right down the length of the field to me, getting under the Fokker's wings and lifting it like a kite before we had gone a hundred feet. I did a slow turn then, getting a good look at the field with all the new, green grass starting to show, and adjusting my goggles.

Have you ever looked from an open cockpit to see the wing struts trembling and the ground swinging far below? There is nothing like it. I pulled back on the stick and gave it more throttle and rose and rose until I was looking down on the backs of all the birds and I could not be certain which of the tiny roofs I saw was the house where I live or the factory where I work. Then I forgot looking down, and looked up and out, always remembering to

look over my shoulder especially, and to watch the sun where the
S.E. 5a's of the Royal Flying Corps love to hang like dragonflies,
invisible against the glare.

Then I looked away and I saw it, almost on the horizon, an
orange dot. I did not, of course, know then what it was; but I
waved to the other members of the Jagstaffel I command and
turned toward it, the Fokker thrilling to the challenge. It was
moving with the wind, which meant almost directly away from
me, but that only gave the Fokker a tailwind, and we came at
it—rising all the time.

It was not really orange-red as I had first thought. Rather it was
a thousand colors and shades, with reds and yellows and white
predominating. I climbed toward it steeply with the stick drawn
far back, almost at a stall. Because of that I failed, at first, to see
the basket hanging from it. Then I leveled out and circled it at a
distance. That was when I realized it was a balloon. After a
moment I saw, too, that it was of very old-fashioned design with
a wicker basket for the passengers and that someone was in it. At
the moment the profusion of colors interested me more, and I went
slowly spiraling in until I could see them better, the Easter egg
blues and the blacks as well as the reds and whites and yellows.

It wasn't until I looked at the girl that I understood. She was the
passenger, a very beautiful girl, and she wore crinolines and had
her hair in long chestnut curls that hung down over her bare
shoulders. She waved to me, and then I understood.

The ladies of Richmond had sewn it for the Confederate army,
making it from their silk dresses. I remembered reading about it.
The girl in the basket blew me a kiss and I waved to her, trying to
convey with my wave that none of the men of my command would
ever be allowed to harm her; that we had at first thought that her
craft might be a French or Italian observation balloon, but that for
the future she need fear no gun in the service of the Kaiser's
Flugzeugmeisterei.

I circled her for some time then, she turning slowly in the basket
to follow the motion of my plane, and we talked as well as we
could with gestures and smiles. At last when my fuel was running
low I signaled her that I must leave. She took, from a container
hidden by the rim of the basket, a badly shaped, corked brown
bottle. I circled even closer, in a tight bank, until I could see the
yellow, crumbling label. It was one of the very early soft drinks,
an original bottle. While I watched she drew the cork, drank
some, and held it out symbolically to me.

Then I had to go. I made it back to the field, but I landed dead stick with my last drop of fuel exhausted when I was half a kilometer away. Naturally I had the Fokker refueled at once and went up again, but I could not find her balloon.

I have never been able to find it again, although I go up almost every day when the weather makes it possible. There is nothing but an empty sky and a few jets. Sometimes, to tell the truth, I have wondered if things would not have been different if, in finishing the Fokker, I had used the original, flammable dope. She was so authentic. Sometimes toward evening I think I see her in the distance, above the clouds, and I follow as fast as I can across the silent vault with the Fokker trembling around me and the throttle all the way out; but it is only the sun.

HAWK AMONG THE SPARROWS

Dean McLaughlin

The map-position scope on the left side of *Pika-Don*'s
instrument panel showed where he was, but it didn't
show airfields. Right now, Howard Farman needed an airfield. He
glanced again at the fuel gauge. Not a chance of making it to
Frankfurt, or even into West Germany. Far below, white clouds
like a featureless ocean sprawled all the way to the horizon.

Those clouds shouldn't have been there. Less than four hours
ago, before he lifted off the *Eagle*, he'd studied a set of weather
satellite photos freshly televised down from orbit. Southern
France had been almost clear—only a dotting of cottonboll tufts.
It should not have been possible for solid overcast to build up so
fast. For the dozenth time, he flipped through the meteorological
data on his clipboard. No, nothing that could have created such a
change.

That made two things he hadn't been able to figure out. The
second was even stranger. He'd lifted from the *Eagle*'s deck at
midmorning. The French bomb test he'd been snooping had
blinded him for a while—how long he didn't know—and *Pika-
Don* was thrown out of control. The deadman circuit had cut in;
control was re-established. When his sight came back—and it
couldn't have been terribly long—the sun had been halfway down
in the west.

It wasn't possible. *Pika-Don* didn't carry enough fuel to stay up
that long.

Just the same, she had stayed up, and she still had almost half
her load. When he couldn't find the *Eagle* near Gibraltar, he'd
thought there was enough to take him to the American air base at
Frankfurt. (And where could the *Eagle* have gone? What could
have happened to her radar beacon? Could the French blast
have smashed *Pika-Don*'s reception equipment? Everything else

119

seemed to work all right. But he'd made an eyeball search, too. Aircraft tenders didn't just vanish.)

On the map scope, the Rhone valley crawled slowly southward under the north-moving central piplight that marked *Pika-Don*'s inertially computed position. It matched perfectly the radar-scanned terrain displayed on the airspace viewscope on the right-hand side of the instrument panel. Frankfurt was still beyond the horizon, more than four hundred miles off. *Pika-Don* didn't have fuel to cover half that distance.

Well, he wouldn't find an airfield by staying up here, above that carpet of cloud. He eased the throttles back and put *Pika-Don*'s nose down. She'd burn fuel a lot faster down close to the deck, but at Mach 1.5 he could search a lot of ground before the tanks went dry.

Not that he absolutely had to find an airfield. *Pika-Don* could put down almost anywhere if she had to. But an airfield would make it a lot simpler to get a new load of fuel, and it would make less complicated the problems that would come from putting down in a technically still friendly nation.

It was a long way down. He watched the radar-echo altimeter reel downward like a clock thrown into panicked reverse; watched the skin temperature gauge edge up, level out, edge up again as *Pika-Don* descended into thicker air. For the first eighty thousand feet, visibility was perfect, but at twelve thousand feet *Pika-Don* went into the clouds; it was like being swallowed by gray night. Uneasily, Farman watched the radar horizon; these clouds might go down all the way to the ground, and at Mach 1.5 there wouldn't be anything left but a smear if *Pika-Don* hit. She was too sweet an airplane for that. Besides, he was inside.

He broke out into clear air a little under four thousand feet. A small city lay off to his right. He turned toward it. Beaufort, the map scope said. There ought to be some sort of airfield near it. He pulled the throttles back as far as he dared—just enough to maintain airspeed. The Machmeter slipped back to 1.25.

He passed north of the town, scanning the land. No sign of a field. He circled southward, careful to keep his bearing away from the town's center. There'd be trouble enough about his coming down in France—aerial trespass by a nuclear-armed warplane, to start with—without half the townspeople screaming about smashed windows, cracked plaster, and roosters so frightened they stopped laying eggs. The ambassador in Paris was going to earn his paycheck this week.

Still no airfield. He went around again, farther out. Dozens of villages flashed past below. He tore his flight plan, orders, and weather data off their clipboard—crammed the papers into the disposal funnel; wouldn't do to have nosy Frenchmen pawing that stuff, not at all. He substituted the other flight plan—the one they'd given him just in case he had to put down in French or French-friendly territory.

He was starting his third circuit and the fuel gauge was leaning against the red mark when he saw the field. It wasn't much of a place—just a grassy postage stamp with a few old planes in front of three ramshackle sheds and a windsock flopping clumsily over the middle one. He put around, aimed for it, and converted to vertical thrust. Airspeed dropped quickly—there was a momentary surge of wing-surface heating—and then he was hovering only a few miles from the field. He used the deflectors to cover the distance, losing altitude as he went. He jockeyed to a position near the hangars, faced *Pika-Don* into the wind, and let her down.

The engines died—starved of fuel—before he could cut them off.

It took a while to disconnect all the umbilici that linked him into *Pika-Don*'s control and environment systems. Some of the connections were hard to reach. It took a while longer to raise the canopy, climb over the side, and drop to the ground. Two soldiers were waiting for him. They had rifles.

The bigger one—the one with the bushy mustache—spoke dangerously. Farman didn't know French, but their gestures with rifle muzzles were a universal language. He raised his hands. "I'm an American," he said. "I ran out of fuel." He hoped they weren't disciples of the late *grand Charles*. They looked nasty enough.

The two exchanged glances. "*Américain?*" the smaller one asked. He was clean-shaved. His eyes had a deep, hollow look. He didn't sound at all displeased.

Farman nodded vigorously. "Yes. American." He pointed to the fifty-one-star flag on his coverall sleeve. Their faces broke into delighted smiles and they turned their gun muzzles groundward. The small one—he made Farman think of a terrier, and his rifle was absurdly big for him—pointed to a shack beyond the hangars.

At least the natives seemed friendly. Farman went. The area in front of the hangars had been paved—an uneven spread of asphalt. Half a dozen rattletrap airplanes stood in a line, facing out toward the field. Where the pavement met unpaved ground, it was one mud puddle after another. Farman had to be careful where he put his feet; his flight boots had been clean when he took off this morning. The soldiers didn't seem to mind. They splashed cheerfully through the wet and scuffed their heels on the tufts of grass.

The planes were all the same type—biplanes with open cockpits and two-bladed wooden propellers and radial-type piston engines. The kind of planes, Farman thought, that shouldn't even be flying any more. Nevertheless, they were obviously working airplanes, with oil stains on their cowls and the smell of gasoline and patches glued over holes in the fabric of wings and fuselage. A crop-dusting outfit? Did the French have crop-dusting outfits? Then he realized that those things in front of the cockpits were machine guns. Air-cooled machine guns rigged to shoot through the propeller. And those odd, oval-shaped tail assemblies . . .

Some kind of museum?

"That is strange aeroplane you have," the mustached soldier said. His accent was as thick as the grass on the field. "One like it I have not seen."

Farman hadn't known that either of them spoke English. "I'll need to make some phone calls," he said, thinking of the ambassador in Paris. A mechanic was working on one of the planes they passed; he was standing on a wooden packing crate, tinkering with the engine.

A movie outfit, doing a period flick? But he didn't see any cameras.

Another biplane taxied in from the field—a Nieuport, like the others. Its engine racketed like a lawnmower. It joggled and bounced in the chuckholes. There were a lot of chuckholes in the mud at the pavement's fringe. The plane came up on the pavement and the engine cut out. As the propeller turned around to a spasmodic stop, Farman realized that not just the propeller but the whole engine had been spinning. What kind of crazy way to build airplanes was that?

The Nieuport's pilot climbed up out of the cockpit and dropped to the ground. "Guns jammed again!" he yelled loudly, hellishly mad. He flung a small hammer on the ground at his feet.

Three men came out of the hangar carrying packing crates. They set them down around the Nieuport's nose, got up on them, and started working on the guns. The flier pulled off his scarf and draped it over the cockpit's side. He turned away, spoke a few

French words over his shoulder to the mechanics, and walked off.

"Monsieur Blake!" the big soldier hailed. When the flier didn't seem to hear, the soldier ran to him, caught his shoulder. "Monsieur Blake. A countryman." The soldier beside Farman pointed to the flag on Farman's sleeve.

Blake came over, stuffing a goggled cloth helmet into a pocket of his heavy overcoat as he approached. His hand was out in welcome.

"This one has teach all my *Anglais* to me," the big trooper grinned. "Is good, *non*?"

Farman scarcely heard him. All his attention was on this American. "Harry Blake," the man introduced himself. " 'Fraid I won't be able to hear you too good for a while." He swung a glance at his Nieuport's motor and raised hands to his ears to signify deafness. He was young—not more than twenty-two or -three—but he had the mature poise of a man much older. "I'm a Lafayette with this outfit. From Springfield, Illinois. You?"

Farman accepted the hand in numb silence. By calling himself a Lafayette, the flier had obliterated Farman's last incredulous doubt. It wasn't possible—not real. Things like this didn't happen.

"Hey, you don't look so good," Blake said, grabbing his arm with a strong hand.

"I'll be all right," Farman said, but he wasn't really sure.

"Come on." Blake steered Farman into the passageway between two of the hangars. "We've got what you need back here."

The troopers came after them. "Monsieur Blake. This man has only now arrived. He has not reported."

Blake waved them away. "I haven't either. We'll report later. Can't you see when a man's breathed too much oil?"

The soldiers tuned back. Blake's hand steered Farman onward. Puddles slopped under Blake's boots.

Behind the hangars, the path split in two directions. One way led to a latrine whose door swung loose in the breeze. The other led to a shack huddled up to the back of a hangar. It was hard to guess which path was more frequently used. Blake paused at the parting of the ways. "Think you can make it?"

"I'm all right." He wasn't, really. It takes more than a deep breath and a knuckling of the eyes to adjust a man to having lost six and a half decades. Between books about aerial combat he'd devoured as a kid—two wars and all those brushfire skirmishes— he'd read some Heinlein and Asimov. If it wasn't for that, he'd have had nothing to hang on to. It was like a kick in the belly.

"I'll be all right," he said.

"You're sure? You breathe castor oil a few hours a day and it doesn't do a man's constitution much good. Nothin' to be embarrassed about."

Every now and then, Farman had heard castor oil mentioned, mostly in jokes, but he'd never been sure what it did to a man. Now he remembered it had been used in aircraft engines of this time. Suddenly, he understood all. "That's one problem I don't have."

Blake laughed. "It's a problem we all have." He pushed open the shack's door. Farman went inside at his nod. Blake followed. "Onree!" Blake called out. "Two double brandies."

A round little baldpated Frenchman got up from a stool behind the cloth-draped trestle that served as a bar. He poured two glasses almost full of something dark. Blake picked up one in each hand. "How many for you?"

Whatever it was, it looked evil. "One," Farman said, "for a start." Either this youngster was showing off—which didn't seem likely—or it wasn't as deadly as it looked. "A double, that is."

Blake led the way to a table in the far corner, next to a window. It was a plain wood table, stained and scarred. Farman set his glass down and took a chair before he tried a small taste. It was like a trickle of fire all the way down. He looked at the glass as if it had fangs. "What is this stuff?"

Blake had sampled from each glass on the way to the table, to keep them from spilling. Now he was almost halfway through one of them and the other was close to his hand. "Blackberry brandy," he said with a rueful grin. "It's the only cure we've found. Would you rather have the disease?"

Flight medicine, Farman thought, had a long way to go. He put his glass carefully aside. "My plane doesn't use that kind of oil."

Blake was on him right away. "Something new? I thought they'd tried everything."

"It's a different kind of engine," Farman said. He had to do something with his hands. He took a sip of the brandy, choked, regretted it.

"How long you been flying?" Blake asked.

"Ten, twelve years."

Blake had been about to finish his first glass. He set it down untouched, looked straight at Farman. Slowly, a grin came. "All right. A joke's a joke. You going to be flying with us?"

"Maybe. I don't know," Farman said, holding his brandy glass in both hands, perfectly steady—and all the time, deep inside, the small trapped being that was himself screamed silently, *What's happened to me? What's happened?*

It had been a tricky mission, but he'd flown a lot of tricky ones. Ostensibly, he'd been taking part in a systems-test/training exercise off the northwest coast of Africa. High-altitude Mach 4 aircraft, their internal equipment assisted by the tracking and computer equipment on converted aircraft carriers, were attempting to intercept simulated ballistic warheads making re-entry into the atmosphere. He'd lifted from the deck of the airplane tender *Eagle* in the western Mediterranean. Half an hour later he was circling at Big Ten—one-zero-zero thousand feet—on-station north of the Canary Islands when the signal came that sent him on his true mission.

A guidance system had gone wrong at the Cape, said the talker aboard the *Iwo Jima*, and the range-safety system had failed. The misdirected warhead was arching over the Atlantic, farther and higher than programmed. Instead of splashing in the Atlantic, its projected impact-point was deep in the Sahara. It carried only a concrete block, not thermonuclear weaponry, but diplomatic relations with France—which still maintained military bases in this land it had once governed—were troublesome. Standing orders for such an eventuality were that, as a good-faith demonstration, an attempt should be made to intercept it.

Operation Skeetshoot's master computer said Farman's *Pika-Don* was the only plane able to make the interception. No other plane was in the right position. No other plane had enough altitude or fuel load. No other plane had such an advantageous direction of flight at that moment. Farman sent *Pika-Don* streaking toward interception point at full thrust.

As planned.

Nothing had really gone wrong at the Cape. It was a pretext. Washington knew the French were about to test a new-model nuclear bomb. They would explode it above the atmosphere, in the Van Allen belt; the rocket would be launched from their main testing site, the Saharan oasis of Reggan; they would select the moment of launch to coincide with the arrival of a solar proton storm, when subnuclear particles from the storm would blend with the bomb's fission products, rendering surveillance by other nations more difficult and the findings less certain.

The proton storm had been already on its way when Farman left the *Eagle*'s deck. It was being tracked, not only by American installations around the world, but by French stations also. Code message traffic was high between New Caledonia and Reggan. The time of the storm's arrival was known to within five seconds.

Farman hadn't paid much attention to why Washington wanted to snoop the test; the French were, after all, still allies in spite of the frictions between Paris and Washington. Asking questions like that wasn't Farman's job; he was just the airplane driver. But they'd told him anyway, when they gave him the mission. Something about Washington wanting to have up-to-date knowledge of France's independent nuclear capability. Such information was needed, they said, for accurate judgment of how dependent France might still be on America's ability to wage modern war. To Farman, the explanation didn't mean much; he didn't understand much about international politics.

But a warhead dropping into the atmosphere, sheathed in the meteor-flame of its fall—*that* he could understand. And a multi-megaton fireball a hundred miles up, blazing like the sun brought suddenly too close—that, too, he could understand. And a Mach 4 airplane riding her shock-wave across the sky, himself inside watching instruments and flight-path guide scopes, and his thumb on the button that would launch the Lance rockets sheathed against her belly. Those were things he understood. They were his job.

Nor did the mission call for him to do more than that. All that was really necessary was to have *Pika-Don* somewhere in the sky above Reggan when the French bomb went off. *Pika-Don* would do everything else, automatically.

All the planes in Operation Skeetshoot were equipped the same as *Pika-Don*. All of them carried elaborate flight recorders; and because they were fitted to intercept thermonuclear warheads, and their own Lance rockets had sub-kiloton fission tips, those recorders included all the instruments needed to monitor a nuclear explosion—even a unit to measure the still not fully understood magnetohydrodynamic disturbances that played inside a nuclear fireball. (And, it was known from previous tests, there was something unusual about the magnetic fields of French bombs.)

Nor would there be much risk if *Pika-Don* were forced down where French nosypokes could get a look at it. All *Pika-Don* carried was standard equipment—equipment the French already knew about, in configurations and for purposes they also understood. There would be nothing the French could find to support a charge of deliberate snooping, no matter how much they might suspect. Not that the possibility was large; the explosion, after all, would be out in space. There'd be no blast effects, certainly, and very little radiation. Enough to tickle the instruments, was all.

And already the hot line between Washington and Paris would be explaining why an American plane was intruding on French-controlled airspace. Everything had been planned.

Farman watched his instruments, his flight-path guide scopes, his radar. *Pika-Don* slashed the thin air so fast she drew blood. She was up to one-three-zero thousand now; rocket launch point lay five thousand higher, two hundred miles ahead. Reggan moved onto the edge of the inertial-guide map-position scope, ahead and off to the south. The projected trajectory of the warhead was a red line striking downward on the foreview guide scope. An X-slash marked Skeetshoot Control's computed interception point.

Something flared on the radar near Reggan. It rose, slowly for a moment, then asymptotically faster and faster, shining on the radar screen like a bright, fierce jewel. The French rocket. Farman's breath caught as he watched it. The thing was going up. The test was on.

It rose, was level with him, then higher. Suddenly, it quivered like a water drop, and suddenly it was gone from the screen in an expanding black blindness like a hole in the universe; and simultaneously the cockpit was full of unendurable white light. The sky was flaming, so bright Farman couldn't look at it, didn't dare. He had just time enough to think, terrified, *Not in the Van Allen belt!* and then *Pika-Don* was spinning, spinning, spinning like a spindle—light flashing into the cockpit, then blackness, brightness, then blackness again, repeating and repeating faster and faster and faster until light and darkness merged to a flickering brilliance that dazzled not only the eyes but the whole brain. Farman battled the controls, but it was like fighting the Almighty's wrath. The flickering blaze went on and on.

And slowed. Stopped, like the last frame of film in a halted movie projector, and it was only daylight again, and *Pika-Don*'s disabled pilot circuit had cut in. She was flying level, northwest-ward if the compass could be trusted, and if the sun's position could be trusted, the afternoon was more than half gone. Farman was sure that much time had not passed.

The map scope confirmed the compass. So did the airspace radar view. The controls felt all right now, and *Pika-Don* seemed to fly without difficulty. He turned straight north toward the

Mediterranean and came out above it not far from Oran. He curved west then, toward the spot where he'd left the *Eagle*. He watched the foreview guide scope for the Eagle's homing beacon. It didn't show up. He spoke on the radio, got no answer. Equipment damage?

He took *Pika-Don* down to fifty thousand. He used the telescope-view scope on the ships his radar picked out. None was the *Eagle*; old freighters, mostly, and two small warships of a type he'd thought wasn't used any more except by the Peruvian Navy.

His orders said, if he couldn't find his base ship, go to Frankfurt. The big base there could take him. He turned *Pika-Don* northwestward. He crossed the French coast. Overcast covered the land. It shouldn't have been there. Fuel began to run low. It was going into the engines faster than the distance to Frankfurt was narrowing. He tried to cut fuel consumption, but he couldn't cut it enough. He had no choice but to put down in France.

"Look, Mister, either you've got orders to fly with us, or you don't," Blake said. "What outfit are you with?"

It was restricted information, but Farman didn't think it mattered much. "The CIA, I think."

He might as well have said the Seventh Cavalry with General Custer. "Where's your base?" Blake asked.

Farman took another swallow of brandy. He needed it, even if not for the reason Blake thought. It wasn't so bad, this time. He tried to think of a way to explain the thing that had happened to him. "Did you ever read *The Time Machine*?" he asked.

"What's that? A book about clocks?"

"It's a story by H. G. Wells."

"Who's H. G. Wells?"

He wasn't going to make much explanation by invoking H. G. Wells. "It's about a man who . . . who builds a machine that moves through time the way an airplane moves in the air."

"If you're having fun with me, you're doing it good," Blake said.

Farman tried again. "Think of a building—a tall building, with elevators in it. And suppose you don't know about elevators— can't even imagine how they work. And suppose you were on the ground floor, and suppose I came up and told you I was from the twentieth floor."

"I'd say that's doing a lot of supposing," Blake said.

"But you get the idea?"

"Maybe. Maybe not."

"All right. Now imagine that the ground floor is now. Today. And the basement is yesterday. And the second floor is tomorrow, and the third floor is the day after tomorrow, and so on."

"It's a way of thinking about things," Blake said.

Give thanks the elevator had been invented. "Take it one step more, now. Suppose you're on the ground floor, and someone comes down from the twentieth floor."

"He'd of come from somewhere the other side of next week," Blake said.

"That's the idea," Farman said. He took more of the brandy. "What if I told you I . . . just fell down the elevator shaft from sixty-some years up?"

Blake appeared to consider while he started on his second glass. He permitted himself a smile and a chuckle. "I'd say a man's got to be a bit crazy if he wants to fly in this war, and if you want to fight Huns you've come to the right place."

He didn't believe. Well, you couldn't expect him to. "I was born in nineteen fifty-three," Farman told him. "I'm thirty-two years old. My father was born in nineteen twenty. Right now, it's nineteen . . . seventeen?"

"Nineteen *eighteen*," Blake said. "June tenth. Have another brandy."

Farman discovered his glass was empty. He didn't remember emptying it. Shakily, he stood up. "I think I'd better talk to your commanding officer."

Blake waved him back to his chair. "Might as well have another brandy. He hasn't come back yet. My guns jammed and I couldn't get them unjammed, so I came home early. He'll be back when he runs out of bullets or fuel, one or the other."

His back was to the door, so he had to twist around while still talking, to see who came in. The small, razor-mustached man draped his overcoat on a chair and accepted the brandy the barman had poured without having to be asked. "Today, M'sieu Blake, it was a small bit of both." His English had only a flavor of accent. "On coming back, I find I am left with one bullet."

"How was the hunting?"

The Frenchman gave a shrug that was as much a part of France as the Eiffel Tower. "Ah, that man has the lives of a cat, the hide of an old bull elephant, and the skills of a magician."

"Keyserling?" Blake asked.

The newcomer took a chair at the table. "Who else? I have him in my sights. I shoot, and he is gone. It would be a shame to kill this man—he flies superbly!—and I would love to do it very much." He smiled and sipped his brandy.

"This is our CO," Blake said. "Philippe Deveraux. Thirty-three confirmed kills and maybe a dozen not confirmed. The only man on this part of the front with more is Keyserling." He turned to Farman. "I don't think I got your name."

Farman gave it. "He's just over from the States," Blake said. "And he's been funning me with the craziest story you ever heard."

Farman didn't bother to protest. In similar shoes, he'd be just as skeptical. "This Keyserling," he said. "That's Bruno Keyserling?"

He'd read about Keyserling; next to Richthofen, Bruno Keyserling had been the most hated, feared, and respected man in the German air force.

"That's him," Blake said. "There's not a one of us that wouldn't like to get him in our sights." He set his empty glass down hard. "But it won't happen that way. He's gotten better men than us. Sooner or later, he'll get us all."

Deveraux had been delicately sipping his drink. Now he set it down. "We shall talk of it later, M'sieu Blake," he said firmly. He addressed Farman. "You have been waiting for me?"

"Yes. I . . ." Suddenly, he realized he didn't know what to say.

"Don't give him the same you gave me," Blake warned. "Now it's business."

"You are a pilot, M'sieu Farman?" Deveraux asked.

Farman nodded. "And I've got a plane that can fly faster and climb higher than anything you've got. I'd like a try at this Keyserling."

"That could possibly be arranged. But I should warn you, M'sieu . . . Farman, did you say?"

"Howard Farman."

"I should warn you, the man is a genius. He has done things his aeroplane should not be possible to do. He has shot down forty-six, perhaps more. Once three in a day. Once two in five minutes. It has been said the man came from nowhere—that he is one of the gods from the *Nibelungenlied*, come to battle for his fatherland. He . . ."

"You might say I'm from nowhere, too," Farman said. "Me and my plane."

• • •

When Deveraux had finished his brandy and when Blake had downed his fourth, they went out in front of the hangars again. Farman wanted them to see *Pika-Don*. *Pika-Don* would be at least sixty years ahead of any plane they'd ever seen.

Her skids had cut into the turf like knives. Blake and Deveraux examined her from end to end. They walked around her, their boot tips whipping the grass. "Don't touch anything," Farman told them. "Even a scratch in the wrong place could wreck her." He didn't add that the rockets concealed under her belly could vaporize everything within a hundred yards. The false-skin strips that sealed them from the slipstream were supposed to be tamper-proof, but just to be safe Farman placed himself where they would have to go past him to investigate *Pika-Don*'s underside.

Pika-Don was eighty-nine feet long. Her shark-fin wings spanned less than twenty-five. She was like a needle dart, sleek and shiny and razor-sharp on the leading edge of her wings. Her fuselage was oddly flat-bodied, like a cobra's hood. Her airscoops were like tunnels.

Blake crouched down to examine the gear that retracted the skids. Farman moved close, ready to interrupt if Blake started to fool with the rockets. Instead, Blake discovered the vertical thrust vents and lay down to peer up into them. Deveraux put his head inside one of the tail pipes. It was big enough to crawl into. Slowly, Blake rolled out from under and got to his feet again.

"Do you believe me now?" Farman asked.

"Mister," Blake said, looking at him straight, "I don't know what this thing is, and I don't know how you got it here. But don't try to tell me it flies."

"How do you think I got it here?" Farman demanded. "I'll show you. I'll . . ." He stopped. He'd forgotten he was out of fuel. "Ask your ground crews. They saw me bring her down."

Blake shook his head, fist on hips. "I know an aeroplane when I see one. This thing can't possibly fly."

Deveraux tramped toward them from the tail. "This is indeed the strangest zeppelin I have ever been shown, M'sieu. But obviously, a zeppelin so small—so obviously heavy . . . it can hardly be useful, M'sieu."

"I tell you, this is a *plane*. An *air*plane. It's faster than anything else in the air."

"But it has no wings, M'sieu. No propeller. It does not even have wheels on the undercarriage. How can such a thing as this gain airspeed if it has no wheels?"

Farman was speechless with exasperation. Couldn't they see? Wasn't it obvious?

"And why does it have so strong the scent of paraffin?" Deveraux asked.

A Nieuport buzzed over the hangars in a sudden burst of sound. It barrel-rolled twice, turned left, then right, then came down onto the grass. Its engine puttered. Its wires sang in the wind. It taxied across the field toward them.

"That'll be Mermier," Blake said. "He got one."

Two more planes followed. They did no acrobatics—merely turned into the wind and set down. They bounced over the turf toward the hangars. One had lost part of its upper wing. Shreds of cloth flickered in the breeze.

Blake and Deveraux still watched the sky beyond the hangars, but no more planes came. Blake's hand clapped Deveraux's shoulder. "Maybe they landed somewhere else."

Deveraux shrugged. "And perhaps they did not live that long. Come. We shall find out."

They walked to the other end of the flight line where the three planes straggled up on the hardstand. Deveraux hurried ahead and Mermier and then the other two pilots climbed out of their cockpits. They talked in French, with many gestures. Farman recognized a few of the gestures—the universal language of air combat—but others were strange or ambiguous. Abruptly, Deveraux turned away, his face wearing the look of pain nobly borne.

"They won't come back," Blake told Farman quietly. "They were seen going down. Burning." His fist struck the hangar's wall. "Keyserling got Michot. He was the only one of us that had a hope of getting him."

Deveraux came back. His face wore a tight, controlled smile. "M'sieu Farman," he said. "I must ask to be shown the abilities of your machine."

"I'll need five hundred gallons of kerosene," Farman said. That would be enough for a lift-off, a quick crack through the barrier, and a landing. Ten minutes in the air, if he didn't drive her faster than Mach 1.4. Enough to show them something of the things *Pika-Don* could do.

Deveraux frowned, touched his mustache. "Kerosene?"

"Paraffin," Blake said. "Lamp oil." He turned to Farman. "They call it paraffin over here. But five hundred gallons—are you nuts? There isn't an aeroplane flying that needs that much lubricating. Shucks, this whole *escadrille* doesn't use that much *gas* in a week. Besides, it's no good as a lubricant—if it was, you think we'd be using the stuff we do?"

"It's not a lubricant," Farman said. "She burns it. It's fuel. And she burns it fast. She delivers a lot of thrust."

"But . . . five hundred gallons!"

"I'll need that much just for a demonstration flight." He looked straight and firmly into Blake's incredulous eyes and decided not to add that, fully loaded, *Pika-Don* took fifty thousand gallons.

Deveraux smoothed his mustache. "In liters, that is how much?"

"You're going to let him . . . ?"

"M'sieu Blake, do you believe this man a fraud?"

Challenged like that, Blake did not back down. "I think he's funning us. He says he'll show us an aeroplane, and he showed us that . . . that thing over there. And when you want to see how it flies, he says it's out of fuel and asks for kerosene—*kerosene* of all things! Enough to go swimming in! Even if that's what she burns, he doesn't need anywhere near that much. And who ever heard of flying an aeroplane with lamp oil?"

Farman took Blake's arm, joggled it, made him turn. "I know," he said. "I'm telling you things it's hard to believe. In your shoes, I wouldn't believe me, either. All right. But let me have a chance to show you. I want to fight the Germans as much as you do." In his thoughts was the picture of a whole *jagdstaffel* of Albatrosses being engulfed by the fireball of one of *Pika-Don*'s rockets. They'd never even see him coming, he'd come at them so fast; even if they saw him, they wouldn't have a chance. Sitting ducks. Fish in a barrel.

"Mister," Blake said, "I don't know what you want all that kerosene for, but I'm sure of one thing—you don't need it to fly. Because if I was ever sure of anything, I know that thing can't fly."

"M'sieu Blake," Deveraux said, moving in front of the American. "This man may perhaps be mistaken, but I do not think he lies. He has a faith in himself. We have need of such men in this war. If he cannot use the paraffin when we have obtained it for him, it will be given to the chef for his stoves. We shall have lost nothing. But we must let him prove his abilities, if he can, for if there is some portion of truth in his claims, why, it is possible that we have before us the man and the machine that shall hurl Bruno Keyserling from the sky."

Blake gave way grudgingly. "If you're funning us, watch out."

"You'll see," Farman promised, grim. And to Deveraux: "Make it a high-grade kerosene. The best you can get." A jet engine could burn kerosene if it had to, but kerosene wasn't a perfect jet fuel any more than wood alcohol could make good martinis. Kerosene was just the nearest thing to jet fuel he could hope to find in 1918. "And we'll have to put it through some kind of filters."

"M'sieu," Deveraux said. "There is only one kind of paraffin. Either it is paraffin, or it is not."

Two days later, while they were waiting for the kerosene to come, Blake took him up in a Caudron two-seater to show him the landmarks. It was a clear day, with only a little dust haze in the direction of the front. Farman didn't think much of learning the landmarks—*Pika-Don*'s map scope was a lot more accurate than any amount of eyeball knowledge. But the scope wouldn't show him the frontline trenches twisting across the landscape, or the location of the German airfields. It might be useful to know such things. Farman borrowed flying clothes, and they were off.

The Caudron looked like nothing so much as a clumsy box kite, or a paleolithic ancestor of the P-38. Its two racketing engines were suspended between the upper and lower wings, one on either side of the passenger nacelle. The tail empennage was joined to the wings by openwork frames of wire-braced wood that extended back from behind the engines. It had a fragile appearance, but it held together sturdily as it lurched across the field like an uncontrolled baby carriage. Finally, after what seemed an interminable length of bumping and bouncing it lofted into the air at a speed that seemed hardly enough to get a feather airborne. A steady windblast tore at Farman's face. Hastily, he slipped the goggles down over his eyes. The climb to six thousand feet seemed to take years.

Blake didn't turn out of their spiral until they reached altitude, then headed east. The air seemed full of crests and hollows, over which the Caudron rode like a boat on a slow-swelled sea. Now and then, woozily, it swayed. A queasy feeling rooted itself in Farman's midsection, as if his stomach was being kneaded and squeezed.

Airsick? No, it couldn't be that. Anything but that. He was an experienced flier with more than ten thousand hours in the air. He couldn't possibly be airsick now. He swallowed hard and firmly held down.

Blake, in the cockpit behind him, yelled and pointed over the side. Farman leaned over. The rush of air almost ripped his goggles off. Far below, small as a diorama, the trench systems snaked across a strip of barren ground—two latticework patterns cut into the earth, roughly parallel to each other, jaggedly angular like toothpick structures that had been crushed. Between them, naked earth as horribly pocked as the surface of the moon.

The Caudron had been following a rivercourse. The trenchlines came down from the hills to the south, crossed the river, and continued northward into the hills on that side. Ahead, over the German trenches, black puffs of antiaircraft fire blossomed in spasmodic, irregular patterns. Blake banked the Caudron and turned south yelling something over his shoulder about the Swiss border. The antiaircraft barrage slacked off.

Recognizing the front would be no problem, Farman decided. He tried to tell Blake, but the slipstream ripped the words away. He twisted around to say it straight. Something snatched at his sleeve.

He looked. Something had gashed the thick fabric, but there was nothing in sight that could have done it. And for some unaccountable reason Blake was heeling the Caudron over into a dive. The horizon tilted crazily, like water sloshing in a bowl. The Caudron's wire rigging snarled nastily.

"Use the gun!" Blake yelled. He jerked an urgent thumb upward.

There was a machine gun on the upper wing, above and just aft of Farman's cockpit, but for a shocked moment Farman didn't grasp what Blake was talking about. Then a dark airplane shape flashed overhead, so close the buzz of its motor could be heard through the noise of the Caudron's own two engines. The goggled, cruel-mouthed face of its pilot turned to look at them. Blake threw the Caudron into a tight turn that jammed Farman deep in his cockpit. Farman lost sight of the German plane, then found it again. It was coming at them.

It was purple—a dark royal purple—with white trim around the edges of wing and tail, and around the engine cowl. Little flashes of light sparkled from its nose, and Farman heard something—it sounded like thick raindrops—spattering the upper wing close to the passenger nacelle. Tracer bullets flashed past like quick fireflies.

"Use the gun!" Blake yelled again. They were climbing now. They leveled off, turned. The German plane came after them. "Use the gun!"

He was being shot at. It was appalling. Things like that didn't happen. In a moment, Farman was too busy to think about it. Somehow he got his seat belt off and stood up in the cockpit, back to the wind. He fumbled with the machine gun's unfamiliar grips. He found the trigger before he knew what it was. The gun chattered and bucked in his grasp. He looked all over the sky for the purple airplane. It was nowhere in sight. Blake hurled the Caudron through another violent maneuver that almost threw Farman overboard, and suddenly there were three German planes behind them, high, the one with the white trim in front and the others trailing. The one with the white trim shifted a little to the left, turned inward again. It nosed down, gun muzzles flickering.

Farman swung the machine gun to bear on the German. He pressed the trigger. The gun stuttered and a spray of tracers streamed aft as it caught in the slipstream. They passed under the German, not even close.

Aerial gunnery wasn't a thing Farman had ever had to learn. Combat was done with guidance systems, computers, and target-seeking missiles, not antique .30 caliber popguns. He raised the gun and fired another burst. Still too low, and passing behind the German, who was boring close in, weaving up, sidewise, and down as he came. The gun didn't have any sights worth mentioning—no target tracking equipment at all. Farman wrestled with the clumsy weapon, trying to keep its muzzle pointed at the German. It should have been easy, but it wasn't. The German kept dodging. Farman emptied the machine gun without once touching the other plane. He spent an eternity dismounting the empty magazine and clipping another into place, all the time holding on one-handed, while Blake hurled the Caudron through a wild series of gut-wrenching acrobatics.

A section of the cockpit coaming at Farman's knee shattered and disappeared in the wind. He got the gun working again—fired a burst just as the German sidled behind the Caudron's right rudder. Farman's tracers went right through. The rudder exploded in a spray of chips and tatters. The German swung out to the right, gained a few feet altitude, turned in again and down again. His guns hurled blazing streaks. Blake sent the Caudron into a dive, a turn, and a twist that almost somersaulted Farman out of the plane. Abruptly, then, the German was gone. Little scraps were still tearing loose from the rudder, whipped away by the slipstream.

"Where?" Farman shouted, bending down as close to Blake as he could. He meant, where had the German gone, but he wasn't up to asking a question that complicated.

"Skedaddled," Blake yelled up at him. "We've got friends. Look."

Farman looked when Blake aimed his thumb. Five hundred feet above them five Nieuports cruised in neat formation. After a moment, the formation leader waggled his wings and they curved off eastward. Farman looked down and saw they were far behind the French lines, headed northwest. They were flying level and smooth—only the slow, gentle lift and descent of random air currents, like silence at the end of a storm. He sagged down into his cockpit. "You all right?" Blake asked.

"I think so," Farman said. But suddenly, as the Caudron slipped into a downdraft, he wasn't. His stomach wrenched, and he had time enough only to get his head over the cockpit's side before the first gush of vomit came. He was still there, gripping the splintered coaming with both hands, his stomach squeezing itself like a dry sponge, when Blake circled the airfield and slowly brought the Caudron down to a three-point landing. All Farman could think—distantly, with the part of his brain not concerned with his terrible miseries—was how long it had been since anyone, anywhere in the world, had even thought about making a three-point landing.

He wouldn't admit, even to himself, it had been airsickness. But after a while the horizon stopped wheeling around him and he could stand without needing a hand to steady him. He discovered he was very hungry. Blake went down to the mess hall and came back with a half-loaf of black bread and a dented tin of pâté. They went to the shack behind the hangars. Henri gave Blake a bottle of peasant's wine and two glasses. Blake put them down in the middle of the table and sat down across from Farman. He poured, and they went to work on the bread and pâté.

"He was trying to kill us," Farman said. It just came out of him. It had been there ever since the fight. "He was trying to *kill* us."

Blake cut himself another slice of the bread. He gnawed on the leathery crust. "Sure. And I'd of killed him, given the chance. That's what we're supposed to do—him and us, both. Nothing personal at all. I've got to admit I wasn't expecting him, though. They don't often come this side of the lines. But . . ." He made a rueful grimace. "He's a tough one to outguess."

"He?"

Blake stopped gnawing, frowned. "You know who it was, don't you?"

The idea of knowing an enemy's name after such a brief acquaintance was completely strange to Farman. His mouth made motions, but no words came out.

"Bruno Keyserling," Blake said. "He's the only man with an aeroplane painted that way."

"I'm going to get him," Farman said.

"Easier said than done," Blake said. His mouth turned grim. "You'll have to sharpen up your gunnery quite a bit, if you're going to make good on that."

"I'm going to get him," Farman repeated, knuckles white on the table.

The next day it rained. Thick, wet, gray clouds crouched low to the ground and poured down torrents. All patrols were canceled, and the fliers sat in the shack behind the hangars, drinking and listening to the storm as it pelted the shingles. At first light, when he woke and heard the rain, Farman had borrowed a slicker and gone out to *Pika-Don*. She was all right. He'd left her buttoned up tight, and the rain was doing her no harm.

Blake was still the only man Farman could talk with, except for Deveraux. None of the other pilots had more than a smattering of English. When they left the mess hall after a drab lunch, instead of returning to the drinking shack, Blake led him to one of the hangars. There, in a back corner, were stacked wooden boxes of ammunition and others full of the bent-metal sections of disintegrating-link machine-gun belts. Blake showed Farman how to assemble the links and how to check both the links and the cartridges for manufacturing defects. He handed Farman a gauge into which a properly shaped cartridge should fit perfectly, and they spent the next several hours inspecting cartridges and assembling belts of ammunition. It was tedious work. Each cartridge looked just like the one before it. The imperfections were small.

"Do you always do this yourself?" Farman inspected his grimy hands, his split cuticles. He wasn't accustomed to this kind of work.

"Every chance I get," Blake said. "There're enough reasons for a gun to jam without bad ammunition being one of 'em. When you're up there with Keyserling's circus flying rings around you, all you've got are your guns and your engine and your wings, and if any of those go, you go. And it's a long way down."

Farman said nothing for awhile. Rain drummed on the roof. Now and then came the clang of tools being used in another part of the hangar. "How come you're here?" he asked finally. "What's in it for you?"

Blake's busy hands paused. He looked at Farman. "Say that again, slower."

"This here's a French squadron. You're an American. What are you doing here?"

Blake snorted—not quite a chuckle. "Fighting Germans."

Farman wondered if Blake was making fun of him. He tried again. "Sure—but why with a bunch of Frenchmen?"

Blake inspected a cartridge, fitted it into the belt. He picked up another. "Didn't care to transfer," he said. "Could have, when they started bringing U.S. squadrons over. But I like the plane I've got. If I transferred, they'd give me a plane the French don't want and the British don't want, because that's all the American squadrons are getting. Well, I don't want 'em, either." He dropped a cartridge in the reject pile.

"I didn't mean that," Farman said. "You joined before America got into the war—right?"

"Came over in 'sixteen."

"All right. That's what I mean. Why help France?" He couldn't understand why an American would do anything to help the personal kingdom of *le grand Charles*. "You weren't involved," he said. "Why?"

Blake went on inspecting cartridges. "Depends what you mean, involved. I figure I am. Everyone is. The Germans started this war. If we can show the world it doesn't pay to start a war, then there won't be any more. I want that. This is going to be the last war the human race will ever have."

Farman went back to inspecting cartridges. "Don't get your hopes too high," he said. It was as near as he could bring himself to telling Blake how doomed his optimism was. The rain made thunder on the roof like the march of armies.

Late in the afternoon, two days later, three lorries sputtered into the supply area behind the hangars. They brought fuel for the escadrille, but also, crowded among the drums of gasoline were twenty hundred-liter barrels of kerosene which were carefully put aside and trucked down to the mess hall's kitchen and then—when the error was discovered—had to be reloaded and trucked back up to the hangars again.

Farman had managed to rig a crude filtration system for the kerosene. The stuff they cooked with was full of junk. He'd scrounged sheets of silk, and enlisted a crew of mechanics to scrub empty petrol drums until their innards gleamed like the insides of dairy cans. He even succeeded in testing the rig with a bucket of kerosene cadged from the kitchens. The process was glacially slow, and the end product neither looked nor smelled any different from the stuff he started with. But when he tried it in one of *Pika-Don*'s engines, the engine had started and—at low r.p.m.— had delivered thrust and functioned as it should until the tank was sucked dry. More important, when he inspected, none of the injectors had fouled.

He started the filtering process, and stayed with it through the night and all the next day. He had a mechanic to help him, but he had no confidence in the mechanic's understanding of how vital fuel quality was to an engine. It was not a thing an airplane mechanic of this time could be expected to know. Deveraux came around once, inspected the raw material and sniffed the filtered product, and went away again, having said nothing.

Once, between missions, Blake came and sat to watch. Farman showed him the sludge the filters had taken out of the kerosene. Blake scowled. "It's still kerosene," he said. "You can't fly an aeroplane on kerosene any more than you can feed it birdseed. I don't know what you really want it for, but don't expect me to believe it's for flying."

Farman shrugged. "I'll take *Pika-Don* up tomorrow morning. You can tell me what you think tomorrow afternoon. Fair enough?"

"Maybe," Blake said.

"You think I'm a cushmaker, don't you?"

"Possible. What's a cushmaker?"

Blake hadn't heard the story. Maybe it hadn't been invented yet. Farman explained it—the ultra shaggy joke about the cushmaker who, obliged by an admiral to demonstrate his specialty, after commandeering a battleship and tons of elaborate equipment, and after arduous technological efforts, finally dropped a white-hot sphere of steel amid the ice floes of the Antarctic Ocean, where it went *cussh*.

Blake went away, then. "I'll say this. If you're pulling a deal, you're a cool one." He shook his head. "I just don't know about you."

Morning brought high, ragged clouds. They'd make no trouble for the demonstration flight. Farman waited beside *Pika-Don* while Blake took off and slowly climbed to ten thousand feet, circling over the field the whole time. "I think we are ready, M'sieu," Deveraux said, fingering his trim mustache.

Farman turned to his plane. "Better make everybody stand back," he said. Turbine scream wasn't gentle to unprotected ears. He climbed up on the packing crate—pulled himself up *Pika-Don*'s sloped side and dropped into the cockpit. Looking back, he saw the onlookers had retreated about twenty-five feet. He had quite an audience. He grinned. They'd back off a lot farther when he got the engines going.

He got the cockpit hatch down. He checked the seal; it was tight. He went through the pre-ignition cockpit check. He began the engine start-up cycle, felt the momentary vibration and saw the twitch of instruments coming alive. Engine One caught, ragged for an instant, then steady as the tachometer wound around like a clock gone wild. Its scream of power drilled through the cockpit's insulation. Farman started Engine Two, then Engine Three. He brought them up to standby idle. They burned smooth.

Good enough. He didn't have fuel to waste on all the pre-takeoff operations; some were necessary, some not. He did all the necessary ones, turned the jets into the lift vents, and brought them up to full power. By that time, *Pika-Don* was already off the ground. She bobbled momentarily in the light breeze, and rose like a kite on a string. The sprawling fuselage surface prevented him from looking down at the airfield; it didn't matter. They'd be watching, all right—and probably holding shriek-filled ears. He grinned at the trembling instruments in front of him. He wished he could see their eyes, their open mouths. You'd think they'd never seen a plane fly before.

He took *Pika-Don* up to ten thousand feet. Hovering, he tried to find the image of Blake's Nieuport on the airspace view scope. It didn't show. For a worried moment, Farman wondered if something had gone wrong and Blake had gone down. Then the Nieuport flew past him on the left, a little above. It turned to pass in front of him. He could see Blake's goggled face turned toward him.

Even then, there wasn't an image on the radar. Farman swore. Something was wrong with the equipment.

No time to fiddle with the dials now, though. *Pika-Don* was guzzling the kerosene like a drunk on holiday. He converted to lateral flight. As always, it was like the floor dropping out from under him. He moved all three throttles forward, felt the thrust against his back. For a frightened instant, he saw Blake had turned back—was coming straight at him, head-on. He'd warned Blake not to get ahead of him like that. But *Pika-Don* was dropping fast. At speeds less than Mach 0.5 she had the glide capability of a bowling ball. She slashed underneath the Nieuport with a hundred feet to spare. The altimeter began to unwind, faster and faster. The horizon lifted on the forward view scope like a saucer's rim.

He watched the Machmeter. It was edging up. He could feel the drive of the engines, full thrust now, exciting him like they always did, hurling him across the sky. The altimeter steadied, began to rise again. He tipped *Pika-Don*'s prow upward and cracked the barrier in a rocketing fifty-degree climb. Blake's Nieuport was nowhere in sight.

At forty thousand he cut the engines back, leveled off, and started down. He had to search hard for the airfield; without the map scope he couldn't have found it. It was just another green field in a countryside of green fields. At five thousand feet he converted back to vertical thrust and let *Pika-Don* drop to a landing—quickly for most of the distance to save fuel, with a heavy retarding burst in the last thousand feet. He hovered a moment two hundred feet up, picked out a landing spot, and put down. According to the gauges, less than thirty seconds' fuel was left in the tanks.

He dropped to the ground without waiting for a packing crate to be brought. He stood and looked around in disbelief. There was hardly a man in sight, and none of the escadrille's planes remained on the field. He saw them, finally, small specks flying off eastward. He walked back to the hangars, perplexed. Was that all the impression he'd made? He grabbed the first man he found—a mechanic. "What happened?"

The mechanic grinned and made gestures and gabbled in French. Farman shook him and asked again—or tried to—in pidgin French. All he got was more of the same jabber and some gestures in the general direction of the front lines. "I know they went that way," Farman growled and flung the man away. He stalked back to the shack behind the hangars and asked Henri for a Scotch. He drank it, waited five minutes, and had another. He was deep into his fourth when the men came back.

They trooped into the shack, and Henri set a row of glasses on the counter and went down the line with the brandy bottle. As soon as a glass had been filled, a hand snatched it away. Blake came to Farman's table, a brimful glass in his hand, sat down.

"Howard," he said, "I don't know how that thing of yours works. I don't even know if you can call it an aeroplane. But I've got to admit you got it off the ground, and the only thing I ever saw go past me faster was a bullet. Now, if you'll just tell me one thing . . ."

"Anything you want to know," Farman said, abruptly raised from dejection to smugness.

"How can you fly when you don't have the wind on your face?"

Farman started to laugh, but Blake wasn't even smiling. To him, it wasn't an old joke. He was serious.

With effort, Farman controlled his amusement. "I don't need the wind. In fact, if the window broke, I'd probably be killed. I've got instruments that tell me everything I need to know."

He could see the skeptical expression shaping itself on Blake's face. He started to get up, not quite steady because of the Scotches he'd downed. "Come on. I'll show you the cockpit."

Blake waved him down. "I saw the cockpit. You've got so many things in there you don't have time to look outside. I don't know if I'd call it flying. You might as well be sitting at a desk."

Sometimes, Farman had thought the same thought. But all those instruments were necessary to fly a thing like *Pika-Don*. He wondered if he'd have taken up flying if he'd known it would be like that. "Or maybe a submarine?" he asked, not entirely sarcastic. "The the thing is, did I fly circles around you, or didn't I?"

Blake's reply was a rueful shrug. "First, you hung there like a balloon. If I hadn't seen you, I wouldn't believe it. Then all of a sudden you were coming at me like something out of a cannon. I got to admit you had me scared. I never saw anything move like that thing of yours. By the time I got turned around you were out of sight. If we'd been dogfighting, you could of put a string of bullets through me from end to end, and I couldn't of got a shot off."

A shadow intruded onto the table between them. They looked up. "Indeed, M'sieu Farman," Deveraux said, "your machine's speed gives it the ability to attack without the risk of being attacked itself. I will not pretend to understand how it can fly with such small wings, nor how it can rise directly into the air, but I have seen it do these things. That is enough. I must apologize that we could not be here to applaud you when you landed."

So he'd made an impression after all. "Where'd you go? I thought you didn't have any patrols scheduled until this afternoon."

Deveraux pulled out a chair and sat down beside Blake. With delicate care, he placed a half-full wineglass in front of him. "That is true, M'sieu. But we heard the sound of big guns at the front, and our duty is to be in the air at such times, until the matter is clarified, doing such things as will assist our men in the trenches."

"I didn't hear any guns," Farman said. "When I got back here, it was as quiet as a bar mitzvah in Cairo."

He realized almost at once, seeing their faces, that the metaphor had no meaning for them. Well, they hadn't heard of Social Security, either.

"It is curious," Deveraux said. "When we are come to the front, it is as you say—most quiet. The guns have stopped, and we see no aircraft but our own. We search for fifty kilometers along the front. There is no evidence of even small actions. When we come back, I message to commanders at the front, and they tell me there has been no action. Nor have guns in their sectors been made use of—theirs or the Boche—though it is curious . . . some do say that they have heard guns being used in other sectors. And you can see"—he pointed to the window, the clear sky—"it could not have been thunder."

He said it all with the innocent mystification of a small boy, still not sure of all the things in the universe. Farman suddenly laughed and Deveraux blinked, startled.

"Sorry," Farman said. "I just realized. It wasn't guns you heard. It was me."

"You, M'sieu? What jest is this?"

"No joke. What you heard was my plane. It makes a shock wave in the air, just like an explosion's." He looked at their faces. "You don't believe me."

Deveraux's wineglass was empty. Blake stood up, empty brandy glass in hand. He reached for Deveraux's glass, but the Frenchman put his hand in the way. Blake went to the bar with only his own glass. Farman nursed his drink.

"I do not pretend to understand this aeroplane of yours," Deveraux said. "But now that you have shown its abilities . . ."

"Some of them," Farman said. They'd only seen an iceberg tip of what *Pika-Don* could do.

"Yes. But now we have seen," Deveraux said. "I will agree, it is possible your machine could outmatch Bruno Keyserling."

"I know she can," Farman said.

"Perhaps," Deveraux said with a small smile, but very firm. "But I agree—it should be tried. If you will tell us where to mount the guns on your machine . . ."

"I don't need guns," Farman said. "Don't want them."

"But M'sieu, an aeroplane *must* have guns. Without guns, it is like a tiger without teeth and claws."

The thought of machine guns stuck on *Pika-Don*'s prow was a horror. "I've got my own weapons," Farman said. Blake came back, sat down heavily. His glass slopped a little on the table. "Machine guns would . . . they'd destroy her aerodynamic integrity. They'd . . . she probably couldn't even fly with them sticking out in the wind."

"Aerody . . . *what* integrity?" Blake snorted. "What are you talking about?"

Farman leaned forward. "Look. You've seen my plane. All right. Now—you've seen those overlapping strips along her belly, between the ports the skids retract into?"

"I have noticed," Deveraux said.

"There's a rocket under each one of them," Farman said. "Just one of those can wipe out a whole squadron."

"Ah? How many rockets? Eight?"

"Six," Farman said. "How many squadrons have the Germans got in this sector?"

"Two jagdstaffels," Deveraux said. "They are quite enough." He shook his head. "But M'sieu, the men who planned the equipping of your aeroplane did not understand the needs of combat. It is assuming a marksman's skill beyond human abilities to believe that with only six of these rockets you could expect to be effective against enemy aircraft. One must remember, they are not motionless targets, like balloons. It is difficult enough to strike a balloon with rockets—balloons do not move—but to destroy an aeroplane . . . that cannot be done. Often I have expended all my ammunition—hundreds of rounds—without so much as touching my opponent. That you would imagine going into combat with a mere six possibilities of striking your target . . . this is folly. It is not worth the effort."

"They're not just things I shoot off," Farman said. Did he have to explain everything? "In fact, my plane's so fast any weapons system that depends on human senses couldn't possibly work. My rockets find their targets themselves. They are . . ."

He saw the utter disbelief on their faces. "Look," he said, "I've shown you my plane can do everything I told you it could. It flies faster and climbs faster than anything you ever saw. Now, if you'll give me enough fuel to take her up against Keyserling, I'll show you what my rockets can do. They'll wipe him out of the sky like a blob of smoke in a high wind."

"Bruno Keyserling is a very skilled and deadly man," Deveraux said. "A man impossible to kill. We have tried—all of us. He has killed many of our own men, and he will send more of us down in flames before this war ends. I would suggest you be not so confident of yourself and your equipment."

"Just give me enough kerosene for a mission," Farman said. "One mission. Let me worry about the rest of it." He wasn't worried at all. A dogfight between World War I model planes and something from 1985 would be like a wrestling match between a man and a gorilla.

"But M'sieu, you *have* the paraffin," Deveraux said, mildly puzzled. "You have almost two thousand liters."

Farman shook his head. "I burned that. There's just about enough left to fill that glass of yours."

Deveraux looked down at his empty wineglass. "M'sieu, you must be joking."

"No joke," Farman said. "*Pika-Don* flies fast and climbs like a rocket, but you don't get something for nothing—law of conservation of energy, if you know what that is. She drinks fuel like a sewer."

There was a silence—a silence, Farman realized, not only at their own table, but all through the shack. Maybe these fliers understood more English than he thought. Blake downed a large swallow of brandy.

"How much do you need for a mission?" he asked.

"Ten thousand gallons will do for a short one," Farman said. "An hour—hour and a half."

There was another long silence. "M'sieu," Deveraux said at last, "I have wide discretion in the requisition of the usual

materials. I am trying to balance in my mind the possible
destruction of Bruno Keyserling—which is a thing we all desire—
against the difficulty I must expect in explaining my request for so
much kitchen fuel. And I remain in doubt you will be able to
accomplish as successful as you claim. So I must ask—have I your
word of honor as an American that you must have this paraffin to
fly your machine?"

"You've got it, on a stack of Bibles."

"The good old USA is alive with con men," Blake said.

"M'sieu Blake," Deveraux said reproachfully, "we must not
assume that a man tells lies because he claims ability to do a thing
we cannot do ourselves. He is optimistic, yes. But that is a fault
of almost all the young men who come to us. If we do not put him
to the test, we shall not know if he could do the thing he claims
or not."

Blake made a sour twist of his mouth. "All right. But how are
you going to explain wanting forty thousand liters of kerosene?"

Deveraux cocked his head to one side, as if listening to a voice
no one else could hear. "I think I shall merely tell a part of the
truth. That we wish to try a weapon suggested by one of our men,
a weapon which makes use of paraffin."

"Such as?" Blake asked.

"If they want details," Farman said, leaning forward, "tell them
you're putting it in old winebottles and cramming a rag in the
neck. And before you drop the bottle on the Germans you set fire
to the rag. The bottle breaks when it hits, and spills burning
kerosene over everything."

Blake and Deveraux looked at each other. Delight animated
their faces. "Now that's something I think might work," Blake
said, rubbing his jaw. "Why didn't somebody think of it before?"

It was the first time Farman had heard him enthusiastic about
something. This, at least, was a weapon they could understand.
"It might work," he said. "But gasoline does it better. It's called
Molotov cocktail."

"M'sieu Farman," Deveraux said, "I think we shall try that,
also." He stood up, wineglass in hand. "Henri!" he called. "More
wine!"

Early that afternoon, two men came to the airfield fresh from
training school. Boys, really; neither could have been more than
seventeen. They were eager to get into the war—looked discon-
solate as they came away from reporting to Deveraux. "They'll

have to spend a day or two learning their way around," Blake
said, a twisty smile curling his mouth. "Some guys just can't wait
to get killed."

Their Nieuports were straight from the factory, new as pennies.
The smell of dope and varnish surrounded them like an
aura. Blake worked his way around them, a point-by-point
inspection. The new men would be assigned to his flight. He
peered intently at struts and wires and fabric surfaces. "Good
aeroplanes," he said finally. Then it was time for him to go out on
patrol. Three other men went with him. Farman watched them
take off. They disappeared eastward. He went back and saw about
readying his jerry-built filtration plant for the job of turning ten
thousand gallons of cooking oil into aviation fuel.

At first light next morning, the new men stood beside their
planes and watched the escadrille fly out on dawn patrol. They
looked like children not invited to play. Farman went and checked
Pika-Don; there was sign of a gummy deposit in her tail pipes, but
a close inspection of her compressor blades showed they were
clean, and none of the fuel injectors was fouled. He buttoned her
up again and headed for the drinking shack. Until he got his
shipment of kerosene, he'd have nothing to do.

The escadrille came back three hours later. If there'd been any
Germans in the sky that morning, they'd made themselves hard to
find. There'd been no action. Six planes refueled at once and went
out again. Deveraux took the new men out on an orientation flight.
In the afternoon, Blake and another pilot took the new men out for
a mock dogfight. When they came back, Farman was waiting at
the edge of the field; he had an idea he felt foolish for not having
thought of sooner—to make a start on the long kerosene
upgrading job by borrowing a barrel or two of the raw material
from the mess hall. He needed Blake to translate and haggle for
him.

As Blake taxied up onto the hardstand, Farman saw the tattered
fabric fluttering from the right upper wing. He ran over as Blake
cut the motor. "Hey! You've been in a fight!"

Blake dropped down from the cockpit. He stripped off helmet
and goggles and gloves. Farman repeated his question. Blake
grinned and pointed to his ears and shook his head. Farman
pointed at the shredded wing.

"Yeah. I've been in a fight," Blake said, his voice loud as if he
was trying to talk through the noise his motor had made.

Farman looked out at the other planes taxiing in from the field.

They're all right," Blake said. "We jumped a Brandenburg—
what he was doing way off there behind the lines, don't ask me.
I got the observer interested in me"—he nodded at the damaged
wing—"and Jacques moved in and put a few in the engine. Simple
enough."

The other planes of the flight came up on the hardstand, and the
mechanics moved in to turn them around and chock the wheels.
The pilots climbed out, and the new men crowded around the
other veteran—Jacques, Farman assumed. They pumped his arm
and slapped his back and jabbered jubilantly. Jacques managed to
break free of them long enough to reach Blake. He grabbed both
Blake's arms and spoke with a warm grin. Blake looked a little
embarrassed by the attention and managed, finally, to shrug off
Jacques' hands without offending. By then the new men had
closed in again. A rapid four-way conversation broke out.

Blake got loose again after a minute. "They never saw an
aeroplane shot down before." He grinned. "Wasn't much of a
shoot-down, really. Jacques put a few in the engine, and it just sort
of went into a glide." He nodded at the three men; they were still
talking energetically. "I guess they liked the show, even if they
don't understand some of it. They're wanting to know why we
didn't go on shooting after Jacques got the engine."

It sounded like a reasonable thing to ask. "Well, why didn't
you?" He remembered to speak loud.

Blake shrugged. "Why kill 'em? There's enough people getting
killed. They were out of the war as soon as their propeller
stopped."

"Well, yes. Sure. But . . ."

"Oh, we made sure they landed close to a convoy on the road,
so they'd be captured all right," Blake said. "Didn't want a pair
of Huns running loose behind the lines."

"But they were Germans. The enemy."

Blake punched a finger into Farman's ribs. "Once Jacques got
their engine, they were just a couple of poor guys in an aeroplane
that couldn't fly any more. We got no fight with guys like that. It's
the man they worked for we're against. The Kaiser. Besides, that
guy in the rear cockpit still had a lot of bullets in his machine gun,
and he was sort of mad at us. I figure we were smart to keep our
distance."

The new men had a few more training flights the next day, and
the day after that they went out with the dawn patrol. The patrol
met a flight of German machines led by Keyserling's white-

trimmed purple Albatross. It was a fast, cruel scrap. Only one o
the new men came back.

"We shouldn't of put 'em on service so quick," Blake said
nodding across the shack toward where the survivor was slowl
drinking himself into numbness; he'd been in shock ever since h
climbed out of his cockpit. "But we've got to have men. It take
three months to train a man enough so he's got a chance in th
air—and Keyserling and his circus kill 'em in five minutes. Lik
swatting a fly." He picked up his brandy and downed it whole.

Deveraux came and put a hand on Blake's shoulder. "It is true,
he said. "One might wish we did not so desperately need men t
fight. But we fight a war to preserve civilization, and for that it i
necessary that some good men die. And so we have lost one ma
today. And one other machine is damaged. Do not forget
Keyserling has lost two men in this morning's battle, and three o
his aeroplanes will need considerable work before they fly again
We have done well, this day."

"Yeah. Sure. But he was just a kid," Blake said. His open han
banged on the table. Glasses rattled. "A poor, dumb kid. As gree
as—"

"To keep a civilization is worth a few lives, M'sieu Blake."
Deveraux squeezed Blake's shoulder, held the grip a moment, le
his hand slip away. He moved off to talk with the men at anothe
table.

"Civilization," Blake muttered.

"Stick around," Farman said. If he lived long enough, Blak
would know of Dachau, Bataan, Hiroshima, 'Nam, and th
bloody mess France herself would make of her African colonies
And lots more.

"You haven't seen anything yet," Farman said.

The kerosene began to come two days later. It came spasmod
ically, in odd-sized lots: one day a demijohn arrived; the next, hal
a lorry load. Kerosene, to these people, was not a strategicall
vital petrochemical; it was a fluid used in lamps and stoves. I
couldn't just be commanded up from the nearest supply dump i
anything like the quantities a supersonic jet had to have. Genghi
Khan's army might have been similarly inept at meeting a sudden
inexplicable demand for a few thousand pounds of gunpowder.

June became July. The summer sun burned warm. There wa
talk of heavy fighting to the north, in a place called Bois d
Belleau. Farman worked at the makeshift filters day after day. Th

smell of warm kerosene was a weight in his lungs, an ache in his brain. Some evenings, he was too sickened to eat.

The weeks blended into each other. He didn't have much idle time; there was always more kerosene to be poured into the system, or a filter to be changed and the clogged filter to be scraped and scrubbed and carefully examined for flaws before being used again. After a while, he stopped looking up when he heard the sound of airplane motors.

But in that time he saw airplanes lose power as they left the ground, stall, and nose stiffly into the turf. Their wings snapped like jackstraws. He saw a tattered plane coming back from a dogfight; it fell apart over the field and its pilot died in the wreck. He saw a man bring his plane down, taxi off the field, and die from loss of blood with the engine still puttering. And there were many times when he saw men watch the sky, searching for planes that would not come back, ever.

Some nights, he heard the big guns thunder at the front, like a grumbling storm just beyond the horizon. Muzzle flash and shellburst blazed in the sky.

Several days came when no new loads of kerosene arrived. He used that time to learn what he could about the Germans—their tactics, their formations, the capabilities of their planes. Not much of the information was useful—he'd expected that; matched against *Pika-Don*, they'd be almost motionless targets. But with only ten thousand gallons to fly on, it would be a good idea to know where he'd be most likely to find them. He wouldn't have much more time in the air than just enough to lift off, aim and launch rockets, and return to base. He started planning the mission.

"They stay mostly on their own side of the lines," he said to Deveraux. "All right. When I go up, I don't want you to have any planes on that side. I want to be sure any planes I find over there are theirs, not yours. I'll be going too fast to look at 'em close."

"You ask more than is possible, or even wise," Deveraux said. Breeze ruffled grass on the field. The Frenchman's scarf flapped and fluttered. "It is necessary always to have patrols in all sectors to protect our reconnaissance aeroplanes. If we do not patrol, the reconnaissance aeroplanes would be attacked. They could not do their missions. Perhaps it would be possible to remove patrols from one sector for a few hours—one in which none of our observation missions will be flying. Is not that as much as you shall need?"

"Not quite," Farman said. "I don't think you've thought it all the way through. You cover the front between the Swiss border and the Vosges Mountains. Right?"

"There are several escadrilles with which we share that duty."

"Yeah. Well, that's not important except they'll have to be warned off, too. What I'm asking now is, how many miles of front are you covering? Fifty? Seventy-five?"

"It is fifty kilometers," Deveraux said.

"All right. I'll be flying at about Mach 2. At that speed, I can cover that much distance in three minutes. It takes me twenty miles just to get turned around. I can patrol the whole front, all by myself. You don't need to have anybody else out there."

Deveraux's face wore a scowlish mask. "So fast? I must assume you do not exaggerate, M'sieu."

"At sixty thousand feet, I could do it twice that fast," Farman said. "But I'm going to cruise at forty. Air's too thick for full power flying that low down. I'd burn like a meteor."

"Of course, M'sieu."

Farman couldn't be sure if Deveraux believed him or not.

"But I must say, it would seem you have not considered all the necessities," the Frenchman went on. "Even if you are able to patrol all the sectors, that would be true only should you not find a Boche patrol. Then you would move to attack it, and *voilà*, you would cease to patrol. You would be engaged in combat, M'sieu. And it is not uncommon for the Boche to have four or five flights in the air at one time. Who would be protecting our observation missions while you are fighting?"

"I don't even want any observation flights on that side of the lines while I'm flying," Farman said. "Because I'm going to wipe that sky clean like a blackboard. If you have observation planes over there, they might get it, too. So you don't need to have any patrols out to protect 'em. Anyway, it won't take me more than five minutes from the time I've spotted a flight until I've launched rockets, and then I'll be free to go back on patrol. That's not much more than if I'd took time out for a smoke."

They heard, then, very faint but growing, the sound of aircraft motors. Deveraux turned to search the eastward sky for the approaching planes. "And have you thought, M'sieu, what the Boche would be doing while you are shooting these rockets of yours? Bruno Keyserling and his men are aviators of consummate skill. They would not fly calmly, doing nothing, while you attack them. And even should your rockets each find a target, that would

till be only one of their aeroplanes for each rocket. You have, I
believe you said, only six."

"They won't even see me coming, I'll jump 'em so fast,"
Farman said. "They won't have time to do anything but look
surprised. And one of my rockets can . . ." He made a wipe-out
gesture. "Look. All I'm asking—keep your planes on this side of
the lines for a couple of hours. With only ten thousand gallons, I
won't be able to stay out even that long. Am I asking too much?
Two hours?"

The returning planes were in sight now. There were three of
them, strung out, the one in the rear far behind the other two,
losing altitude, regaining it, losing it again. Farman didn't know
how many had gone out on that particular patrol—he hadn't been
paying much attention to such things—but it was rare for a patrol
of only three planes to go out. There would be some empty chairs
in the mess, this evening.

The first plane came down to land. Its lower wing was shredded
close to the fuselage—loose fabric fluttered like torn flags—and
the landing gear wheel on that side wobbled oddly. As it touched
down, the whole gear collapsed. The wing dipped—caught the
ground—and flung the machine into a tangle of broken struts, tail
high in the air. Men ran across the field. Farman caught a glimpse
of the pilot's arm, waving for help. A thin black thread of smoke
began to rise. A moment later it was a fierce inferno. No one could
get near it. There wasn't a sign of the man. The second plane
landed and taxied across the grass unheeded.

Deveraux turned to Farman again. "No, M'sieu," he said.
"You do not ask too much. It is we who ask too much of men."

Farman boosted *Pika-Don* from the field while dawn was still a
growing light in the east and all the land was gray. She lifted
sluggishly; well, the gunk he was feeding her was a poor sub-
stitute for her usual diet. He took her to eight thousand feet
before converting to lateral flight. She was down to four before
he cracked the barrier and down to three and a half before she
bottomed out and started to climb. The Machmeter moved past
1.25. He raised *Pika-Don*'s nose and drove her at the sky.

She broke into sunlight at twenty thousand feet. The sun was
cold and the air was as clean as clear ice. Somewhere in the
darkness below two armies faced each other as they had faced
each other for four years. At forty thousand feet he leveled off and
began his loiter pattern—a slim-waisted figure eight course,

looping first to the south, then to the north—overflying the German lines from the Swiss border to the Vosges Mountains. He watched the airspace view scope for the pips that would be German aircraft.

Almost always, on good flying days, the Germans sent up patrols a few minutes before sunrise, to intercept the reconnaissance planes the French almost always sent over on good flying days. Bruno Keyserling would be leading one of those patrols. Farman watched particularly the area surrounding the German airfield. The Germans would climb quickly to fighting altitude; as soon as their altitude and motion dissociated them from the ground, *Pika-Don*'s radars would pick them out. He watched the scope, followed his loiter pattern, and waited for the German planes to appear.

Two circuits later, he was still up there. The scope showed the shaded contours of the land, but that was all. Not one German plane—no planes at all, even though the whole escadrille had flown out ahead of him to watch the fight he'd promised. He had fuel enough for six or eight more circuits—it was going faster than he'd counted on—before there'd be only enough to get him back to the field.

And more weeks of filtering kerosene? Not if he could help it. He made two more circuits—still nothing. He put *Pika-Don*'s needle prow downward. If they wouldn't come up and fight, he'd go after them. He checked the German field's position on the map scope. He could fly down straight to the end of its runway, and he had six rockets. One would be enough. Two would destroy it utterly.

He was down below twenty thousand feet when he saw the airplanes. They were flying on a northerly course, as he was, patrolling above the German lines in a Junck's row formation—each plane above, behind, and to the side of the one below it; an upright, diagonal line. A quick glance at the radar scope: not a hint of those planes.

Nuts with the airfield. Not with those planes over there. Flying where they were, using that formation, they had to be Germans. Farman pulled out of this attack dive, immelmanned into a corkscrew turn that would take him back and place him behind their formation. He lost sight of them in that maneuver, but the map scope showed him where they had to be; they didn't have the speed to move far while he was getting into position.

Behind them now, he turned again and drove toward them. Still nothing on the airspace scope, but he knew where they were. He tried the target-tracking radar—the one in the middle of the instrument panel. They didn't show there, either.

But he knew where they were, and in another moment he saw them again. Little black specks, like gnats, only gnats didn't fly in formation. And one rocket anywhere near them . . .

Still they didn't show on the target-tracking scope. It would have to be an eyeball launch, then. He primed the proximity detonators on rockets one and six. There still was no sign that they'd seen him. They didn't even seem to move against the sky.

He launched the rockets at four miles. The distance was a guess—without help from his radars, a guess was all he could do, but the German planes were still only specks. It didn't matter. The rockets were built to heat-seek a target from ten times that distance. He felt the shock as the rockets struck from their sheaths even as he sent *Pika-Don* screaming straight up, engines suddenly at full thrust, and over on her back, and a half-roll, and he was at forty-five thousand feet. Rockets one and six sketched their ionized tracks on the airspace scope, all the way to the edge.

The edge was somewhere beyond the crest of the Vosges Mountains. Farman couldn't understand it. He'd sent those rockets straight as bullets into that formation, proximities primed and warheads armed. They should have climbed right up those Germans' tail pipes and fireballed and wiped those planes from the sky like tinder touched by flame. It hadn't happened.

He brought *Pika-Don* around. On the map scope he found again the position where the German planes had been. They didn't show on the airspace view—what could possibly be wrong with the radar—but they would still be close to where he'd seen them last, and he still had four rockets left. On the airspace scope, the tracks of rockets one and six ended in tiny sparks as their propellants exhausted and their automatic destructs melted them to vapor. He turned *Pika-Don*'s nose down. He armed the warheads, primed the proximities. This time he wouldn't miss.

He saw the Germans planes from ten miles away. He launched rockets two and five from a distance of five miles. Two seconds later, he launched three and four and turned away in a high-G immelmann. His G-suit seized him like a hand—squeezed, relaxed, and squeezed again as he threw *Pika-Don* into a long, circling curve. The airspace scope flickered, re-oriented itself. His four rockets traced bright streaks across its face.

Explode! he thought. *Explode!*

They didn't. They traced their paths out to the scope's edge. Their destruct mechanisms turned them to vapor. Ahead of him now, again, he could see the disorganized swarm of the jagd-staffel. He hadn't touched one of them. And they still didn't show on the airspace scope.

Farman swore with self-directed disgust. He should have thought of it. Those planes were invisible to radar. They didn't have enough metal among them to make a decent tin can, so his radar equipment rejected the signals they reflected as static. For the same reason, the proximities hadn't worked. The rockets could have passed right through the formation—probably had—without being triggered. As far as the proximities were concerned, they'd flown through empty air. He might as well have tried to shoot down a cloud.

He turned west, back to base. He located the field with the map scope. He had enough fuel to get there, and some to spare. A thought trickled through his mind about the dinosaurs—how their bodies had been perfectly adapted to the world they lived in, and when the world changed their bodies had not been able to adjust to the changes. So they died.

Pika-Don was like that—a flying *Tyrannosaurus rex* whose world now gave it only insects for food.

"Yeah. We saw the whole action," Blake said. He sat with his back against the hangar wall, a wine bottle close to his hand. The sun was bright and the fields were green. A light breeze stirred.

The escadrille had come back a half hour after Farman landed. Farman had hesitated, but then went out to face Deveraux. He was not eager for the confrontation.

Deveraux was philosophically gentle. "You have seen now, M'sieu, the rockets you carried were not an adequate armament for combat situations. Now, if you will show our mechanics where you think it would be best to mount the machine guns they . . ."

"*Pika-Don* flies faster than bullets," Farman said. He kicked at a ridge of dirt between wheel ruts. The dirt was hard, but it broke on the third try. "I even heard of a guy that got ahead of his own bullets and shot himself down. And his plane was a lot slower than mine." He shook his head—looked back toward where *Pika-Don* crouched low to the ground, sleek and sinister-looking, totally useless. "Might as well let her rot there."

He kicked the loosened clod off into the grass.

About eleven o'clock, Blake got a bottle of wine from Henri. It was plain peasant's wine, but that was all right. They sat in the narrow noontide shade of a hangar and worked on it.

"You've got to get in close before you shoot," Blake said. "I don't know where you learned combat, but it didn't look like you learned much. You flew at their formation so fast they wouldn't of seen you until you broke right through 'em, but you shot those rockets from a couple of miles away. You can't hit anything at that kind of range."

"I thought I could," Farman said. "And with the kind of warheads they had, it's a good idea to have a few miles distance when they go off."

"You don't think you're funning me with that, do you?" Blake said. He sat up straight—looked at Farman. "Nothing scatters shrapnel that wide."

Farman helped himself from the bottle. "My rockets would have done more than just scatter shrapnel, if they'd gone off."

"Not much good if you've got to shoot 'em from so far off you can't hit the target," Blake said.

It was no use trying again to explain target-seeking missiles. Anyway, they hadn't worked. He'd finally figured that out, too. Their heat-seeking elements had been designed to track on a hot jet's exhaust, or the meteor-flame of a ballistic warhead. All the German planes were putting out was the feeble warmth of a piston engine. That wasn't enough. If he was going to do any good in this war, it wasn't going to be with *Pika-Don*. "Harry, I want you to check me out on your plane."

"Huh?"

"My plane's useless. She hasn't any teeth left," Farman said. "If I'm going to do any more fighting, it's going to be in a plane like yours. I've got more flying hours than all of you put together, but I don't have any cockpit time in your—" He almost called them box kites. "I want you to show me how it flies."

Blake shrugged. "One plane's pretty much like another. They've all got their tricks—like these Nieuports, you don't want to do much diving in them; takes the fabric off the top wings every time. But aside from that the only way you get the feel is by flying 'em."

They walked out to Blake's Nieuport. It looked about as airworthy as a Model T Ford. Farman had a little trouble climbing up until Blake showed him the footholds. It was cramped in the cockpit, and the wicker seat was hard. Blake stood on a packing crate and leaned over the coaming.

Farman put his hand on the stick. That was what it was—an erect rod sticking up between his knees. He'd never seen one like it before. He tried moving it, and it moved with the smoothness of a spoon in a gluepot. "Do you have to fight it like this all the time?" he asked.

"Takes some getting used to," Blake said. "It's easier when she's flying, though."

Farman turned his attention to the instruments. They were a haphazard assortment of circular dials, unevenly distributed, and except for one big dial straight in front of him there was no apparent priority of position given to the more important ones— whichever ones they were. They were all identified, the words lettered across their faces, but the words were French.

"That's the oil pressure," Blake said, tapping the glass in front of a dial. "And that's r.p.m., and that's fuel mixture."

"Oil pressure. Is that important?"

Blake looked at him strangely. "You say you've been flying . . . how long? And you don't know oil pressure?"

"I've never flown a piston engine craft," Farman said. "Pika-Don has a different kind. Is it important?"

"Your engine doesn't work too good without it."

"And—fuel mixture, did you say?" Farman asked, putting his finger to the dial Blake had indicated. He was careful not to ask if it was important, though he wasn't sure what difference it made. Mixed with what, he wondered to himself.

"Right," Blake said. "And this here's your compass—don't trust it too far—and that's the altimeter, and here's the gas gauge."

At least those were instruments Farman understood. But he frowned at the altimeter. "Is that the highest this can fly?"

"Those are meters, not feet," Blake said. "This crate can go up as high as I can breathe. Sixteen . . . eighteen thousand feet." He pointed into the cockpit again. "This here's the switch, and that's the throttle, and that's the mixture control."

Farman touched them, one by one, trying to get their feel. His hand encountered a small plumb bob dangling from a cord. "Good-luck charm?" he asked.

Blake laughed. "Yeah, it's good luck all right. Without it I could be flying upside down and not know it."

"Don't you have a turn-and-bank indicator?" Farman wondered.

"Mister, that *is* my turn-and-bank indicator."

"Oh," Farman said, feeling foolish. But how could he have known?

"And these here," Blake went on, unnoticing, "that one tightens the flying wires, and that one the landing wires."

"What kind of wires?"

"Some wires you want tight when you're flying, and some others when you're coming in to land. If you don't, you stand a good chance of coming apart at the wrong time."

"Oh." Flying a Nieuport wasn't going to be as easy as he'd thought. It would be like trying to ride horseback after driving cars all your life. "My plane doesn't have wires."

"What holds it together?" Blake asked.

Farman ignored him. He was thinking about driving a car, and some of his confidence came back. This Nieuport was a lot different from *Pika-Don,* but her engine wasn't too much different from the one in the BMW he'd had in another place and time—more primitive, maybe, but it worked on the same principles. He could handle a gasoline engine all right.

"Where's the starter?" he asked.

Blake frowned, as if he didn't understand. Then a wry grin cracked his face. He nodded forward—pointed to the propeller's blade. "Right there," he said.

Half a minute later Farman was looking forward through the blur of a spinning propeller. He felt the blast of air on his face, and the stench of exhaust made him want to retch. The oil-pressure gauge worked up. He experimented with throttle settings and fuel-mixture adjustments, trying to learn something about how it handled. It occurred to him that his BMW had two or three times the horsepower this thing had.

Blake handed him a helmet and goggles. Farman put them on. "Taxi her around a bit, until you get the feel," Blake yelled through the engine's blatting. Farman nodded, and Blake bent to pull the chocks from in front of the wheels; one side and then—slipping quickly underneath—the other. The Nieuport lurched forward even before Farman advanced the throttle. It bumped clumsily over the grass.

The thing had no brakes, so when he advanced the throttle again she hurtled forward, bumping and thumping across the field. The airspeed indicator began to show readings. The bumping got worse. He edged the throttle forward a little more. Except for the jouncing and that awful smell, it wasn't much different from driving a car.

The tail came up. It startled him, and it was almost by reflex—seeing the horizon lift in front of him—that Farman pulled the stick back. The bumping stopped as if it were shut off. The engine's sound changed, and airspeed began to slacken. The silly Model T was airborne. He shoved the throttle forward and tried to level out. It shouldn't have been flying at this speed—he'd driven his BMW faster than this, and his BMW was a lot more streamlined.

He was beyond the field's edge now, with a rise of ground ahead of him. He tried to turn, but the Nieuport resisted. He pulled the stick back to clear the hill's crest. The airspeed meter started to unwind. He got over the hill with a few yards to spare, but airspeed was falling back toward zero. He tried to level out again; it wasn't easy to do without an artificial horizon on the instrument panel. The real horizon was rocking back and forth, up and down, and drifting sidewise. He tried turning the other way, and she turned easily but she also nosed down. He hauled back on the stick, swearing loudly. How any man could fly a crazy, contrary thing like this was more than he could understand.

The ground wheeled under him. The engine's sound changed, became a snarl, then a sputter. Wildly, he looked for a place to put down, but there was nothing but orchard under him as far as he could see—which wasn't far because the plane had nosed down again. A queasy, liquid feel began in his stomach, and the stench from the engine didn't help it any.

The engine chose that moment to quit. For a long time—it couldn't really have been more than a few seconds—the only sound was the whisper of air against the wings. Then the Nieuport stalled and plunged down among the trees. Branches snapped and the wings buckled. The Nieuport came to rest midway between the treetops and the ground. It dangled there, swaying a little in the gentle breeze. After a while, Farman thought to turn off the ignition, to reduce the danger of fire. After another while, he began to think about how to climb down.

He met Blake and half a dozen other men before he got out of the orchard. They went back to the Nieuport. Blake looked up at the wreck among the tree branches, made an angry noise that might have been extremely basic English, or it might not, and walked away.

Farman started to go after him but then thought better of it. Another tree branch cracked and the Nieuport sagged a few feet closer to the ground. Farman looked up at the mess one more time, then turned away and followed Blake. It was a long walk back to the field.

Blake was given another Nieuport. The escadrille had several replacements ready—craft that had been sent down from an escadrille in the Somme region that had switched to Spads. The older Nieuports were still good enough for this less active section of the front. Blake spent the rest of the day and all the next with the mechanics, checking it out.

Farman spent the time poking around *Pika-Don*, trying to figure a way she could still be used. There was a space where a Vickers gun could be fitted if he took out the infrared sensor unit, but working out a trigger linkage was beyond him; every cubic inch inside *Pika-Don* was occupied by one or another piece of vital equipment. And at Mach 2 an orifice the size of a .30-caliber muzzle might be enough to blow the plane apart.

The only other thing he could think of was that the radars were powerful enough to fry a man dead, but it didn't seem likely that Bruno Keyserling would hold still for the hour or two needed for the job.

He gave up. *Pika-Don* was useless. Reluctantly, he resigned himself to asking Deveraux for assignment to a flight school. It would mean swallowing a lot of pride, but if he was going to shoot Keyserling out of the sky, he'd have to learn how to fly a Nieuport.

When the escadrille came back from a patrol, he went out to talk with the Frenchman. Deveraux came toward him, helmet bunched in a still-gloved hand. "I am sorry, M'sieu," he said gravely. He laid his empty hand on Farman's shoulder. "Your friend . . . your countryman . . ."

The patrol had run into a flock of Albatrosses, Keyserling in the lead. No one had seen Blake go down, but several planes had been seen falling, burning like meteors. When the dogfight broke off and the flight had re-formed, Blake wasn't with them.

Farman's mind became like cold iron as he heard Deveraux recite the plain, unchangeable facts. It shouldn't have struck him so hard, but Blake was a man he'd known, a man he'd talked with. All the other men here, even Deveraux, were strangers.

"Did anyone see a parachute?"

"M'sieu, such things do not work," Deveraux said. "We do not use them. They catch on the wires. For men in the balloons, perhaps such things can be used, but not for us. Our aeroplane is hit in its vitals, we go down."

"You shouldn't build them with so many wires, then."

Deveraux's reply was a Gallic shrug. "Perhaps not, M'sieu. But they are what hold our aeroplanes together."

"The German planes, too?" Farman asked in a suddenly different voice.

"Of course, M'sieu."

"Get me some kerosene," Farman said.

"Paraffin? Of course, M'sieu. And if you will show the mechanics where to fasten the machine guns they . . ."

Farman shook his head. "I don't need guns. Just get me the kerosene. I'll do the rest. And when I'm done with 'em on this front, I'll go up the line and clean out the rest of 'em."

"Of course, M'sieu," Deveraux said without irony.

Not that Farman cared. This time he'd do what he said he could do. He knew it. "Ten thousand gallons," he said.

Mid-August came, and *Pika-Don* was fueled again. Reports and rumors had been coming down from other sectors of the front that American troops were somewhere in the fighting.

Pika-Don lifted into a sky as clean as polished glass. Later in the day there might be a scatter of cumulus tufts, but it was not yet midmorning. "It is not a good day for fighting," Deveraux had said. "One can make use of the clouds."

It would be a good day for observation planes, though, so the German patrols would be out. And, Farman thought savagely, there'd be fighting enough. He'd see to that.

Once he'd shifted to lateral flight, he didn't try for altitude. *Pika-Don* would guzzle fuel faster at low levels, but he didn't figure the mission to take long. The German field was less than thirty miles away. He fixed its location on the map scope and sent *Pika-Don* toward it at full thrust. *Pika-Don* began to gain altitude, but at ten thousand feet, with the Machmeter moving up past 1.75 he leveled her off and turned her downward along a trajectory that would bring her to ground level just as he reached the German field.

It was almost perfectly calculated. He saw the field ahead of him. It was small—he'd seen pastures that were bigger—and he started to pull out of his descent. He passed over the field with just enough altitude to clear the trees on the far side. It took less than a second—the Machmeter said 2.5, and skin temperature was going up fast. He took *Pika-Don* a few hundred feet up and brought her around—lined her up on the field with the map scope's help—and brought her down again for another pass. This time she flew straight at the open mouth of a hangar in the middle of a row of hangars on the far side of the field.

He brought *Pika-Don* around one more time, but this time he stayed a thousand feet up and kept off to one side of the field. He looked down and felt the satisfaction of a kid who'd just stomped an anthill. Wreckage was still flying through the air. He didn't need rockets. He didn't need machine guns. All he had to have was *Pika-Don* herself.

He turned her south toward the Swiss border. He had seen only a few planes on the ground, which meant that most of them were out on patrol.

Heading south, he took *Pika-Don* up to eighteen thousand feet. On a day like this, with no clouds to hide in, the best altitude for a German patrol would be up close to the operational ceiling. Even if no altitude advantage could be gained, at least the advantage would not be lost to a higher-flying French patrol.

The map scope showed the Swiss border. Farman brought *Pika-Don* around. The front was not hard to find. It was a sinuous gash across the land, like a bloodless wound. He followed it north, staying to the German side. He watched the sky ahead of him.

He flew the course to the Vosges Mountains at Mach 1.5, partly to save fuel and to minimize the skin-temperature problem; flying this low, the air was a lot thicker than *Pika-Don* was built to fly in. His main reason, though, was that even at Mach 1.5 he was flying through a lot of airspace. With no more sophisticated target-finding equipment than his own bare eyes, he could pass within a mile or less of a German patrol and not see it. Flying as slowly as he could improved his chances.

The mountains rose ahead of him. They weren't very high mountains; their crests lay well below him. He caught sight of the German patrol as he turned *Pika-Don* for another run south.

They were a few hundred yards higher than he was, and so small with distance he'd have thought they were birds except that birds didn't fly this high, nor did birds fly in a neatly stacked Junck's row formation. They hung suspended in the sky, like fleck-marks on a window, and if it hadn't been for their formation he wouldn't have known their direction of flight. They were flying south, as he was now—patrolling the front, as he was.

And they were close—too close. If he turned toward them they'd be inside the radius of his turn. He'd cross their path in front of them like a black cat, warning them. He mind-fixed their position on the map scope and turned away.

Come at them from eight o'clock, he decided. That would be the best angle. On the outward arc of his circle he took *Pika-Don* up to thirty thousand feet. Then, as *Pika-Don* started to come around for the approach, he started down, full thrust in all three engines. The Machmeter climbed to 2.0, then 2.5. It edged toward 3.0, trembling. It would mean a heating problem in this soup-thick air, but it wouldn't be for long.

The patrol was almost exactly where he'd seen it before. There hadn't been time for it to move far. With only a small correction *Pika-Don* was driving down toward it like a lance, target-true. The insect-speck planes became recognizable shapes, then rapidly expanded. They ballooned to their full size in a flash and he was almost on top of them.

At the last instant, he moved the controls just enough to avoid collision—passed behind them so close he had a glimpse of round knobs bulging from the cockpits just behind the upper wings—pilots' helmeted heads—and yes! at the bottom of the stack leading the flight, the purple Albatross of Bruno Keyserling.

Then the whole flight was somewhere behind him. Farman reduced thrust and put *Pika-Don* into a steep climb, over on her back, and down again to level out into the airspace he'd flown through before.

It was all changed. The sky was full of junk, as if someone had emptied a barrel of trash. Fluttering wing sections, bashed fuselages, masses of twisted wreckage without any shape he could recognize. He saw a wingless fuselage falling a-tumble, like a crippled dragonfly. It was all purple, with bits of white on the shattered engine cowl. *Got him!*

And there wasn't a whole plane left in the sky. They hadn't been built to survive the impact of *Pika-Don*'s shock wave. Just like the hangars at their field which had exploded when he buzzed them.

He started to curve southward again. He'd tasted blood, wanted more. He'd hardly begun the turn when a whump shook *Pika-Don* and the sky wheeled crazily and the engine function instruments erupted with a Christmas tree of red lights as if engine two had gobbled something that didn't digest too well. (Part of an airplane?

art of a man?) Some of the lights flashed panic, others glared
rmly at his eyes. The horizon outside was tipping up on edge,
lling over, tipping up again. The controls felt numb in his hands.

arman knew the drill. When a plane as hot as this one went bad,
ou got out if you could. At Mach 2 you could hit the ground in
ss than thirty seconds. He slapped the eject button—felt the
ckets blast him upward. A moment later the instrument panel
roke away and the seat's firm pressure on his back and thighs
ere gone. He was tumbling like a wobbling top in midair,
ddenly no longer enclosed in several million dollars' worth of
rplane. There was the teeth-cracking shock of his chute coming
pen, and abruptly the confusion of too many things happening
o fast stopped. He looked all around for some trace of *Pika-Don*,
ut there wasn't any.

He tugged at the shrouds to spill air from the chute and drift him
estward toward the French lines. The wind was doing some of it,
ut not enough. A line of planes came toward him. He held his
reath, thinking of a school of sharks nosing in toward a man cast
verboard. But then he saw the French markings on their wings
nd sides. They were Nieuports, and the pilot of the leading plane
aved. Farman waved back. The flight came on. It circled him
nce and then curved off. They stayed in sight, though, following
im down. When flak bursts started to puff around him, they went
own to strafe the German trenches.

He spilled another dollop of air from his chute. He was over the
rench lines now. He could see the men in the trenches looking up
t him. He floated down toward them, closer and closer. Then,
ery abruptly, he was down—down among the trenches and
arbed wire of the French Seventh Army. He sprawled in the
reasy mud of a shell hole. The chute started to drag him, but it
aught on a tangle of wire and collapsed.

He got to his hands and knees, fumbling with the parachute
arness. A bullet snapped past his ear. He flattened. The Nieu-
orts dived on the German trenches again.

He struggled out of the harness and started to crawl in the
irection of the nearest trench. It wasn't far. He scraped the dirt
ith his belt buckle all the way. Bullets whipped past him like
eadly mosquitoes. The soldiers in the trenches reached out to pull
im down.

They hugged him. They mobbed around him. There must have
een thousands of men in that trench to celebrate the man who'd

brought down Bruno Keyserling. Someone pressed a cup of wine into his hands—a soldier in dirty clothes, with mud on his brow and a matted beard. Farman drank gratefully.

After a while, he sat down and just sat there, dead inside. He looked at the dirt wall a few inches from his eyes. The empty cup dangled from his hand. *Pika-Don* was gone, and nothing he could do would rebuild her. Suddenly he was just an ordinary man. He couldn't even fly any more. *Pika-Don* had been the only plane in this age that he knew how to fly, and *Pika-Don* was gone.

He wasn't aware of the passage of time, but only of the heat and dust and the smell of a trench that had been lived in too long by unwashed men. He didn't know what he was going to do. But after a time, the wine began to have its effect. A trickle of life came back into him.

Slowly, he got to his feet. The start of a smile quirked his mouth. On second thought, no, he wasn't just an ordinary man.

The war would be over in a few months. Maybe he didn't know what he'd do, but . . .

The soldier who'd given him the wine was standing a few feet away. Farman held himself crisply erect. It occurred to him that man probably didn't know a word of English.

"How do I get back to America?" he asked, and grinned at the soldier's incomprehension.

A man from the future ought to have *some* advantage over the natives!

CUSTER'S LAST JUMP

Steven Utley
and
Howard Waldrop

Smithsonian Annals of Flight 39: *The Air
War in the West*
Chapter 27: "The Krupp Monoplane"

INTRODUCTION

Its wings still hold the tears from many bullets. The ailerons are
still scorched black, and the exploded Henry machine rifle is bent
awkwardly in its blast port.

The right landing skid is missing, and the frame has been
restraightened. It stands in the left wing of the Air Museum today,
next to the French Devre jet and the X-FU-5 Flying Flapjack, the
world's fastest fighter aircraft.

On its rudder is the swastika, an ugly reminder of days of glory
fifty years ago.

A simple plaque describes the aircraft. It reads:

CRAZY HORSE'S KRUPP MONOPLANE
(Captured at the raid on Fort Carson, January 5, 1882)

GENERAL

1. To study the history of this plane is to delve into one of the
most glorious eras of aviation history. To begin: the aircraft was
manufactured by the Krupp plant in Haavesborg, Netherlands.
The airframe was completed August 3, 1862, as part of the third
shipment of Krupp aircraft to the Confederate States of America

under terms of the Agreement of Atlanta of 1861. It was originally
equipped with power plant #311 Zed of 87¼ horsepower,
manufactured by the Jumo plant at Nordmung, Duchy of Austria,
on May 3 of the year 1862. Wingspan of the craft is twenty-three
feet; its length is seventeen feet three inches. The aircraft arrived
in the port of Charlotte on September 21, 1862, aboard the
transport *Mendenhall*, which had suffered heavy bombardment
from GAR picket ships. The aircraft was possibly sent by rail to
Confederate Army Air Corps Center at Fort Andrew Mott,
Alabama. Unfortunately, records of rail movements during this
time were lost in the burning of the Confederate archives at
Ittebeha in March 1867, two weeks after the Truce of Haldeman
was signed.

2. The aircraft was damaged during a training flight in
December 1862. Student pilot was Flight Subaltern (Cadet)
Neldoo J. Smith, CSAAC; flight instructor during the ill-fated
flight was Air Captain Winslow Homer Winslow, on interservice
instructor-duty loan from the Confederate States Navy.

Accident forms and maintenance officer's reports indicate that
the original motor was replaced with one of the new 93½
horsepower Jumo engines which had just arrived from Holland by
way of Mexico.

3. The aircraft served routinely through the remainder of Flight
Subaltern Smith's training. We have records[141] which indicate that
the aircraft was one of the first to be equipped with the Henry
repeating machine rifle of the chain-driven type. Until December
1862, all CSAAC aircraft were equipped with the Sharps repeating rifles of the motor-driven, low-voltage type on wing or turret
mounts.

As was the custom, the aircraft was flown by Flight Subaltern
Smith to his first duty station at Thimblerig Aerodrome in
Augusta, Georgia. Flight Subaltern Smith was assigned to Flight
Platoon 2, 1st Aeroscout Squadron.

4. The aircraft, with Flight Subaltern Smith at the wheel,
participated in three of the aerial expeditions against the Union
Army in the Second Battle of the Manassas. Smith distinguished
himself in the first and third missions. (He was assigned aerial
picket duty south of the actual battle during his second mission.)
On the first, he is credited with one kill and one probable (both
bi-wing Airsharks). During the third mission, he destroyed one
aircraft and forced another down behind Confederate lines. He
then escorted the craft of his immediate commander, Air Captain

Dalton Trump, to a safe landing on a field controlled by the Confederates. According to Trump's sworn testimony, Smith successfully fought off two Union craft and ranged ahead of Trump's crippled plane to strafe a group of Union soldiers who were in their flight path, discouraging them from firing on Trump's smoking aircraft.

For heroism on these two missions, Smith was awarded the Silver Star and Bar with Air Cluster. Presentation was made on March 3, 1863, by the late General J.E.B. Stuart, Chief of Staff of the CSAAC.

5. Flight Subaltern Smith was promoted to flight captain on April 12, 1863, after distinguishing himself with two kills and two probables during the first day of the Battle of the Three Roads, North Carolina. One of his kills was an airship of the Moby class, with a crew of fourteen. Smith shared with only one other aviator the feat of bringing down one of these dirigibles during the War of Secession.

This was the first action the 1st Aeroscout Squadron had seen since Second Manassas, and Captain Smith seems to have been chafing under inaction. Perhaps this led him to volunteer for duty with Major John S. Mosby, then forming what would later become Mosby's Raiders. This was actually sound military strategy: the CSAAC was to send a unit to southwestern Kansas to carry out harassment raids against the poorly defended forts of the Far West. These raids would force the Union to send men and materiel sorely needed at the southern front far to the west, where they would be ineffectual in the outcome of the war. That this action was taken is pointed to by some[142] as a sign that the Confederate States envisioned defeat and were resorting to desperate measures four years before the Treaty of Haldeman.

At any rate, Captain Smith and his aircraft joined a triple flight of six aircraft each, which, after stopping at El Dorado, Arkansas, to refuel, flew away on a westerly course. This is the last time they ever operated in Confederate states. The date was June 5, 1863.

6. The Union forts stretched from a medium-well-defended line in Illinois to poorly garrisoned stations as far west as the Wyoming Territory and south to the Kansas–Indian Territory border. Southwestern Kansas was both sparsely settled and garrisoned. It was from this area that Mosby's Raiders, with the official designation 1st Western Interdiction Wing, CSAAC, operated.

A supply wagon train had been sent ahead a month before from Fort Worth, carrying petrol, ammunition, and material for shelters. A crude landing field, hangars, and barracks awaited the eighteen craft.

After two months of reconnaissance (done by mounted scouts due to the need to maintain the element of surprise, and, more importantly, by the limited amount of fuel available) the 1st WIW took to the air. The citizens of Riley, Kansas, long remembered the day: their first inkling that Confederates were closer than Texas came when motors were heard overhead and the Union garrison was literally blown off the face of the map.

7. Following the first raid, word went to the War Department headquarters in New York, with pleas for aid and reinforcements for all Kansas garrisons. Thus the CSAAC achieved its goal in the very first raid. The effects snowballed; as soon as the populace learned of the raid, it demanded protection from nearby garrisons. Farmers' organizations threatened to stop shipments of needed produce to eastern depots. The garrison commanders, unable to promise adequate protection, appealed to higher military authorities.

Meanwhile, the 1st WIW made a second raid on Abilene, heavily damaging the railways and stockyards with twenty-five-pound fragmentation bombs. They then circled the city, strafed the Army Quartermaster depot, and disappeared into the west.

8. This second raid, and the ensuing clamor from both the public and the commanders of western forces, convinced the War Department to divert new recruits and supplies, with seasoned members of the 18th Aeropursuit Squadron, to the Kansas-Missouri border, near Lawrence.

9. Inclement weather in the fall kept the 18th AS and the 1st WIW grounded for seventy-two of the ninety days of the season. Aircraft from each of these units met several times; the 1st is credited with one kill, while pilots of the 18th downed two Confederate aircraft on the afternoon of December 12, 1863.

Both aircraft units were heavily resupplied during this time. The Battle of the Canadian River was fought on December 18, when mounted reconnaissance units of the Union and Confederacy met in Indian territory. Losses were small on both sides, but the skirmish was the first of what would become known as the Far Western Campaign.

10. Civilians spotted the massed formation of the 1st WIW as early as 10 A.M. Thursday, December 16, 1863. They headed northeast, making a leg due north when eighteen miles south of Lawrence. Two planes sped ahead to destroy the telegraph station

at Felton, nine miles south of Lawrence. Nevertheless, a message of some sort reached Lawrence; a Union messenger on horseback was on his way to the aerodrome when the first flight of Confederate aircraft passed overhead.

In the ensuing raid, seven of the nineteen Union aircraft were destroyed on the ground and two were destroyed in the air, while the remaining aircraft were severely damaged and the barracks and hangars demolished.

The 1st WIW suffered one loss: during the raid a Union clerk attached for duty with the 18th AS manned an Agar machine rifle position and destroyed one Confederate aircraft. He was killed by machine rifle fire from the second wave of planes. Private Alden Evans Gunn was awarded the Congressional Medal of Honor posthumously for his gallantry during the attack.

For the next two months, the 1st WIW ruled the skies as far north as Illinois and as far east as Trenton, Missouri.

THE FAR WESTERN CAMPAIGN

1. At this juncture, the two most prominent figures of the next nineteen years of frontier history enter the picture: the Oglala Sioux Crazy Horse, and Lieutenant Colonel (Brevet Major General) George Armstrong Custer. The clerical error giving Custer the rank of Brigadier General is well known. It is not common knowledge that Custer was considered by the General Staff as a candidate for Far Western Commander as early as the spring of 1864, a duty he would not take up until May 1869, when the Far Western Command was the only theater of war operations within the Americas.

The General Staff, it is believed, considered Major General Custer for the job for two reasons: they thought Custer possessed those qualities of spirit suited to the warfare necessary in the Western Command, and that the Far West was the ideal place for the twenty-three-year-old Boy General.

Crazy Horse, the Oglala Sioux warrior, was with a hunting party far from Oglala territory, checking the size of the few remaining buffalo herds before they started their spring migrations. Legend has it that Crazy Horse and the party were crossing the prairies in early February 1864 when two aircraft belonging to the 1st WIW passed nearby. Some of the Sioux jumped to the ground, believing that they were looking on the Thunderbird and its mate. Only Crazy Horse stayed on his pony and watched the aircraft disappear into the south.

He sent word back by the rest of the party that he and two of his young warrior friends had gone looking for the nest of the Thunderbird.

2. The story of the 1st WIW here becomes the story of the shaping of the Indian wars, rather than part of the history of the last four years of the War of Secession. It is well known that increased alarm over the Kansas raids had shifted War Department thinking: the defense of the Far West changed in importance from a minor matter in the larger scheme of war to a problem of vital concern. For one thing, the Confederacy was courting the emperor Maximilian of Mexico, and through him the French, to entering the war on the Confederate side. The South wanted arms, but most necessarily to break the Union submarine blockade. Only the French navy possessed the capability.

The Union therefore sent the massed 5th Cavalry of Kansas and attached to it the 12th Air Destroyer Squadron and the 2nd Airship Command.

The 2nd Airship Command, at the time of its deployment, was equipped with the small pursuit airships known in later days as the "torpedo ship," from its double-pointed ends. These ships were used for reconnaissance and light interdiction duties, and were almost always accompanied by aircraft from the 12th ADS. They immediately set to work patrolling the Kansas skies from the renewed base of operations at Lawrence.

3. The idea of using Indian personnel in some phase of airfield operations in the west had been proposed by Mosby as early as June 1863. The C of C, CSA, disapproved in the strongest possible terms. It was not a new idea, therefore, when Crazy Horse and his two companions rode into the airfield, accompanied by the sentries who had challenged them far from the perimeter. They were taken to Major Mosby for questioning.

Through an interpreter, Mosby learned they were Oglala, not Crows sent to spy for the Union. When asked why they had come so far, Crazy Horse replied, "To see the nest of the Thunderbird."

Mosby is said to have laughed[143] and then taken the three Sioux to see the aircraft. Crazy Horse was said to have been stricken with awe when he found that men controlled their flight.

Crazy Horse then offered Mosby ten ponies for one of the craft. Mosby explained that they were not his to give, but his Great

Father's, and that they were used to fight the Yellowlegs from the Northeast.

At this time, fate took a hand: the 12th Air Destroyer Squadron had just begun operations. The same day Crazy Horse was having his initial interview with Mosby, a scout plane returned with the news that the 12th was being reinforced by an airship combat group; the dirigibles had been seen maneuvering near the Kansas-Missouri border.

Mosby learned from Crazy Horse that the warrior was respected, if not in his own tribe, then with other Nations of the North. Mosby, with an eye toward those reinforcements arriving in Lawrence, asked Crazy Horse if he could guarantee safe conduct through the northern tribes and land for an airfield should the present one have to be abandoned.

Crazy Horse answered, "I can talk the idea to the people; it will be for them to decide."

Mosby told Crazy Horse that if he could secure the promise, he would grant him anything within his power.

Crazy Horse looked out the window toward the hangars. "I ask that you teach me and ten of my brother-friends to fly the Thunderbirds. We will help you fight the Yellowlegs."

Mosby, expecting requests for beef, blankets, or firearms, was taken aback. Unlike the others who had dealt with the Indians, he was a man of his word. He told Crazy Horse he would ask his Great Father if this could be done. Crazy Horse left, returning to his village in the middle of March. He and several warriors traveled extensively that spring, smoking the pipe, securing permissions from the other Nations for safe conduct for the Gray white men through their hunting lands. His hardest task came in convincing the Oglala themselves that the airfield could be built in their southern hunting grounds.

Crazy Horse, his two wives, seven warriors, and their women, children, and belongings rode into the CSAAC airfield in June 1864.

4. Mosby had been granted permission from Stuart to go ahead with the training program. Derision first met the request within the southern General Staff when Mosby's proposal was circulated. Stuart, though not entirely sympathetic to the idea, became its champion. Others objected, warning that ignorant savages should not be given modern weapons. Stuart reminded them that some of the good Tennessee boys already flying airplanes could neither read nor write.

Stuart's approval arrived a month before Crazy Horse and his band made camp on the edge of the airfield.

5. It fell to Captain Smith to train Crazy Horse. The Indian became what Smith in his journal[144] describes as "the best natural pilot I have seen or it has been my pleasure to fly with." Part of this seems to have come from Smith's own modesty; by all accounts, Smith was one of the finer pilots of the war.

The operations of the 12th ADS and the 2nd Airship Command ranged closer to the CSAAC airfield. The dogfights came frequently and the fighting grew less gentlemanly. One 1st WIW fighter was pounced by three aircraft of the 12th simultaneously: they did not stop firing even when the pilot signaled that he was hit and that his engine was dead. Nor did they break off their runs until both pilot and craft plunged into the Kansas prairie. It is thought that the Union pilots were under secret orders to kill all members of the 1st WIW. There is some evidence[145] that this rankled with the more gentlemanly of the 12th Air Destroyer Squadron. Nevertheless, fighting intensified.

A flight of six more aircraft joined the 1st WIW some weeks after the Oglala Sioux started their training: this was the first of the ferry flights from Mexico through Texas and Indian territory to reach the airfield. Before the summer was over, a dozen additional craft would join the Wing, this before shipments were curtailed by Juarez's revolution against the French and the ouster and execution of Maximilian and his family.

Smith records[146] that Crazy Horse's first solo took place on August 14, 1864, and that the warrior, though deft in the air, still needed practice on his landings. He had a tendency to come in overpowered and to stall his engine out too soon. Minor repairs were made on the skids of the craft after his flight.

All this time Crazy Horse had flown Smith's craft. Smith, after another week of hard practice with the Indian, pronounced him "more qualified than most pilots the CSAAC in Alabama turned out"[147] and signed over the aircraft to him. Crazy Horse begged off. Then, seeing that Smith was sincere, he gave the captain many buffalo hides. Smith reminded the Indian that the craft was not his: during their off hours, when not training, the Indians had been given enough instruction in military discipline as Mosby, never a stickler, thought necessary. The Indians had only a rudimentary idea of government property. Of the seven other Indian men, three were qualified as pilots; the other four were given gunner positions in the Krupp bi-wing light bombers assigned to the squadron.

Soon after Smith presented the aircraft to Crazy Horse, the captain took off in a borrowed monoplane on what was to be the daily weather flight into northern Kansas. There is evidence[148] that it was Smith who encountered a flight of light dirigibles from the 2nd Airship Command and attacked them single-handedly. He crippled one airship; the other was rescued when two escort planes of the 12th ADS came to its defense. They raked the attacker with withering fire. The attacker escaped into the clouds.

It was not until 1897, when a group of schoolchildren on an outing found the wreckage, that it was known that Captain Smith had brought his crippled monoplane within five miles of the airfield before crashing into the rolling hills.

When Smith did not return from his flight, Crazy Horse went on a vigil, neither sleeping nor eating for a week. On the seventh day, Crazy Horse vowed vengeance on the men who had killed his white friend.

6. The devastating Union raid of September 23, 1864, caught the airfield unawares. Though the Indians were averse to fighting at night, Crazy Horse and two other Sioux were manning three of the four craft which got off the ground during the raid. The attack had been carried out by the 2nd Airship Command, traveling at twelve thousand feet, dropping fifty-pound fragmentation bombs and shrapnel canisters. The shrapnel played havoc with the aircraft on the ground. It also destroyed the mess hall, enlisted barracks, and three teepees.

The dirigibles turned away and were running fast before a tail wind when Crazy Horse gained their altitude.

The gunners on the dirigibles filled the skies with tracers from their light .30–30 machine rifles. Crazy Horse's monoplane was equipped with a single Henry .41–40 machine rifle. Unable to get in close killing distance, Crazy Horse and his companions stood off beyond the range of the lighter Union guns and raked the dirigibles with heavy machine rifle fire. They did enough damage to force one airship down twenty miles from its base, and to ground two others for two days while repairs were made. The intensity of fire convinced the airship commanders that more than four planes had made it off the ground, causing them to continue their headlong retreat.

Crazy Horse and the others returned and brought off the second windfall of the night; a group of 5th Cavalry raiders were to have

attacked the airfield in the confusion of the airship raid and burn
everything still standing. On their return flight, the four craft
encountered the cavalry unit as it began its charge across ground.

In three strafing runs, the aircraft killed thirty-seven men and
wounded fifty-three, while twenty-nine were taken prisoner by the
airfield's defenders. Thus, in his first combat mission for the
CSAAC, Crazy Horse was credited with saving the airfield against
overwhelming odds.

7. Meanwhile, Major General George A. Custer had distinguished himself at the Battle of Gettysburg. A few weeks after the
battle, he enrolled himself in the GAR jump school at Watauga,
New York. Howls of outrage came from the General Staff. Custer
quoted the standing order: "any man who volunteered and of
whom the commanding officer approved" could be enrolled.
Custer then asked, in a letter to C of S, GAR, "how any military
leader could be expected to plan maneuvers involving parachute
infantry when he himself had never experienced a drop, or found
the true capabilities of the parachute infantryman?"[149] The Chief
of Staff shouted down the protest. There were mutterings among
the General Staff[150] to the effect that the real reason Custer wanted
to become jump-qualified was so that he would have a better
chance of leading the invasion of Atlanta, part of whose contingency plans called for attacks by airborne units.

During the three-week parachute course, Custer became ac-
quainted with another man who would play an important part in
the Western Campaign, Captain (Brevet Colonel) Frederick W.
Benteen. Upon graduation from the jump school, Brevet Colonel
Benteen assumed command of the 505th Balloon Infantry, stationed at Chicago, Illinois, for training purposes. Colonel Benteen
would remain commander of the 505th until his capture at the
Battle of Montgomery in 1866. While he was prisoner of war, his
command was given to another, later to figure in the Western
Campaign, Lieutenant Colonel Myles W. Keogh.

Custer, upon his successful completion of jump school, returned to his command of the 6th Cavalry Division and participated throughout the remainder of the war in that capacity. It was
he who led the successful charge at the Battle of the Cape Fear
which smashed Lee's flank and allowed the 1st Infantry to overrun
the Confederate position and capture the southern leader. Custer
distinguished himself and his command up until the cessation of
hostilities in 1867.

8. The 1st WIW, CSAAC, moved to a new airfield in Wyoming

Territory three weeks after the raid of September 24. At the same time, the 2nd WIW was formed and moved to an outpost in Indian territory. The 2nd WIW raided the Union airfield, took it totally by surprise, and inflicted casualties on the 12th ADS and 2nd AC so devastating as to render them ineffectual. The 2nd WIW then moved to a second field in Wyoming Territory. It was here, following the move, that a number of Indians, including Black Man's Hand, were trained by Crazy Horse.

9. We leave the history of the 2nd WIW here. It was redeployed for the defense of Montgomery. The Indians and aircraft in which they trained were sent north to join the 1st WIW. The 1st WIW patrolled the skies of Indiana, Nebraska, and the Dakotas. After the defeat of the 12th ADS and the 2nd AC, the Union forestalled attempts to retaliate until the cessation of southern hostilities in 1867.

We may at this point add that Crazy Horse, Black Man's Hand, and the other Indians sometimes left the airfield during periods of long inactivity. They returned to their nations for as long as three months at a time. Each time Crazy Horse returned, he brought one or two pilot or gunner recruits with him. Before the winter of 1866, more than thirty percent of the 1st WIW were Oglala, Sansarc Sioux, or Cheyenne.

The South, losing the war of attrition, diverted all supplies to Alabama and Mississippi in the fall of 1866. None were forthcoming for the 1st WIW, though a messenger arrived with orders for Major Mosby to return to Texas for the defense of Fort Worth, where he would later direct the Battle of the Trinity. That Mosby was not ordered to deploy the 1st WIW to that defense has been considered by many military strategists as a "lost turning point" of the battle for Texas. Command of the 1st WIW was turned over to Acting Major (Flight Captain) Natchitoches Hooley.

10. The loss of Mosby signaled the end of the 1st WIW. Not only did the nondeployment of the 1st to Texas cost the South that territory, it also left the 1st in an untenable position, which the Union was quick to realize. The airfield was captured in May 1867 by a force of five hundred cavalry and three hundred infantry sent from the Battle of the Arkansas, and a like force, plus aircraft, from Chicago. Crazy Horse, seven Indians, and at least five Confederates escaped in their monoplanes. The victorious Union troops were surprised to find Indians in the field. Crazy Horse's people were eventually freed; the army thought them to have been hired by the Confederates to hunt and cook for the airfield. Mosby

had provided for this in contingency plans long before; he had not wanted the Plains tribes to suffer for Confederate acts. The army did not know, and no one volunteered the information, that it had been Indians doing the most considerable amount of damage to the Union garrisons lately.

Crazy Horse and three of his Indians landed their craft near the Black Hills. The Cheyenne helped them carry the craft, on travois, to caves in the sacred mountains. Here they mothballed the planes with mixtures of pine tar and resins and sealed up the caves.

11. The aircraft remained stored until February 1872. During this time, Crazy Horse and his Oglala Sioux operated, like the other Plains Indians, as light cavalry, skirmishing with the army and with settlers up and down the Dakotas and Montana. George Armstrong Custer was appointed commander of the new 7th Cavalry in 1869. Stationed first at Chicago (Far Western Command Headquarters), they later moved to Fort Abraham Lincoln, Nebraska.

A column of troops moved against Indians on the warpath in the winter of 1869. They reported a large group of Indians encamped on the Washita River. Custer obtained permission for the 505th Balloon Infantry to join the 7th Cavalry. From that day on, the unit was officially Company I (Separate troops), 7th US Cavalry, though it kept its numerical designation. Also attached to the 7th was the 12th Airship Squadron, as Company J.

Lieutenant Colonel Keogh, acting commander of the 505th for the last twenty-one months, but who had never been on jump status, was appointed by Custer as commander of K Company, 7th Cavalry.

It is known that only the 505th Balloon Infantry and the 12th Airship Squadron were used in the raid on Black Kettle's village. Black Kettle was a treaty Indian, "walking the white man's road." Reports have become garbled in transmission: Custer and the 505th believed they were jumping into a village of hostiles.

The event remained a mystery until Kellogg, the Chicago newspaperman, wrote his account in 1872.[151] The 505th, with Custer in command, flew the three (then numbered, after 1872, named) dirigibles No. 31, No. 76, and No. 93, with seventy-two jumpers each. Custer was in the first "stick" on Airship 76. The three sailed silently to the sleeping village. Custer gave the order to hook up at 5:42 Chicago time, 4:42 local time, and the 505th jumped into the village. Black Kettle's people were awakened when some of the balloon infantry crashed through their teepees;

others died in their sleep. One of the first duties of the infantry was to moor the dirigibles; this done, the gunners on the airships opened up on the startled villagers with their Gatling and Agar machine rifles. Black Kettle himself was killed while waving an American flag at Airship No. 93.

After the battle, the men of the 505th climbed back up to the moored dirigibles by rope ladder, and the airships departed for Fort Lincoln. The Indians camped downriver heard the shooting and found horses stampeded during the attack. When they came to the village, they found only slaughter. Custer had taken his dead (three, one of whom died during the jump by being drowned in the Washita) and wounded (twelve) away. They left 307 dead men, women, and children, and 500 slaughtered horses.

There were no tracks leading in and out of the village except those of the frightened horses. The other Indians left the area, thinking the white men had magicked it.

Crazy Horse is said[152] to have visited the area soon after the massacre. It was this action by the 7th which spelled their doom seven years later.

12. Black Man's Hand joined Crazy Horse; so did other former 1st WIW pilots soon after Crazy Horse's two-plane raid on the airship hangars at Bismarck, in 1872. For that mission, Crazy Horse dropped twenty-five-pound fragmentation bombs tied to petrol canisters. The shrapnel ripped the dirigibles, the escaping hydrogen was ignited by the burning petrol: all—hangars, balloons, and maintenance crews—were lost.

It was written up as an unreconstructed Confederate's sabotage; a somewhat ignominious former Southern major was eventually hanged on circumstantial evidence. Reports by sentries that they heard aircraft just before the explosions were discounted. At the time, it was believed the only aircraft were those belonging to the army, and the carefully licensed commercial craft.

13. In 1874, Custer circulated rumors that the Black Hills were full of gold. It has been speculated that this was used to draw miners to the area so the Indians would attack them; then the cavalry would have unlimited freedom to deal with the red man.[153] Also that year, those who had become agency Indians were being shorted in their supplies by members of the scandal-plagued Indian Affairs Bureau under President Grant. When these left the reservations in search of food, the cavalry was sent to "bring them back." Those who were caught were usually killed.

The Sioux ignored the miners at first, expecting the gods to deal with them. When this did not happen, Sitting Bull sent out a party of two hundred warriors, who killed every minor they encountered. Public outrage demanded reprisals; Sheridan wired Custer to find and punish those responsible.

14. Fearing what was to come, Crazy Horse sent Yellow Dog and Red Chief with a war party of five hundred to raid the rebuilt Fort Phil Kearny. This they did successfully, capturing twelve planes and fuel and ammunition for many more. They hid these in the caverns with the 1st WIW craft.

The army would not have acted as rashly as it did had it known the planes pronounced missing in the reports on the Kearny raid were being given into the hands of experienced pilots.

The reprisal consisted of airship patrols which strafed any living thing on the plains. Untold thousands of deer and the few remaining buffalo were killed. Unofficial counts list as killed a little more than eight hundred Indians who were caught in the open during the next eight months.

Indians who jumped the agencies and who had seen or heard of the slaughter streamed to Sitting Bull's hidden camp on the Little Big Horn. They were treated as guests, except for the Sansarcs, who camped a little way down the river. It is estimated there were no less than ten thousand Indians, including some four thousand warriors, camped along the river for the Sun Dance ceremony of June 1876.

A three-pronged-pincers movement for the final eradication of the Sioux and Cheyenne worked toward them. The 7th Cavalry, under Keogh and Major Marcus Reno, set out from Fort Lincoln during the last week of May. General George Crook's command was coming up the Rosebud. The gunboat *Far West*, with three hundred reserves and supplies, steamed to the mouth of the Big Horn River. General Terry's command was coming from the northwest. All Indians they encountered were to be killed.

Just before the Sun Dance, Crazy Horse and his pilots got word of the movement of Crook's men up the Rosebud, hurried to the caves, and prepared the craft for flight. Only six planes were put in working condition in time. The other pilots remained behind while Crazy Horse, Black Man's Hand, and four others took to the skies. They destroyed two dirigibles, soundly trounced Crook, and chased his command back down the Rosebud in a rout. The column had to abandon its light-armored vehicles and fight its way back, on foot for the most part, to safety.

15. Sitting Bull's vision during the Sun Dance is well known.[154]

He told it to Crazy Horse, the warrior who would see that it came true, as soon as the aviators returned to camp.

Two hundred fifty miles away, "Chutes and Saddles" was sounded on the morning of June 23, and the men of the 505th Balloon Infantry climbed aboard the airships *Benjamin Franklin, Samuel Adams, John Hancock,* and *Ethan Allen.* Custer was first man on stick one of the *Franklin.* The *Ethan Allen* carried a scout aircraft which could hook up or detach in flight; the bi-winger was to serve as liaison between the three armies and the airships.

When Custer bade good-bye to his wife Elizabeth that morning, both were in good spirits. If either had an inkling of the fate which awaited Custer and the 7th three days away on the bluffs above a small stream, they did not show it.

The four airships sailed from Fort Lincoln, their silver sides and shark-tooth mouths gleaming in the sun, the eyes painted on the noses looking west. On the sides were the crossed sabers of the cavalry; above, the numeral 7; below, the numerals 505. It is said that they looked magnificent as they sailed away for their rendezvous with destiny.[155]

16. It is sufficient to say that the Indians attained their greatest victory over the army, and almost totally destroyed the 7th Cavalry, on June 25–26, 1876, due in large part to the efforts of Crazy Horse and his aviators. Surprise, swiftness, and the skill of the Indians cannot be discounted, nor can the military blunders made by Custer that morning. The repercussions of that summer day rang down the years and the events are still debated. The only sure fact is that the US Army lost its prestige, part of its spirit, and more than four hundred of it finest soldiers in the battle.

17. While the demoralized commands were sorting themselves out, the Cheyenne and Sioux left for the Canadian border. They took their aircraft with them on travois. With Sitting Bull, Crazy Horse and his band settled just across the border. The aircraft were rarely used again until the attack on the camp by the combined Canadian-US Cavalry offensive in 1879. Crazy Horse and his aviators, as they had done so many times before, escaped with their aircraft, using one of the planes to carry their remaining fuel. Two of the nine craft were shot down by a Canadian battery.

Crazy Horse, sensing the end, fought his way, with men on horseback and the planes on travois, from Montana to Colorado. After learning of the deaths of Sitting Bull and Chief Joseph, he took his small band as close as he dared to Fort Carson, where the cavalry was massing to wipe out the remaining American Indians.

He assembled his men for the last time. He made his proposal; all concurred and joined him for a last raid on the army. The five remaining planes came in low, the morning of January 5, 1882, toward the army airfield. They destroyed twelve aircraft on the ground, shot up the hangars and barracks, and ignited one of the two ammunition dumps of the stockade. At this time, army gunners manned the William's machine cannon batteries (improved by Thomas Edison's contract scientists) and blew three of the craft to flinders. The war gods must have smiled on Crazy Horse: his aircraft was crippled, the machine rifle was blown askew, the motor slivered, but he managed to set down intact. Black Man's Hand turned away; he was captured two months later, eating cottonwood bark in the snows of Arizona.

Crazy Horse jumped from his aircraft as most of Fort Carson ran toward him; he pulled two Sharps repeating carbines from the cockpit and blazed away at the astonished troopers, wounding six and killing one. His back to the craft, he continued to fire until more than one hundred infantrymen fired a volley into his body.

The airplane was displayed for seven months at Fort Carson before being sent to the Smithsonian in Pittsburgh, where it stands today. Thus passed an era of military aviation.

—Lt. Gen. Frank Luke, Jr.
USAF, Ret.

From the December 2, 1939, issue of *Collier's Magazine*
Custer's Last Jump?
A. R. Redmond

Few events in American history have captured the imagination so thoroughly as the Battle of the Little Big Horn. Lieutenant Colonel George Armstrong Custer's devastating defeat at the hands of Sioux and Cheyenne Indians in June 1876 has been rendered time and again by such celebrated artists as George Russell and Frederic Remington. Books, factual and otherwise, which have been written around or about the battle would fill an entire library wing. The motion-picture industry has on numerous occasions drawn upon "Custer's last jump" for inspiration; latest in a long line of movieland Custers is Erroll Flynn, who appears with Olivia de Havilland and newcomer Anthony Quinn in Warner Brothers' soon-to-be-released *They Died with Their Chutes On*.

The impetuous and flamboyant Custer was an almost legendary

figure long before the Battle of Little Big Horn, however. Appointed to West Point in 1857, Custer was placed in command of Troop G, 2nd Cavalry, in June 1861, and participated in a series of skirmishes with Confederate cavalry throughout the rest of the year. It was during the First Battle of Manassas, or Bull Run, that he distinguished himself. He continued to do so in other engagements—at Williamsburg, Chancellorsville, Gettysburg— and rose rapidly through the ranks. He was twenty-six years old when he received a promotion to Brigadier General. He was, of course, immediately dubbed the Boy General. He had become an authentic war hero when the Northerners were in dire need of nothing less during those discouraging months between First Manassas and Gettysburg.

With the cessation of hostilities in the East when Bragg surrendered to Grant at Haldeman, the small hamlet about eight miles from Morehead, Kentucky, Custer requested a transfer of command. He and his young bride wound up at Chicago, which was manned by the new 7th US Cavalry.

The war in the West lasted another few months; the tattered remnants of the Confederate Army staged last desperate stands throughout Texas, Colorado, Kansas, and Missouri. The final struggle at the Trinity River in October 1867 marked the close of conflict between North and South. Those few Mexican military advisers left in Texas quietly withdrew across the Rio Grande. The French, driven from Mexico in 1867 when Maximilian was ousted, lost interest in the Americas when they became embroiled with the newly united Prussian states.

During his first year in Chicago, Custer familiarized himself with the airships and aeroplanes of the 7th. The only jump-qualified general officer of the war, Custer seemed to have felt no resentment at the ultimate fate of mounted troops boded by the extremely mobile flying machines. The Ohio-born Boy General eventually preferred traveling aboard the airship *Benjamin Franklin,* one of the eight craft assigned to the 505th Balloon Infantry (Troop I, 7th Cavalry, commanded by Brevet Colonel Frederick Benteen) while his horse soldiers rode behind the very capable Captain (Brevet Lt. Col.) Myles Keogh.

The War Department in Pittsburgh did not know that various members of the Plains Indian tribes had been equipped with aeroplanes by the Confederates, and that many had actually flown against the Union garrisons in the West. (Curiously enough, those tribes which held out the longest against the army—most notably

the Apaches under Geronimo in the deep Southwest—were those
that did not have aircraft.) The problems of transporting and
hiding, to say nothing of maintaining planes, outweighed the
advantages. A Cheyenne warrior named Brave Bear is said to have
traded his band's aircraft in disgust to Sitting Bull for three horses.
Also, many of the Plains Indians hated the aircraft outright, as
they had been used by the white men to decimate the great buffalo
herds in the early 1860s.

Even so, certain Oglalas, Minneconjous, and Cheyenne did
reasonably well in the aircraft given them by CS Army Air Corps
Major John S. Mosby, whom the Indians called the "Gray White
Man" or "Many-Feathers-in-Hat." The Oglala war chief Crazy
Horse led the raid on the Bismarck hangars (1872) four months
after the 7th Cavalry was transferred to Fort Abraham Lincoln,
Dakota Territory, and made his presence felt at the Rosebud and
Little Big Horn in 1876. The Cheyenne Black Man's Hand,
trained by Crazy Horse himself, shot down two army machines at
the Rosebud and was in the flight of planes that accomplished the
annihilation of the 505th Balloon Infantry during the first phase of
the Little Big Horn fiasco.

After the leveling of Fort Phil Kearny in February 1869, Custer
was ordered to enter the Indian territories and punish those who
had sought sanctuary there after the raid. Taking with him 150
parachutists aboard three airships, Custer left on the trail of a large
band of Cheyenne.

On the afternoon of February 25, Lieutenant William van W.
Reily, dispatched for scouting purposes in a Studebaker bi-
winger, returned to report that he had shot up a hunting party near
the Washita River. The Cheyenne, he thought, were encamped on
the banks of the river some twenty miles away. They appeared not
to have seen the close approach of the 7th Cavalry as they had not
broken camp.

Just before dawn the next morning, the 505th Balloon Infantry,
led by Custer, jumped into the village, killing all inhabitants and
their animals.

For the next five years, Custer and the 7th chased the hostiles
of the plains back and forth between Colorado and the Canadian
border. Relocated at Fort Lincoln, Custer and an expedition of
horse soldiers, geologists, and engineers discovered gold in the
Black Hills. Though the Black Hills still belonged to the Sioux
according to several treaties, prospectors began to pour into the
area. The 7th was ordered to protect them. The Blackfeet,

Minneconjous, and Hunkpapa—Sioux who had left the warpath on the promise that the Black Hills, their sacred lands, were theirs to keep for all time—protested, and when protest brought no results, took matters into their own hands. Prospectors turned up in various stages of mutilation, or not at all.

Conditions worsened over the remainder of 1875, during which time the United States Government ordered the Sioux out of the Black Hills. To make sure the Indians complied, airships patrolled the skies of the Dakota Territory.

By the end of 1875, plagued by the likes of Crazy Horse's Oglala Sioux, it was decided that there was but one solution to the Plains Indian problem—total extermination.

At this point, General Phil Sheridan, Commander in Chief of the United States Army, began working on the practical angle of this new policy toward the red men.

In January 1876, delegates from the Democratic Party approached George Armstrong Custer at Fort Abraham Lincoln and offered him the party's presidential nomination on the condition that he pull off a flashy victory over the red men before the national convention in Chicago in July.

On February 19, 1876, the Boy General's brother Thomas, commander of Troop C of the 7th, climbed into the observer's cockpit behind Lieutenant James C. Sturgis and took off on a routine patrol. Their aeroplane, a Whitney pushertype, did not return. Ten days later its wreckage was found sixty miles west of Fort Lincoln. Apparently, Sturgis and Tom Custer had stumbled on a party of mounted hostiles and, swooping low to fire or drop a handbomb, suffered a lucky hit from one of the Indian's firearms. The mutilated remains of the two officers were found a quarter mile from the wreckage, indicating that they had escaped on foot after the crash but were caught.

The shock of his brother's death, combined with the Democrats' offer, was to lead Lieutenant Colonel G.A. Custer into the worst defeat suffered by an officer of the United States Army.

Throughout the first part of 1876, Indians drifted into the Wyoming Territory from the east and south, driven by mounting pressure from the army. Raids on small Indian villages had been stepped up. Waning herds of buffalo were being systematically strafed by the airships. General Phil Sheridan received reports of tribes gathering in the vicinity of the Wolf Mountains, in what is now southern Montana, and devised a strategy by which the hostiles would be crushed for all time.

Three columns were to converge upon the massed Indians from the north, south, and east, the west being blocked by the Wolf Mountains. General George Crook's dirigibles, light tanks, and infantry were to come up the Rosebud River. General Alfred Terry would push from the northeast with infantry, cavalry, and field artillery. The 7th Cavalry was to move from the east. The Indians could not escape.

Commanded by Captain Keogh, Troops A, C, D, E, F, G, and H of the 7th—about 580 men, not counting civilian teamsters, interpreters, Crow and Arikara scouts—set out from Fort Lincoln five weeks ahead of the July 1 rendezvous at the junction of the Big Horn and Little Big Horn rivers. A month later, Custer and 150 balloon infantrymen aboard the airships *Franklin*, *Adams*, *Hancock*, and *Allen* set out on Keogh's trail.

Everything went wrong from that point onward.

The early summer of 1876 had been particularly hot and dry in the Wyoming Territory. Crook, proceeding up the Rosebud, was slowed by the tanks, which theoretically traveled at five miles per hour but kept breaking down from the heat and from the alkaline dust which worked its way into the engines through chinks in the three-inch armor plate. The crews roasted. On June 13, as Crook's column halted beside the Rosebud to let the tanks cool off, six monoplanes dived out of the clouds to attack the escorting airships *Paul Revere* and *John Paul Jones*. Caught by surprise, the two dirigibles were blown up and fell about five miles from Crook's position. The infantrymen watched, astonished, as the Indian aeronauts turned their craft toward them. While the foot soldiers ran for cover, several hundred mounted Sioux warriors showed up. In the ensuing rout, Crook lost forty-seven men and all his armored vehicles. He was still in headlong retreat when the Indians broke off their chase at nightfall.

The 7th Cavalry and the 505th Balloon Infantry linked up by liaison craft carried by the *Ethan Allen* some miles southeast of the hostile camp on the Little Big Horn on the evening of June 24. Neither they, nor Terry's column, had received word of Crook's retreat, but Keogh's scouts had sighted a large village ahead.

Custer did not know that this village contained not the five or six hundred Indians expected, but between eight and ten *thousand*, of whom slightly less than half were warriors. Spurred by his desire for revenge for his brother Tom, and filled with glory at the thought of the Democratic presidential nomination, Custer decided to hit the Indians before either Crook's or Terry's columns could reach the village. He settled on a scaled-down version of Sheridan's tri-pronged movement, and dispatched Keogh to the south and Reno to the east, with himself and the 505th attacking from the north. A small column was to wait downriver with the pack train. On the evening of June 24, George Armstrong Custer waited, secure in the knowledge that he, personally, would deal the Plains Indians their mortal blow within a mere twenty-four hours.

Unfortunately, the Indians amassed on the banks of the Little Big Horn—Oglala, Minneconjous, Arapaho, Hunkpapas, Blackfeet, Cheyenne, and so forth—had the idea that white men were on the way. During the Sun Dance ceremony the week before, the Hunkpapa chief Sitting Bull had had a dream about soldiers falling into his camp. The hostiles, assured of victory, waited.

On the morning of June 25, the *Benjamin Franklin, Samuel Adams, John Hancock,* and *Ethan Allen* drifted quietly over the hills toward the village. They were looping south when the Indians attacked.

Struck by several spin-stabilized rockets, the *Samuel Adams* blew up with a flash that might have been seen by the officers and men riding behind Captain Keogh up the valley of the Little Big Horn. Eight or twelve Indians had, in the gray dawn, climbed for altitude above the ships.

Still several miles short of their intended drop zone, the balloon infantrymen piled out of the burning and exploding craft. Though each ship was armed with Gatling rifles fore and aft, the airships were helpless against the aeroplanes' bullets and rockets. Approximately one hundred men, Custer included, cleared the ships. The Indian aviators made passes through them, no doubt killing several in the air. The *Franklin* and *Hancock* burned and fell to the earth across the river from the village. The *Allen*, dumping water ballast to gain altitude, turned for the Wolf Mountains. Though riddled by machine rifle fire, it did not explode and settled to earth about fifteen miles from where now raged a full-scale battle between increasingly demoralized soldiers and battle-maddened Sioux and Cheyenne.

Major Reno had charged the opposite side of the village as soon as he heard the commotion. Wrote one of his officers later:

A solid wall of Indians came out of the haze which had hidden the village from our eyes. They must have outnumbered us ten to one, and they were ready for us . . . Fully a third of the column was down in three minutes.

Reno, fearing he would be swallowed up, pulled his men back across the river and took up a position in a stand of timber on the riverward slope of the knoll. The Indians left a few hundred braves to make certain Reno did not escape and moved off to Reno's right to descend on Keogh's flank.

The hundred-odd parachute infantrymen who made good their escape from the airship were scattered over three square miles. The ravines and gullies cutting up the hills around the village quickly filled with mounted Indians who rode through unimpeded by the random fire of disorganized balloon infantrymen. They swept them up, on the way to Keogh. Keogh, unaware of the number of Indians and the rout of Reno's command, got as far as the north bank of the river before he was ground to pieces between two masses of hostiles. Of Keogh's command, less than a dozen escaped the slaughter. The actual battle lasted about thirty minutes.

The hostiles left the area that night, exhausted after their greatest victory over the soldiers. Most of the Indians went north to Canada; some escaped the mass extermination of their race which was to take place in the American West during the next six years.

Terry found Reno entrenched on the ridge the morning of the twenty-seventh. The scouts sent to find Custer and Keogh could not believe their eyes when they found the bodies of the 7th Cavalry six miles away.

Some of the men were not found for another two days. Terry and his men scoured the ravines and valleys. Custer himself was about four miles from the sight of Keogh's annihilation; the Boy General appeared to have been hit by a piece of exploding rocket shrapnel and may have been dead before he reached the ground. His body escaped the mutilation that befell most of Keogh's command, possibly because of its distance from the camp.

Custer's miscalculation cost the army 430 men, four dirigibles (plus the Studebaker scout from the *Ethan Allen*), and its prestige. An attempt was made to make a scapegoat of Major Reno, blaming his alleged cowardice for the failure of the 7th. Though Reno was acquitted, grumblings continued until the turn of the century. It is hoped the matter will be settled for all time by the opening, for private research, of the papers of the late President

Phil Sheridan. As Commander in Chief, he had access to a mountain of material which was kept from the public at the time of the court of inquiry of 1879.

Extract from *Huckleberry Among the Hostiles:*
A Journal
by Mark Twain, edited by Bernard Van Dyne
Hutton and Company, New York, 1932.

EDITOR'S NOTE: In November 1886 Clemens drafted a tentative outline for a sequel to *The Adventures of Huckleberry Finn,* which had received mixed reviews on its publication in January 1885, but which had nonetheless enjoyed a second printing within five months of its release. The proposed sequel was intended to deal with Huckleberry's adventures as a young man on the frontier. To gather research material firsthand, Mark Twain boarded the airship *Peyton* in Cincinnati, Ohio, in mid-December 1886, and set out across the Southwest, amassing copious notes and reams of interviews with soldiers, frontiersmen, law enforcement officers, ex-hostiles, at least two notorious outlaws, and a number of less readily categorized persons. Twain had intended to spend four months out west. Unfortunately, his wife, Livy, fell gravely ill in late February 1887; Twain returned to her as soon as he received word in Fort Hood, Texas. He lost interest in all writing for two years after her death in April 1887. The proposed novel about Huckleberry Finn as a man was never written: we are left with 110,000 words of interviews and observations and an incomplete journal of the author's second trek across the American West.— BvD.

February 2: A more desolate place than the Indian Territory of Oklahoma would be impossible to imagine. It is flat the year 'round, stingingly cold in winter, hot and dry, I am told, during the summer (when the land turns brown save for scattered patches of greenery which serve only to make the landscape all the drearier; Arizona and New Mexico are devoid of greenery, which is to their credit—when those territories elected to become barren wastelands they did not lost heart halfway, but followed their chosen course to the end).

It is easy to see why the United States Government swept the few Indians into Godforsaken Oklahoma and ordered them to remain there under threat of extermination. The word "Godforsaken" is the vital clue. The white men who "gave" this land to the few remaining tribes for as long as the wind shall blow—which it certainly does in February—and the grass shall grow (which it does, in Missouri, perhaps) were Christians who knew better than to let heathen savages run loose in parts of the country still smiled upon by our heavenly malefactor.

February 4: Whatever I may have observed about Oklahoma from the cabin of the *Peyton* has been reinforced by a view from the ground. The airship was running into stiff winds from the north, so we put in at Fort Sill yesterday evening and are awaiting calmer weather. I have gone on with my work.

Fort Sill is located seventeen miles from the Cheyenne Indian reservation. It has taken me all day to learn (mainly from one Sergeant Howard, a gap-toothed, unwashed Texan who is apparently my unofficial guardian angel for whatever length of time I am to be marooned here) that the Cheyenne do not care much for Oklahoma, which is still another reason why the government keeps them there. One or two ex-hostiles will leave the reservation every month, taking with them their wives and meager belongings, and Major Rickards will have to send out a detachment of soldiers to haul the erring ones back, either in chains or over the backs of horses. I am told the reservation becomes particularly annoying in the winter months, as the poor boys who are detailed to pursue the Indians suffer greatly from the cold. At this, I remarked to Sergeant Howard that the red man can be terribly inconsiderate, even ungrateful, in view of all the blessings the white man has heaped upon him—smallpox and that French disease, to name two. The good sergeant scratched his head and grinned, and said, "You're right, sir."

I'll have to make Howard a character in the book.

February 5: Today, I was taken by Major Rickards to meet a Cheyenne named Black Man's Hand, one of the participants of the alleged massacre of the 7th Cavalry at the Little Big Horn River in '76. The major had this one Cheyenne brought in after a recent departure from the reservation. Black Man's Hand had been shackled and left to dwell upon his past misdeeds in an unheated hut at the edge of the airport, while two cold-benumbed privates stood on guard before the door. It was evidently feared this one savage would, if left unchained, do to Fort Sill that which he (with a modicum of assistance from four or five hundred of his race) had done to Custer. I nevertheless mentioned to Rickards that I was interested in talking to Black Man's Hand, as the Battle of the

Little Big Horn would perfectly climax Huckleberry's adventures in the new book. Rickards was reluctant to grant permission but gave in abruptly, perhaps fearing I would model a villain after him.

Upon entering the hut where the Cheyenne sat, I asked Major Rickards if it were possible to have the Indian's manacles removed, as it makes me nervous to talk to a man who can rattle his chains at me whenever he chooses. Major Rickards said no and troubled himself to explain to me the need for limiting the movement of this specimen of ferocity within the walls of Fort Sill.

With a sigh, I seated myself across from Black Man's Hand and offered him one of my cigars. He accepted it with a faint smile. He appeared to be in his forties, though his face was deeply lined.

He was dressed in ragged leather leggings, thick calf-length woolen pajamas, and a faded army jacket. His vest appeared to have been fashioned from an old parachute harness. He had no hat, no footgear, and no blanket.

"Major Rickards," I said, "this man is freezing to death. Even if he isn't, I am. Can you provide this hut with a little warmth?"

The fretting major summarily dispatched one of the sentries for firewood and kindling for the little stove sitting uselessly in the corner of the hut.

I would have been altogether comfortable after that could I have had a decanter of brandy with which to force out the inner chill. But Indians are notoriously incapable of holding liquor, and I did not wish to be the cause of this poor wretch's further downfall.

Black Man's Hand speaks surprisingly good English. I spent an hour and a half with him, recording his remarks with as much attention paid to accuracy as my advanced years and cold fingers permitted. With luck, I'll be able to fill some gaps in his story before the *Peyton* resumes its flight across this griddle-cake countryside.

Extract from *The Testament of Black Man's Hand*.
[NOTE: For the sake of easier reading, I have substituted a number of English terms for those provided by the Cheyenne Black Man's Hand.—MT]

I was young when I first met the Oglala mystic Crazy Horse and was taught by him to fly the Thunderbirds which the one called the Gray White Man had given him. [The Gray White Man—John S.

Mosby, Major CSAAC—MT.] Some of the older men among the People [as the Cheyenne call themselves, Major Rickards explains; I assured him that such egocentricity is by no means restricted to savages—MT] did not think much of the flying machines and said, "How will we be able to remain brave men when this would enable us to fly over the heads of our enemies, without counting coup or taking trophies?"

But the Oglala said, "The Gray White Man has asked us to help him."

"Why should we help him?" asked Two Pines.

"Because he fights the blueshirts and those who persecute us. We have known for many years that the men who cheated us and lied to us and killed our women and the buffalo are men without honor, cowards who fight only because there is no other way for them to get what they want. They cannot understand why we fight with the Crows and Pawnees—to be brave, to win honor for ourselves. They fight because it is a means to an end, and they fight us only because we have what they want. The blueshirts want to kill us all. They fight to win. If we are to fight them, we must fight with their own weapons. We must fight to win."

The older warriors shook their heads sorrowfully and spoke of younger days when they fought the Pawnees bravely, honorably, man-to-man. But I and several other young men wanted to learn how to control the Thunderbirds. And we knew Crazy Horse spoke the truth, that our lives would never be happy as long as there were white men in the world. Finally, because they could not forbid us to go with the Oglala, only advise against it and say that the Great Mystery had not intended us to fly, Red Horse and I and some others went with Crazy Horse. I did not see my village again, not even at the big camp on the Greasy Grass [Little Big Horn—MT] where we rubbed out Yellow Hair. I think perhaps the blueshirts came after I was gone and told Two Pines that he had to leave his home and come to this flat dead place.

The Oglala Crazy Horse taught us to fly the Thunderbirds. We learned a great many things about the Gray White Man's machines. With them, we killed yellowleg flyers. Soon I tired of the waiting and the hunger. We were raided once. It was a good fight. In the dark, we chased the Big Fish [the Indian word for dirigibles—MT] and killed many men on the ground.

I do not remember all of what happened those seasons. When we were finally chased away from the landing place, Crazy Horse had us hide the Thunderbirds in the Black Hills. I have heard the yellowlegs did not know we had the Thunderbirds; that they thought they were run by the gray white men only. It did not matter; we thought we had used them for the last time.

Many seasons later, we heard what happened to Black Kettle's village. I went to the place some time after the battle. I heard that Crazy Horse had been there and seen the place. I looked for him but he had gone north again. Black Kettle had been a treaty man: we talked among ourselves that the yellowlegs had no honor.

It was the winter I was sick [1872. The Plains Indians and the US Army alike were plagued that winter by what we would call the influenza. It was probably brought by some itinerant French trapper—MT] that I heard of Crazy Horse's raid on the landing place of the Big Fish. It was news of this that told us we must prepare to fight the yellowlegs.

When I was well, my wives and I and Eagle Hawk's band went looking for Crazy Horse. We found him in the fall. Already the army had killed many Sioux and Cheyenne that summer. Crazy Horse said we must band together, we who knew how to fly the Thunderbirds. He said we would someday have to fight the yellowlegs among the clouds as in the old days. We only had five Thunderbirds which had not been flown many seasons. We spent the summer planning to get more. Red Chief and Yellow Dog gathered a large band. We raided the Fort Kearny and stole many Thunderbirds and canisters of powder. We hid them in the Black Hills. It had been a good fight.

It was at this time Yellow Hair sent out many soldiers to protect the miners he had brought in by speaking false. They destroyed the sacred lands of the Sioux. We killed some of them, and the yellowlegs burned many of our villages. That was not a good time. The Big Fish killed many of our people.

We wanted to get the Thunderbirds and kill the Big Fish. Crazy Horse had us wait. He had been talking to Sitting Bull, the Hunkpapa chief. Sitting Bull said we should not go against the yellowlegs yet, that we could only kill a few at a time. Later, he said, they would all come. That would be a good day to die.

The next year they came. We did not know until just before the Sun Dance [about June 10, 1876—MT] that they were coming. Crazy Horse and I and all those who flew the Thunderbirds went to get ours. It took us two days to get them going again, and we had only six Thunderbirds flying when we flew to stop the blueshirts. Crazy Horse, Yellow Dog, American Gun, Little Wolf, Big Tall, and I flew that day. It was a good fight. We killed

two Big Fish and many men and horses. We stopped the
Turtles-which-kill [that would be the light armored cars Crook had
with him on the Rosebud River—MT] so they could not come
toward the Greasy Grass where we camped. The Sioux under
Spotted Pony killed more on the ground. We flew back and hid the
Thunderbirds near camp.

When we returned, we told Sitting Bull of our victory. He said
it was good, but that a bigger victory was to come. He said he
had had a vision during the Sun Dance. He saw many soldiers and
enemy Indians fall out of the sky on their heads into the village.
He said ours was not the victory he had seen.

It was some days later we heard that a yellowlegs Thunderbird
had been shot down. We went to the place where it lay. There was
a strange device above its wing. Crazy Horse studied it many
moments. Then he said, "I have seen such a thing before. It
carries Thunderbirds beneath one of the Big Fish. We must get our
Thunderbirds. It will be a good day to die."

We hurried to our Thunderbirds. We had twelve of them fixed
now, and we had on them, besides the quick rifles [Henry machine
rifles of calibers .41–40 or .30–30—MT], the roaring spears [Hale
spin-stabilized rockets, of two-and-a-half-inch diameter—MT].
We took off before noonday.

We arrived at the Greasy Grass and climbed into the clouds,
where we scouted. Soon, to the south, we saw the dust of many
men moving. But Crazy Horse held us back. Soon we saw why;
four Big Fish were coming. We came at them out of the sun. They
did not see us till we were on them. We fired our roaring sticks,
and the Big Fish caught fire and burned. All except one, which
drifted away, though it lost all its fat. Wild Horse, in his
Thunderbird, was shot but still fought on with us that morning.
We began to kill the men on the Big Fish when a new thing
happened. Men began to float down on blankets. We began to kill
them with our quick rifles as they fell. Then we attacked those
who reached the ground, until we saw Spotted Pony and his men
were on them. We turned south and killed many horse soldiers
there. Then we flew back to the Greasy Grass and hid the
Thunderbirds. At camp, we learned that many pony soldiers had
been killed. Word came that more soldiers were coming.

I saw, as the sun went down, the women moving among the
dead Men-Who-Float-Down, taking their clothing and supplies.
They covered the ground like leaves in the autumn. It had been a
good fight.

Extract From *The Seventh Cavalry: A History*
Colonel E. R. Burroughs
USA, Ret.

So much has been written about that hot June day in 1876, so much guesswork applied where knowledge was missing. Was Custer dead in his harness before he reached the ground? Or did he stand and fire at the aircraft strafing his men? How many reached the ground alive? Did any escape the battle itself, only to be killed by Indian patrols later that afternoon or the next day? No one really knows, and all the Indians are gone now, so history stands a blank.

Only one thing is certain: for the men of the 7th Cavalry there was only the reality of the exploding dirigibles, the snap of their chutes deploying, the roar of the aircraft among them, the bullets, and those terrible last moments on the bluff. Whatever the verdict of their peers, whatever the future may reveal, it can be said that they did not die in vain.

A LITTLE NIGHT FLYING

Bob Shaw

The dead cop came drifting in toward the Birmingham control zone at a height of some three thousand meters. It was a winter night, and the subzero temperatures that prevailed at that altitude had solidified his limbs, encrusted the entire body with black frost. Blood flowing through shattered armor had frozen into the semblance of a crab, with its claws encircling his chest. The body, which was in an upright position, rocked gently on stray currents, performing a strange aerial shuffle. And at its waist a pea-sized crimson light blinked on and off, on and off, its radiance gradually fading under a thickening coat of ice.

Air Police Sergeant Robert Hasson felt more exhausted and edgy than he would have felt after an eight-hour crosswind patrol. He had been in the headquarters block since lunchtime, dictating and signing reports, completing forms, trying to wrest from the cashier's office the expenses that had been due to him two months earlier. And then, just as he was about to go home in disgust, he had been summoned to Captain Nunn's office for yet another confrontation over the Welwyn Angels case. The four on remand—Joe Sullivan, Flick Bugatti, Denny Johnston, and Toddy Thoms—were sitting together at one side of the office, still in their flying gear.

"I'll tell you what disturbs me most about this whole affair," Bunny Ormerod, the senior barrister, was saying with practiced concern. "It is the utter indifference of the police. It is the callousness with which the tragic death of a child is accepted by the arresting officers." Ormerod moved closer to the four Angels, protectively, identifying with them. "One would think it was an everyday occurrence."

Hasson shrugged. "It is, practically."

Ormerod allowed his jaw to sag, and he turned so that the brooch recorder on his silk blouse was pointing straight at Hasson. "Would you care to repeat that statement?"

Hasson stared directly into the recorder's watchful iris. "Practically every day, or every night, some moron straps on a CG harness, goes flying around at five or six hundred kilometers an hour, thinking he's Superman, and runs into a pylon or a towerblock. And you're dead right—I don't give a damn when they smear themselves over the sides of buildings." Hasson could see Nunn becoming agitated behind his expanse of desk, but he pressed on doggedly. "It's only when they smash into other people that I get worked up. And then I go after them."

"You hunt them down."

"That's what I do."

"The way you hunted down these children."

Hasson examined the Angels coldly. "I don't see any children. The youngest in that gang is sixteen."

Ormerod directed a compassionate smile toward the four black-clad Angels. "We live in a complex and difficult world, Sergeant. Sixteen years isn't a very long time for a youngster to get to know his way around it."

"Balls," Hasson commented. He looked at the Angels again and pointed at a heavy-set, bearded youth who was sitting behind the others. "You—Toddy—come over here."

Toddy's eyes shuttled briefly. "What for?"

"I want to show Mr. Ormerod your badges."

"Naw. Don't want to," Toddy said smugly. " 'Sides, I like it better over here."

Hasson sighed, walked to the group, caught hold of Toddy's lapel, and walked back to Ormerod as if he were holding nothing but the piece of simulated leather. Behind him he heard frantic swearing and the sound of chairs falling over as Toddy was dragged through the protective screen of his companions. The opportunity to express his feelings in action, no matter how limited, gave Hasson a therapeutic satisfaction.

Nunn half rose to his feet. "What do you think you're doing, Sergeant?"

Hasson ignored him, addressing himself to Ormerod. "See this badge? The big *F* with wings on it? Do you know what it means?"

"I'm more interested in what your extraordinary behavior means." One of Ormerod's hands was purposely, but with every appearance of accident, blocking his recorder's field of view. Hasson knew that this was because of recent legislation under which the courts refused to consider any recorded evidence unless the entire spool was presented—and Ormerod did not want a shot of the badge.

"Have a look at it." Hasson repeated his description of the badge for the benefit of the soundtrack. "It means that this quote child unquote has had sexual intercourse in free fall. And he's proud of it. Aren't you, Toddy?"

"Mr. Ormerod?" Toddy's eyes were fixed pleadingly on the barrister's face.

"For your own good, Sergeant, I think you should let go of my client," Ormerod said. His slim hand was still hovering in front of the recorder.

"Certainly." Hasson snatched the recorder, plucking a hole in Ormerod's blouse as he did so, and held the little instrument in front of the Angel's array of badges. After a moment he pushed Toddy away from him and gave the recorder back to Ormerod with a flourish of mock courtesy.

"That was a mistake, Hasson." Ormerod's aristocratic features had begun to show genuine anger. "You've made it obvious that you are taking part in a personal vendetta against my client."

Hasson laughed. "Toddy isn't your client. You were hired by Joe Sullivan's old man to get him out from under a manslaughter charge, and big, simple Toddy just happens to be in the same bag."

Joe Sullivan, sitting in the center of the other three Angels, opened his mouth to retort, but changed his mind. He appeared to have been better rehearsed than his companions.

"That's right," Hasson said to him. "Remember what you were told, Joe—let the hired mouth do all the talking." Sullivan shifted resentfully, staring down at his blue-knuckled hands, and remained silent.

"It's obvious we aren't achieving anything," Ormerod said to Nunn. "I'm going to hold a private conference with my clients."

"Do that," Hasson put in. "Tell them to peel off those badges, won't you? Next time I might pick out an even better one." He waited impassively while Ormerod and two policemen ushered the four Angels out of the room.

"I don't understand you," Nunn said as soon as they were alone. "Exactly what did you think you were doing just now? That boy has only to testify that you manhandled him . . ."

" 'That boy,' as you call him, knows where we could find the Fireman. They all do."

"You're being too hard on them."

"You aren't." Hasson knew at once that he had gone too far, but he was too obstinate to begin retracting the words.

"What do you mean?" Nunn's mouth compressed, making him look womanly but nonetheless dangerous.

"Why do I have to talk to that load of scruff up here in your office? What's wrong with the interview rooms downstairs? Or are they only for thugs who haven't got Sullivan money behind them?"

"Are you saying I've taken Sullivan's money?"

Hasson thought for a moment. "I don't believe you'd do that, but you let it make a difference. I tell you those four have flown with the Fireman. If I could be left alone for half an hour with any one of them I'd . . ."

"You'd get yourself put away. You don't seem to understand the way things are, Hasson. You're a skycop—and that means the public doesn't want you around. A hundred years ago motorists disliked traffic cops for making them obey a few common-sense rules; now everybody can fly, better than the birds, and they find this same breed of cop up there with them, spoiling it for them, and they *hate* you."

"I'm not worried."

"I don't think you're worried about police work either, Hasson. Not really. I'd say you're hooked on cloud-running every bit as much as this mythical Fireman, but you want to play a different game."

Hasson became anxious, aware that Nunn was leading up to something important. "The Fireman is real—I've seen him."

"Whether he is or not, I'm grounding you."

"You can't do that," Hasson blurted instinctively.

Nunn looked interested. "Why not?"

"Because . . ." Hasson was striving for the right words, any words, when the communicator sphere on Nunn's desk lit up redly, signaling a top-priority message.

"Go ahead," Nunn said to the sphere.

"Sir, we're picking up an automatic distress call," it replied with a male voice. "Somebody drifting out of control at three thousand meters. We think it must be Inglis."

"Dead?"

"We've interrogated his compack, sir. No response."

"I see. Wait till the rush hour is over and send somebody up for him. I'll want a full report."

"Yes, sir."

"I'm going up for him now," Hasson said, moving toward the door.

"You can't go through the traffic streams at this hour." Nunn got to his feet and came around the desk. "And you're grounded. I mean that, Hasson."

Hasson paused, knowing that he had already stretched to the limit the special indulgence granted to members of the Air Patrol. "If that's Lloyd Inglis up there, I'm going up to get him right now. And if he's dead, I'm grounding myself. Permanently. Okay?"

Nunn shook his head uncertainly. "Do you want to kill yourself?"

"Perhaps." Hasson closed the door and ran toward the tackle room.

He lifted off from the roof of the police headquarters into a sky that was ablaze with converging rivers of fire. Work-weary commuters pouring up from the south represented most of the traffic, but there were lesser tributaries flowing from many points of the compass into the vast aerial whirlpool of the Birmingham control zone. The shoulder lights and ankle lights of thousands upon thousands of fliers shifted and shimmered, changes of parallax causing spurious waves to progress and retrogress along the glowing streams. Vertical columns of brilliance kept the opposing elements apart, creating an appearance of strict order. Hasson knew, however, that the appearance was to some extent deceptive. People who were in a hurry tended to switch off their lights to avoid detection and fly straight to where they were going, regardless of the air corridors. The chances of colliding with another illegal traveler were vanishingly small, they told themselves, but it was not only occasional salesmen late for appointments who flew wild. There were the drunks and the druggies, the antisocial, the careless, the suicidal, the thrill seekers, the criminal—a whole spectrum of types who were unready for the responsibilities of personal flight, in whose hands a countergravity harness could become an instrument of death.

Hasson set his police flare units at maximum intensity. He climbed cautiously, dye gun at the ready, until the lights of the city were spread out below him in endless glowing geometries. When the information display projected onto the inner surface of his visor told him he was at a height of two hundred meters, he began paying particular attention to his radar. This was the altitude at which rogue fliers were most numerous. He continued rising steadily, controlling the unease that was a normal reaction to being suspended in darkness from which, at any moment, other beings could come hurtling toward him at lethal velocity. The aerial river of travelers was now visible as separate laminae, uppermost levels moving fastest, which slipped over each other like luminous gauze.

A farther eight hundred meters and Hasson began to relax slightly. He was turning his attention to the problem of homing in on Inglis when his proximity alarm sounded and the helmet radar flashed a bearing. Hasson twisted to face the indicated direction. The figure of a man flying without lights, angled for maximum speed, materialized in the light of Hasson's flare units. Veteran of a thousand such encounters, Hasson had time to calculate a miss distance of about ten meters. Within the fraction of a second available to him, he aimed his gun and fired off a cloud of indelible dye. The other man passed through it—glimpse of pale, elated face and dark, unseeing eyes—and was gone in a noisy flurry of turbulence. Hasson called headquarters and gave details of the incident, adding his opinion that the rogue flier was also guilty of drug abuse. With upward of a million people airborne in the sector at that very moment, it was unlikely that the offender would ever be caught, but his flying clothes and equipment had been permanently branded and would have to be replaced at considerable expense.

At three thousand meters Hasson switched to height maintenance power, took a direction-finder reading on Inglis's beacon, and began a slow horizontal cruise, eyes probing the darkness ahead. His flares illuminated a thickening mist, placing him at the center of a sphere of foggy radiance and making it difficult to see anything beyond. This was close to the limit for personal flying without special heaters, and Hasson became aware of the cold that was pressing in on him, searching for a weakness in his defenses. The traffic streams far below looked warm and safe.

A few minutes later, Hasson's radar picked up an object straight ahead. He drew closer until, by flarelight, he could make out the figure of Lloyd Inglis performing its grotesque shuffle through the currents of dark air. Hasson knew at once that his friend was dead, but he circled the body, keeping just outside field interference distance, until he could see the gaping hole in Inglis's chest plate. The wound looked as though it had been inflicted by a lance.

A week earlier, Hasson and Inglis had been on routine patrol over Bedford when they had detected a pack of about eight flying without lights. Inglis had loosed off a miniflare, which burst just beyond the group, throwing them briefly into silhouette, and both men had glimpsed the slim outline of a lance. The transportation of *any* solid object by a person using a CG harness was illegal, because of the danger to other air travelers and people on the ground, and the carrying of weapons was rare even among rogue fliers. It seemed likely that they had chanced on the Fireman. Spreading their nets and snares, Hasson and Inglis had flown subsequent low-level chase, two people had died—one of them a young woman, also flying without lights, who had strayed into a head-on collision with one of the gang. The other had been a pack leader who had almost cut himself in two on a radio mast. At the end of it all the two policemen had had to show for their efforts had been four unimportant members of the Welwyn Angels. The Fireman, the lance carrier, had gotten away to brood about the incident, safe in his anonymity.

Now, as he studied the frozen body of his former partner, Hasson understood that the Fireman had been inspired to revenge. His targets would have been identified for him in the news coverage given to the arrest of Joe Sullivan. Swearing in his bitterness and grief, Hasson tilted his body, creating a horizontal component in the lift force exerted by his CG harness. He swooped in on the rigid corpse, locked his arms around it and, immediately, both bodies began to drop as their countergravity fields canceled each other out. No stranger to free fall, Hasson efficiently attached a line to an eye on Inglis's belt and pushed the dead man away from him. As the two separated to beyond field interference distance, the upward rush of air around them gradually ceased. Hasson checked his data display and saw that he had fallen little more than a hundred meters. He paid the line out from a dispenser at his waist until Inglis's body was at a convenient towing distance, then he flew west, aiming for a point at which it would be safe to descend through the commuter levels. Far beneath him the traffic of the Birmingham control zone swirled like a golden galaxy, but Hasson—at the center of his own spherical universe of white, misty light—was isolated from it, cocooned in his own thoughts.

Lloyd Inglis—the beer-drinking, book-loving spendthrift—was

dead. And before him there had been Singleton, Larmor, and McMeekin. Half of Hasson's original squad of seven years ago had died in the course of duty—and for what? It was impossible to police a human race that had been given its three-dimensional freedom with the advent of the CG harness. Putting a judo hold on gravity, turning the Earth's own attractive force back against itself, had proved to be the only way to fly. It was easy, inexpensive, exhilarating—and impossible to regulate. There were eighty million personal fliers in Britain alone, each one a superman impatient of any curb on his ability to follow the sunset around the curve of the world. Aircraft had vanished from the skies almost overnight, not because the cargo-carrying ability was no longer needed, but because it was too dangerous to fly them in a medium that was crowded with aerial jaywalkers. The nocturnal rogue flier, the dark Icarus, was the folk hero of the age. What, Hasson asked himself, was the point in being a skycop? Perhaps the whole concept of policing, of being responsible for others, was no longer valid. Perhaps the inevitable price of freedom was a slow rain of broken bodies drifting to Earth as their powerpacks faded and . . .

The attack took Hasson by surprise.

It came so quickly that the proximity alarm and the howling of air displaced by the attacker's body was virtually simultaneous. Hasson turned, saw the black lance, jackknifed to escape it, received a ferocious glancing blow, and was sent spinning—all in the space of a second. The drop caused by the momentary field interference had been negligible. He switched off his flares and flight lights in a reflexive action and struggled to free his arms from the towline, which was being lapped around him by his own rotation. When he had managed to stabilize himself he remained perfectly still and tried to assess the situation. His right hip was throbbing painfully from the impact, but as far as he could tell, no bones had been broken. He wondered if his attacker was going to be content with having made a single devastating pass, or if this was the beginning of a duel.

"You were quick, Hasson," a voice called from the darkness. "Quicker than your wingman. But it won't do you any good."

"Who are you?" Hasson shouted as he looked for a radar bearing.

"You know who I am. I'm the Fireman."

"That's a song." Hasson kept his voice steady as he began

spreading his snares and nets. "What's your real name? The one your area psychiatrist has on his books."

The darkness laughed. "Very good, Sergeant Hasson. Playing for time and trying to goad me and learn my name all at once."

"I don't need to play for time—I've already broadcast a QRF."

"By the time anybody gets here you'll be dead, Hasson."

"Why should I be? Why do you want to do this?"

"Why do you hunt my friends and ground them?"

"They're a menace to themselves and to everybody else."

"Only when you make them fly wild. You're kidding yourself, Hasson. You're a skycop, and you like hounding people to death. I'm going to ground you for good—and those nets won't help you."

Hasson stared vainly in the direction of the voice. "Nets?"

There was another laugh, and the Fireman began to sing. *"I can see you in the dark,' cause I'm the Fireman; I can fly with you and you don't even know I'm there. . . ."* The familiar words were growing louder as their source drew near, and abruptly Hasson made out the shape of a big man illuminated by the traffic streams below and by starlight from above. He looked fearsome and inhuman in his flying gear.

Hasson yearned for the firearm that was denied to him by British police tradition, and then he noticed something. "Where's the lance?"

"Who needs it? I let it go." The Fireman spread his arms and—even in the dimness, even with the lack of spatial reference points—it became apparent that he was a giant, a man who had no need of weapons other than those that nature had built into him.

Hasson thought of the heavy lance plummeting down into a crowded suburb three thousand meters below, and a cryogenic hatred stole through him, reconciling him to the forthcoming struggle, regardless of its outcome. As the Fireman came closer, Hasson whirled a net in slow circles, tilting his harness to counteract the spin the net tried to impart to him. He raised his legs in readiness to kick, and at the same time finished straightening out the towline, which made Inglis's body a ghastly spectator to the event. Hasson felt nervous and keyed up, but not particularly afraid now that the Fireman had discarded his lance. Aerial combat was not a matter of instinct; it was something that had to be learned and practiced, and therefore the professional always had the edge on the amateur, no matter how gifted or strongly motivated the latter might be. For example, the Fireman

had made a serious mistake in allowing Hasson to get his legs fully
drawn up into the position from which the power of his thighs
could be released in an explosive kick.

Unaware of his blunder, the Fireman edged in slowly, vectoring
the lift of his harness with barely perceptible shoulder movements.
He's a good flier, Hasson thought, *even if he isn't so good on
combat theory and . . .*

The Fireman came in fast—but not nearly as fast as he should
have done. Hasson experienced something like a sense of luxury
as he found himself with time to place his kick exactly where he
wanted it. He chose the vulnerable point just below the visor,
compensated for the abrupt drop that occurred as both CG fields
canceled out, and unleashed enough energy to snap a man's neck.
Somehow the Fireman got his head out of the way in time and
caught hold of Hasson's outstretched leg. Both men were falling
now, but at an unequal rate, because Hasson was tethered to
Inglis, whose CG field was too far away to have been canceled. In
the second before they parted, the Fireman applied the leverage of
his massive arms and broke Hasson's leg sideways at the knee.

Pain and shock obliterated Hasson's mind, gutting him of all
strength and resolve. He floated in the blackness for an indeter-
minate period, arms moving uncertainly, face contorted in a silent
scream. The great spiral nebula far below continued to spin, but a
dark shape was moving steadily across it, and part of Hasson's
mind informed him that there was no time for indulgence in
natural reactions to injury. He was hopelessly outclassed on the
physical level, and if life were to continue it would only be
through the exercise of intelligence. But how was he to think when
pain had invaded his body like an army and was firing mortar
shells of agony straight into his brain?

For a start, Hasson told himself, *you have to get rid of Lloyd
Inglis.* He began reeling in his comrade's body with the intention
of unhooking it, but almost immediately the Fireman spoke from
close behind him.

"How did you like it, Hasson?" The voice was triumphant.
"That was to show you I can beat you at your own game. Now
we're going to play my game." Hasson tried drawing the line in
faster. Inglis's body bobbed closer and finally came within
interference radius. Hasson and Inglis began to fall. The Fireman
dived in on them instantly, hooked an arm around Hasson's body,
and all three dropped together. The whirlpool of fire began to
expand beneath them.

"This is *my* game," the Fireman sang through the gathering slipstream. *"I can ride you all the way to the ground, 'cause I'm the Fireman."*

Hasson, knowing the tactics of aerial chicken, shut out the pain from his trailing leg and reached for his master switch, but hesitated without throwing it. In two-man chicken the extinguishing of one CG field restored the other one to its normal efficacy, causing a fierce differential, which tended to drag one opponent vertically away from the other. The standard countermove was for the second man to kill his own field at the same time so that both bodies would continue to plunge downward together until somebody's nerve broke and forced him to reactivate his harness. In the present game of death, however, the situation was complicated by the presence of Inglis, the silent partner who had already lost. His field would continue negating those of the other two, regardless of what they did, unless . . .

Hasson freed an arm from the Fireman's mock-sexual embrace and pulled Inglis's body in close. He groped for the dead man's master switch but found only a smooth plaque of frozen blood. The jeweled horizons were rising rapidly on all sides now, and the circling traffic stream was opening like a carnivorous flower. Air rushed by at terminal velocity, deafeningly. Hasson fought to break the icy casting away from the switch on Inglis's harness, but at that moment the Fireman slid an arm around Hasson's neck and pulled his head back.

"Don't try to get away from me," he shouted into Hasson's ear. "Don't try to chicken out—I want to see how well you bounce."

They continued to fall.

Hasson, encumbered by his nets, felt for the buckle of the belt, which held, among other things, the towline dispenser. He fumbled it open with numb fingers and was about to release Inglis's body when it occurred to him that he would gain very little in doing so. An experienced chicken player always delayed breaking out of field interference until the last possible instant, leaving it so late that even with his harness set at maximum lift he hit the ground at the highest speed he could withstand. The Fireman probably intended going to the limit this time, leaving Hasson too disabled to prevent himself from being smashed on impact. Getting rid of Inglis's body would not change that.

They had dropped almost two thousand meters and in just a few seconds would be penetrating the crowded commuter levels. The Fireman began to whoop with excitement, grinding himself against Hasson like a rutting dog. Holding Inglis with his left hand, Hasson used his right to loop the plasteel towline around the Fireman's upraised thigh and to pull it into a hard knot. He was still tightening the knot as they bombed down into the traffic flow. Lights flashed past nearby, and suddenly the slow-spinning galaxy was above them. Patterns of street lamps blossomed beneath, with moving ground cars clearly visible. This, Hasson knew, was close to the moment at which the Fireman had to break free if he was to shed enough downward velocity before reaching ground level.

"Thanks for the ride," the Fireman shouted, his voice ripping away in the slipstream. "Got to leave you soon."

Hasson switched on his flares and then jerked the towline violently, bringing it to the Fireman's attention. The Fireman looked at the loop around his thigh. His body convulsed with shock as he made the discovery that it was he and not Hasson who was linked to the dead and deadly skycop. He pushed Hasson away and began clawing at the line. Hasson swam free in the wind, knowing that the line would resist even the Fireman's giant strength. As Hasson felt his CG field spread its invisible wings, he turned to look back. He saw the two bodies, one of them struggling frantically, pass beyond the range of his flares on their way to a lethal impact with the ground.

Hasson had no time to waste in introspection—his own crash landing was about to occur, and it would require all his skill and experience to get him through it alive—but he was relieved to find that he could derive no satisfaction from the Fireman's death. Nunn and the others were wrong about him.

Even so, he thought, during the final hurtling seconds, *I've hunted like a hawk for far too long. This is my last flight.*

He prepared himself, unafraid, for the earth's blind embrace.

DAVID DRAKE

__NORTHWORLD__ 0-441-84830-3/$3.95

The consensus ruled twelve hundred worlds—but not Northworld. Three fleets had been dispatched to probe the enigma of Northworld. None returned. Now, Commissioner Nils Hansen must face the challenge of the distant planet. There he will confront a world at war, a world of androids...all unique, all lethal.

__SURFACE ACTION__ 0-441-36375-X/$3.95

Venus has been transformed into a world of underwater habitats for Earth's survivors. Battles on Venus must be fought on the ocean's exotic surface. Johnnie Gordon trained his entire life for battle, and now his time has come to live a warrior's life on the high seas.

THE FLEET Edited by David Drake and Bill Fawcett

The soldiers of the Human/Alien Alliance come from different worlds and different cultures. But they share a common mission: to reclaim occupied space from the savage Khalian invaders.

> __BREAKTHROUGH__ 0-441-24105-0/$3.95
> __COUNTERATTACK__ 0-441-24104-2/$3.95
> __SWORN ALLIES__ 0-441-24090-9/$3.95